A HILL OF MANY DREAMS

Books by Richard Llewellyn

A HILL OF MANY DREAMS

BRIDE OF ISRAEL, MY LOVE

THE NIGHT IS A CHILD

WHITE HORSE TO BANBURY CROSS

BUT WE DIDN'T GET THE FOX

THE END OF THE RUG

DOWN WHERE THE MOON IS SMALL

SWEET MORN OF JUDAS' DAY

A MAN IN A MIRROR

UP, INTO THE SINGING MOUNTAIN

CHEZ PAVAN

MR. HAMISH GLEAVE

A FLAME FOR DOUBTING THOMAS

A FEW FLOWERS FOR SHINER

NONE BUT THE LONELY HEART

HOW GREEN WAS MY VALLEY

Juveniles

WARDEN OF THE SMOKE AND BELLS

THE FLAME OF HERCULES

THE WITCH OF MERTHYN

Richard Llewellyn

A Hill of Many Dreams

DOUBLEDAY & COMPANY, INC., GARDEN CITY, NEW YORK, 1974

Library of Congress Cataloging in Publication Data
Llewellyn, Richard.
   A hill of many dreams.

  I. Title.
PZ3.L7714Hi [PR6023.L47]   823'.9'12

ISBN 0-385-03313-3

Library of Congress Catalog Card Number 73–10547

For
SuSu

A HILL OF MANY DREAMS

Paul Denis remembered, though long after, while he talked to Bilara, that he thought he saw the idea in form and substance, opening behind his eyes almost as a blossom of light, standing that noon in hot Israeli sunshine, sniffing pinescent, watching a sunray flinging miles of diamonds in the Mediterranean's blue, praying for strength to do as he dreamed, sure in his soul that he could and in gentlest way ready to laugh aloud up at an eagle flashing gold burnish in black wings. He imagined he felt some of that freedom, a buoyant smart of happiness, or, certainly tingling in his bones, a sense of wonder that far beyond regret, one life was shogged, and another begun.

The surveyor's zigzag of red flags wandering about down there marked the bounds of a property he had yet to walk, and the wide parallels of white rags flapping in noon breeze showed the way of the new road—*his* road!—leading off the Haifa–Nazareth highway, all the way up, among the ruins, round and round the rocks and pinetrees, to the plaza, and on, up, ending at the gates to the heart of his dream.

At farthest peak of the hill highest in all the countryside he wanted to build the house he even now lived in, loved in every detail, patiently collected floor to ceiling down to the smallest item, even the staircase rails, all in moments of rest in tired hours through the years, and now plump for the midwifery of the mason, and the modest art of carpenters, cabinet-makers, ironsmiths, and a caress of the painter, a rap-a-tap-tapping of tilers, the veining artifice of electricians and plumbers, and the silently singing glory of the gardener.

He remembered roughing the black beret over the top of his head, lilting the ebony walking-stick in the middle of the path—the blind suddenly with sight—and slowly, in a sense of luxury, breathing that heavenly pinescent and Mediterranean salt in warm breeze, walking down among the ruins of other time, Ottoman, Crusader, Judean, Phoenician, perhaps even to the reign of David, wondering how many other men had built with the same sense of want, if the same itch had filled those heads—when? But of course it had, or the ruins would not be here, in torn stone, cracked columns, shards of ceramic, glittering glass, all shouting in the voice of other times, building in love. Or why build? A cock bird without a hen? A nid, and no layer? A house, and no woman?

But which woman?

A man can build a house for himself.

How many rooms to wander through, alone?

Since that moment back in New York—was it so long ago? —when she left that note propped against the vase of headless roses, and the words still burned—how do words burn? —how does that drip of acid burn through canvas?—but they did then, did now. You have no time for me and you never said I was necessary. Why did you marry me? All right, so you gave me a lot of things. But things are what I don't want. I'm going with Giorgio. Make up your mind. I want a divorce. It's all cold and gone.

The shock of those first moments still brought the tremor in hands and knees, and still he felt the heat of angry tears, saw the white blaze turning Van Gogh's apple orchard into pale blue waste. What do women want? A man has to work, any time, all the time, travel, go here, go there, talk, persuade, sell, make some money, sell some more. Buy her jewelry, clothes, new furniture. Take her on trips. Buy anything. It should be enough.

But no.

You and your work. Business luncheons, but never dinner at home. Never, in all those years, unless she entertained her friends, and then he had to be on time, or it went on without him. Once, Molly Guggenheim, when he came in late, said she thought it was a shame, poor man, working all hours, and getting a warmed-over meal, and Nelda said, Listen, you mind your business and I'll mind mine. If I say dinner's nine o'clock, I don't mean eleven-thirty. You don't like it, go on home. That was the last of Molly.

Sol rang him next day and said, Look, I was sorry about last night. But when the gals start on the lip, how in hell do you know where it's going to wind up? And he said, You think I was worried? Yesterday, by nine forty-five, I made fifty-five thousand dollars. Think a cold dinner worries me?

But it did. What kind of a woman was that? He began thinking about it after that talk with Sol.

Paul, you're just not living right, he said. What the hell, you earn all kinds of money, you can't get something to eat, your own house? Boy, better not happen to me.

But he loved her. Or did he love the idea of being in love?

You deal in art, the shrink said. She appealed to the esthetic, the sense of beauty in you. She was beautiful, yes. She looked the way a successful man's wife ought. She could wear clothes. Paris, twice a year at least, stock up, wonderful appearance, give him the chokes. Not enough. You and your damned work. He could hear it. She wrote dammed.

No matter. Education gets lost in bed. That was where he missed her. Missed? Hungered, in a god-damned wilderness. Why does one woman matter so much more than a thousand others?

But dear Giorgio got there. That *klutz*. At first he understood he worked for a menswear company, but then *Esquire* did a piece about the string of export outlets he controlled, with color plates and models in monobiks, and cuts of the pad on Sutton Place, and the two Cadillacs, the weekend haunt on Long Island, all the icing on the bun. Nelda swallowed it. Not a month after, she left the note. Giorgio's office gave only a European address, another menswear company, and the detective agency quit after ten days for want of a lead. Nobody knew where she went.

He decided then to do more thinking about himself, and less about others. Before, he never thought about much more than business, and the investment portfolio. He did well enough, and there was no need to worry about the divorce settlement. She was happy with what she had in the bank and her jewelry, and his lawyer said, Leave it that way.

It was the loneliness that hit. Even if she was no companion, and the dinner got burned, well, what the hell, he could go to the club, or the Bull & Bear, or the St. Regis, and have a meal, and then go home to her, warm in bed, and wonderful. She always turned to him, and raised a knee, and the warmth of her, the marvel, drowned any other thought. At those times, deep into her, kissing her breasts, he had a sense that he was blessed among men.

But going back to an empty apartment was something else. He wondered what Giorgio did that he did not. It hurt, kept on hurting. The clipping from a paper out on the Coast, reporting she had married, not Giorgio, but some realtor he never heard of, *that* hurt. Now she *was* gone. Before, there was hope. Now, none.

You live too much in fantasy, the shrink said. The world of art lends itself. It's the world of the image. Imagination. You go on imagining, but you don't worry about anyone else. Especially a wife, waiting at home. She's supposed to be there? Only if she chooses. If she feels she has a place, knows she's needed, wants to wait. But if not? *Not.* Accustom yourself.

But no way to be.

How about sailors and engineers and aircrews? Did they find another type of woman? Was there another breed of woman ready to wait, and willing to accept the duty of being themselves, and faithful? Did some women slip out of the category? Or was the shrink right in saying she resented being treated as a utensil to be racked away until needed? She never said anything. She stayed in bed, and that last morning, when he asked, What's wrong? She turned away from him, and said, Us.

What's that mean? he asked the white back in pale blue satin, and she said, I believe you only want me to die, and suddenly he was so angry the words stayed in the sac of his throat, and he walked across the park in cold rage, repenting on Park Avenue, and sending her roses. That was the morning of the note, and those were the roses she tore the heads off. He never thought of the park after that, except as a place of rage.

The cold life.

You take refuge in your infantilisms, the shrink said. You learned how to sell. You talk well enough in your own line of business. You write a good catalog. But emotionally you rate about ten to twelve years of age, with an IQ of a hundred and thirty. Quite a gap. You try to make a case for yourself. You either misquote to please yourself, or you exaggerate. Protecting the ego.

But for all those years he represented collectors and artists all over the world, and never knew he went anywhere or met anyone. All places were the same. Only people were different.

You never made the effort to find out how to treat *her*, the shrink said. She was only another limb. You used her. Used up part of your energy? Indulged in erotic daydreams? Harem syndrome? Male dominance? Creep into bed, and fuck. Is that all? A hundred years ago, fine. Not today. These times, they take off.

Thoughts, memories, niggling through the hours. Nothing beat off the thoughts. Even two years with the shrink. All right, he got up there by getting his own way. But it was always a fair deal, both sides. After all, they always came back. He was *the* number one. The living artist knew he got a better price. The collector was always happy to double an investment. Artists die, and what they leave behind is unique of its kind. There can never be any more, and so the price goes up. Art is art, and merchandise is only that. Everybody gets a living. Well, all right. Mercenary. But in business, it has to be. It was all for the good of the trade. Publish the prices. Make no secret. Let everybody know where the items went. Most collectors were never less than happy to see prices go all the way up, and their names in print. They liked their friends to know how their investments were paying off. When prices were right, they came to him to sell, and he always knew where to place the items, and on the right terms. Not always the sum the newspapers quoted, but something profitably near, and the new price was basis for the next sale. Although, not always.

Melsom came through the side door that morning with a

large, thick rumple of brown paper underarm, and that, he knew now, was precursor to shambles, catastrophe, any other word meaning disaster, in the soul, spirit, professional sense of rectitude, or honor.

Listen, son, Mr. Blantyre told him, more than thirty years ago in the old gallery, and he heard the gentle voice of that most honorable gentleman now. You must always think ahead. Not just for your sake, but for your client. He's parting with money on your advice. If he finds your advice leads to loss, he'll go elsewhere and you suffer a bruise to your name. It never heals. That moment, you begin to die. Never think of price first. Always think ten years ahead. Is this artist going to command a place in the sales world? Is this piece of paint, this stone, this bronze going up in the market? Is the artist to be trusted? He trusts you with his work? Fine. But can you trust *him?* Is he going to grow? Is he a new Cézanne, Modigliani, Van Gogh? Is he another Picasso? I just got beat to him. It took a couple of others to sell him. But always remember. Picasso was a brilliant draughtsman. He could use a pencil. Before you fool with abstract artists, ask to see what they've done with the pencil. Crayon. Black and white. That's where you find the real craftsman. Most abstracts are rubbish. Patternings. No ideas. Even apes and retarded children'll give you as good. Why should you sell them? Make money? Lose your reputation? This gallery was founded to present the artist to the client. So-o-o-o, long before I make a sale, I think ten years ahead. Is the client going to be happy? May I congratulate myself on good judgment? Is this artist going to mean anything? Is the price compatible with his stature? Shall I be able to say in ten years, Yes, I was right? Will the client thank me for doubling, tripling, his investment? My son, these things you have to keep solidly in mind. Study the catalogs. Attend to the smallest detail. Get to know the artists. Be kind to them. They keep you in business. They are your bread and butter. They have a rough time. Remember it. Always keep that little box in the desk. A twenty-dollar bill can often seem as though the Lord God had interceded. Artists are sensitive people. They are *not* horses. They live on nerves. *And* food. Remember it.

He never forgot. He had an encyclopedic memory. He memorized catalogs and auction lists, prices, artists' and collectors' biographies, the contents of galleries and private collections, and he knew the works of the majority of dead "name" artists from the beginning, and most of the available work of modern artists anywhere, and when Melsom unwrapped that crackle of brown paper, and brought out, one after the other, five portraits in tissue and a plastic envelope, each unmistakably by Giotto, he folded his hands, and sat, elbows on knees, looking at the Rowlandson cartoon above his desk, wondering what Mr. Blantyre might have said.

He knew of no Giotto portrait anywhere. The mental tabulator raced, but beyond Assisi, and so few other places, one or two here and there in the national galleries, none of them simple portraits, he was certain that none existed. The obvious answer? A large painting had been cut. Stolen? One of the Nazi piracies? Or the more recent type of church theft?

He heard Mr. Blantyre say, Check your sources, son. Simply listen. Say nothing. You have time. Make sure. You are the dealer. Your name is in question. Protect it.

Five beautiful Giotto portraits. A collector's dream. A dealer's joy.

Melsom had always seemed one of those friendly visitors to the gallery on first nights, ready to munch a *vol-au-vent*, or raise a glass between the heads of others, a certain deference, a face, a name, a buyer at times of small items, a reputation as stand-in critic for some of the magazines, nothing much, but pleasant, and useful as someone to call to find somebody-or-other, and he always had the somebody, the address, telephone number, and what they had done over the past couple of years, whether artists, collectors, or names in the trade. His information was always accurate in New York, London, Paris, Rome, Madrid, and other places.

The portraits came from Madrid. That had been sighting of the plague.

He sniffed forgery. But forgery is also professional. Who is to tell? Who, after all, *is* the authority? In his own gallery, with more than thirty years' experience under the tutelage of Graeme Blantyre, he was acknowledged to be master in realms he had made intrinsically his own, and they were several. Egyptian, Etruscan, medieval European, Neo-Classicist, Islamic, T'ang, Impressionist, Post-Impressionist, Abstract, and others in between without a label.

But if Nelda had still been at home, in peace and beauty, if he still had a wall behind his back, if she were there to raise that knee, he might have thought a good deal more. He could have said, No.

Honesty? He often asked himself the meaning of the word, or how it applied to what he did day after day. Selling helped the painter, sculptor, printmaker, lithographer, and all the connected trades, giving collectors return for investment, or pleasure in owning. But if the items were forgeries? Who was to tell? If the artists were themselves confounded, who was then the authority?

Giotto? Would he rise from his grave to condemn?

He felt himself in a bare, naked place, where the words

crumbled horribly in the gullet, and silence was sound of witch-moans, and Melsom sat there, looking at him, smiling.

If, but only if, Nelda had been at home he might never have smiled back. But her going seemed to make him unsure, in himself, in work, in expression of will.

But, the shrink said, You went right ahead because of the money. How many times had you done it before? She was never dishonest either with herself or with you. You used her as a shield. She knew nothing about what you did. You were knowingly dishonest. Nobody else. Isn't that why you hated her? Wasn't it easier than looking yourself in the eye, and having to confess? Isn't it why you stopped shaving yourself and went to a barber? You had to look at yourself when you shaved. Did you like what you saw? Could you live with yourself?

You, of proudest name and reputation—or so you imagined—throwing away all you had so carefully built on Mr. Blantyre's work of a lifetime, submitting to deals you knew to be, at best, barely honest? If they were honest at all, from the beginning? Or was honest the wrong word?

You never dared go near the auction rooms on some days, the shrink said. You knew there would be eyes, and knowledge sharp as yours. Let the word go out later. Private transaction. Bar gossip, café chatter, and each mind taking note of prices, and commissions, all the smiles in the darker spectrum of avarice, all the voices adulant with envy, attitudes fawning or offensively familiar, some, and yes, too many, bland, suspicious, crafty.

The word was going around. He could feel it on his skin. He knew the trade.

Like those sudden clouds of midges in Central Park, touching face, hands, the sly, undefined, that stung, itchingly, almost frightening, evading the clouting newspaper, sometimes making him run, always springing the sweat.

Every morning, the walk across the park, a quarter past eight, to the gallery on Fifty-seventh, and coffee waiting in the office. Sit down in the big chair to enjoy the news-paper till Bilara brought in the mail. Every morning for years, except when he was out of town. It was always a pleasure to get back. It was a pleasure to go away to get back. The big chair, safety, silence, and the brother-hood of art.

That's what you have to think about, Mr. Blantyre said. Brotherhood. If you can't find it in you to put your arm, let's say, figuratively, about an artist to protect him, you shouldn't be here. Go and find a bazaar. Sell shoes. Snake-bite cure. Wart remover. It's more your line. A gallery is where the artist comes to blossom. Blossoming is a long process. It's painful. Be respectful. Never dare patronize. That's for the ignorant. Remember, there *are* shits in this business. Don't go anywhere near them. Be warned by your nose. A spiritual sense of smell is all you require to train. Once you have that, you may safely trade in the sacred world of true art. It's sacred because it's the gift of few. It's true because you'll recognize it as right from left, or red from green. And always be careful to say "art." Not ever "awt." *Art.* Awt is like *orto.* That's an Italian orchard. Everything's grown in nightsoil. Nothing to do with the magic of the mind, the wondrous movement of the hand, the glory of invented color. You are the guardian. Keeper of the gate. Re*mem*ber.

And he sat there, smiling at Melsom's smile.

Five beautiful Giotto portraits. It was said that Melsom had been attached to the Fine Arts Commission with the Army in Italy, and on up, through Europe, and he knew, it was also said, as much about the museums and galleries as any of their curators, and from experience, his contacts were sharp worldwide, especially in Japan and the United

States. Old friends can make a little money together and still retain a patina of honesty.

Or what was honesty?

Anyway, there was little sense in any enquiry about the original owner. I have a lot more, Melsom said, in that smile. Same class. All sorts of works turn up. Nobody knows why, or where they come from. If they're right, they'll always find the right buyer. You know them better than anyone else. That's why I'm here.

One call was all, and a bottle of champagne in the office sealed the deal. Nobody, not even Melsom, knew the name of the buyer, and the price went fifty-fifty between them, and when he accepted the check, he presented the new owner with a red morocco folio holding a thick wad of parchment and paper documents, dated through the years, all supporting the origin, ownership, and authenticity of the portraits, some, painted by the master, with detail left to his apprentices, and others sketched, and filled in by students, with finishing touches by the master, and the entire bundle, so far as he was concerned, nothing less than a triumph of merciless fraud.

Why had he violated his principles? Why had he permitted nothing less than rape? Why had Mr. Blantyre not raised his voice? And Melsom said, Please be yourself. You're a dealer. I have a private collector. He doesn't want to appear. Cézanne, Picasso, Braque, Seurat. Listen, I'll have them here by a Brink's truck. Monday. You go through the file. Find a buyer. There's more.

Every word stamped in the brain, remembered in shame.

Abstract? Whose opinion counts? Who constitutes himself an authority except by assent of his peers, and acknowledgment by the painters? Because someone able to hold a pen puts himself into the column of a newspaper or a magazine, is he automatically an authority? But they have the readers. The more generous the verbal rubbish, and the less understandable, the more sought-after. The more arcane, the more gratefully the hangers-on pander. They mouth the language, use the terms, revelling in what seems new to say in a language grown sour with misuse, frowzy with cocktail haze and the fagends of trade gossip.

Probably if Nelda had still been at home in peace and beauty, never mind if the dinner burned, or just was not there—he often wondered how a dinner gets burned unless somebody turns up the gas deliberately after the cook left everything on the warmer—just possibly the Melsom deals might not have happened, and certainly would never have led to the others. But it seemed now to have been like a peat fire. The burn went on underneath and out of sight, and nothing to tell, except for a little smoke, a whiff of scent. That was how the deals went, easy as that, a little smoke, at times a whiff. The canvases came in, they went on the easel, a glass of something-or-other, the buyer nodded, listened to the talk, read the documents, wrote a check, and that was another deal.

It was all business. The buyers were satisfied. Prices were almost absurd, but nobody seemed to mind. The more they were asked to pay, the better they liked it, the sooner the deals were made, generally in private, nearly always with a lawyer, or a proxy, and the more wonderful that ensuing calm, perhaps, prayerfully, meaning safety.

That was where silence held the jewels of omnipotence, and the deal followed without further discussion, except the small talk over sherry about this and that.

Madrid on the line, Bilara said, that morning.

She filled the doorway, big, a slim heavyweight, in black always, black as herself, collars and cuffs starched white, a tiny voice, a child's, Alabama in every syllable, heart as big as herself, and a brain and hard commonsense to match. She knew the plays, saw them ahead, told him, or took precautions on her own, and she detested Melsom from the moment she saw him.

He could never get her to say why. Curious girl, Bilara. But those eyes, that seemed as if they had no whites, looked through people, through and all the way out, and she had never been wrong. That cat saw the mouse in any piece of fur, and said so in her own way, generally with the big eyes. No woman ever spoke plainer with the eyes. That sidelong, unblinking black stare transfixed the victim, made him itch without knowing why, pushed him to get out, go, even against his will. It happened that morning of the Madrid call.

Contessa de Zarapeda, in Bilara's painstaking letter-by-letter take-down. Those were minutes he barely remembered, except that a collection of El Greco was offered to him by somebody he never heard of. Recommended by someone else.

It is the Reid Gallery? a woman's languid voice said, that seemed not to worry if it was tonight, tomorrow, or never. I expect to be in New York tonight at seven. I am at the Waldorf. Please, you see me at nine o'clock? I have no time.

But he was in Boston that night, and Bilara made an appointment for ten o'clock the next day at the gallery. By good fortune he had one of the best exhibitions in years of American painters, and even though it was only coffee-time, the place was crowded.

She came in, little-finger thin, flaunting a grey suit designed and cut only for her, patent leather pumps, white shirt, bluish make-up over the eyelids, hair in a bun crowned by a matador's cap, luminescently patrician, instantly hailed in the crowd's silence.

He invited her to the office, and while Bilara brought the champagne, he looked through the papers, customs documents, receipts, all in order, for ten canvases, certified by the curators at Madrid's El Prado, property of a nobleman, Quiepo de Zarapeda, in the province of Málaga, part of his patrimony, and free of all dues. He looked at the photographs, thought for moments, and chose a name, excused himself, and went to the private telephone in the corner of Bilara's office.

The Name knew the market. Bilara made an appointment for just before midday, and in those minutes he knew he must have this woman for wife. She had the beauty, the withdrawn quality of the *aristo* which he wanted to worship, and the glory of some other time was in her, that he always felt when looking at old masters, names, canvases, streaming through the mind, but only as vital field for thought of *her*, in desperation torturing his estimate of himself to find any facet that might appeal to her. She must have met a thousand handsome men of her own kind. She might be married, or engaged. Blood spurted in his mind, thinking. Blood, that he felt. His brain, the thinking part, became tired, and in a void, a dark night, he was aware that nothing mattered. The struggle came to nothing. You had to be born at the right time. Luck had to be with you. Not part-time, because disappointment, ashes, lay there.

He poured a small cognac from the corner bar, felt it burn in a gulp, but it seemed to disperse thought into another kind of despair. Nothing stood in his favor. A gallery, a name in the art world, a respectable fortune, fair health, all these were little to inspire feeling in that sort of woman.

He saw her along the east wall of the general room, jacket open, fist on hip, resting on the right foot and the heel of the left shoe, looking at a Wyeth, and he wanted to kiss all the way up that leg and down the other, and she turned, seeing him, and smiled, pivoting on the heel, walking between people, toward him. He caught no more than a taunt of perfume, and gestured toward the office.

Bilara, talking on the telephone, nodded him over.

Somebody in George Glosworth's insurance office wanted to know about this new consignment, and was it to be stored in the gallery strongroom, and they should have been told, because extant premiums were no cover.

Just a moment, he said. What consignment?

Why, these El Grecos, Mr. Denis. This is millions.

Who told you about them?

It's in the *Times*, sir. You didn't see it?

I didn't even see the El Grecos. No consignment of any sort's going to be stored here. Understand? Ask Mr. Glosworth to get in touch. He's been listening to gossip.

He cracked the receiver down in fury.

Look, he said to her, pointing to the telephone. How does the *Times* know about this deal?

She sat, one knee over the other, beautifully herself, enormous smiling brown eyes, small teats, and opened hands, beautiful as any by Phidias, pink-nailed.

I have many friends, she said, in that languid voice. At the Embassy. Many people last night.

Where are the canvases now?

They are in the Customs. They will be here tomorrow, and God, the languor, the dancing foot, crossed knees, pressure in thighs, a sweet of warmth denied.

I don't want them here. I'll tell you where they'll go in about ten minutes. Ever hear of insurance? Just throwing money away. You want to deal with me? You want to do as I say? Got somebody else in mind?

Again that opening of the hands, a *femme* Bodhisattva, if there was such a thing, a brilliance of dark eyes in cursory sweep of the office, including him, with the furniture, the pictures, and Bilara in the doorway.

I come to you. I think you are the best. I listen to you. I speak with this man. He wants, or he does not. You find somebody else. Or I go to Texas. I have many friends.

The voice reminded him of taking the pit out of a nectarine. Something tender, sweet to the palate, glory of another time, a newer year.

Could I ask you if you'd have lunch with me?

Again the hands' slow ballet.

I would like to have lunch, thank you. But I prefer the hamburger. Just the hamburger. Underdone. Nothing, the onions, the tomato. Potatoes. Nothing. Hamburger. *Real*. It is so *good*.

The gentle voice, but sure as the seasons. An air about her of the ages. He wanted to kiss her feet, to throw off a horror of embarrassment.

Right, he said. I know where they have *the* hamburger. Undressed. No trim. Mustard?

Oh, yes. English mustard. *One* piece of toast. A glass of claret.

Don't you eat in Spain?

Ah, yes. Too much. I prefer *ham*burger. In New York, only the *ham*burger.

Franks?

Widened mouth, shaken head, closed eyes.

Franks, it's sausage? No. *Ham*burger, it's all. So good.

Are you the daughter of the seller?

I am the granddaughter. You have the Consul-General's

certificate, and also the Ambassador is a friend of my family. If it is necessary, they come here.

No need. If you'll let me, I'll get on to Customs and see if we can go out there this afternoon and see them. Instead of bringing them here. Save time and a lot of paper. Do you know anything about these pictures?

I have known them since I was a little girl. We sell to pay tax. They are only a part. Small importance. But it hurts to sell. Today, necessary. They are in my family nearly three hundred years. The same room. When they go, my grand-father cry. For the spaces.

That was about all he remembered. Bilara's dead stare from the doorway made a thistle-bed of his neck. He wanted to talk to her, ask why.

But the Name came in before time, looked over the papers, made notes, phoned his office, and the three went to Rusty's for a hamburger, she going with the Name, he by cab, after having to supervise a couple of sales, and then unable to go out to Customs because of Jonathan Cole's sudden arrival, and an offer of the Cole collection entire, probably the finest private collection of Etruscan art any-where.

I'm going to die pretty soon, Jonathan said, whisky-unctuous, leaning on the umbrella, underlipping the grey mustache. Had a couple of heart-attacks. That clutch was never much more than a 'surance set-up. I paid for them all over again in premiums. I want to sell. Go around the world. Hell with it. All you can do is look at the goddam things. Let somebody else. Any idea what's the price? Less capital gains?

Outright sale, let's say, overnight? Or hang on for an auction, here or London? Three, four months maybe?

Outright, overnight. I just want the cabbage. I don't have

long to use it. Throw it around. Ever think of it? Who gets to throw it around any more? We had a rotten life. My father. His father. They did everything. I was never able to. Never. Hanging on. Paying this. Paying that. Just to keep the goddam place together. Now I want to throw it around. Just find out how it feels. Get the best you can. Anything over two hundred thousand.

Well, now, that's selling just a little short. Leave it to me?

Bilara took the nod and went to the bar, and Jonathan put the umbrella on his shoulder, sword-style, tipping his hat to the front.

Not only leave it. I left it. I want the hell out. Throw it around. Don't have that long. This for me? You have to be a Southerner, ma'am. Your 'nif'cent health.

Bilara gave him the tumbler and a napkin, and held out the platter.

Great, Jonathan said, and drank, and put a biscuit in his mouth, entire, crunched, chewed.

Bilara. You get bigger every time I see you, baby.

I'm eating good, Mr. Jonathan. Let me take you to the door. Get you a cab.

That's only the beginning, Melsom said, looking at the El Greco check, that night. I have a friend. He doesn't want publicity. He has a superb wall of Manet, Renoir, and Picasso. Sixteen in all. At his house, East Seventy-seventh. When could you go? Tonight? After nine?

Melsom seemed to take command from that moment. Not that he *did*. The cosily deferential manner rarely eroded except in squirmy laughter. He always said *Mister* Denis. *Please*. I leave the whole thing to you.

And the deals went on, the prices were out in space, unpublicized, and nobody seemed to mind. Living artists were happy with the money. That was all-important. Buyers accepted prices seemingly beyond reason because they had a chance to counter taxes, saving in added value against whatever mulct might be in the future. The more they were asked to pay, the better they appeared to like it.

Nobody wanted to know. Nobody needed to.

That feeling of being on the verge of fraud had never before been corrosive, though gradually, through the weeks, months, it softened, passed.

Jumping the heap of rocks at the end of the patio, and picking a way through the rubble across the Plaza-to-be, he felt again that elation of the ride to the sixteenth floor, walking through Waldorf silence toward her suite, with a box of orchids, and wanting to sing. Her maid let him in, tiny, in grey, thin legs, bandy, streamers down her back, and La Contessa clasped her hands over the orchids, waved at the suitcases, and said she had been called back to Madrid, and when would the check be cleared?

No later than tomorrow morning, he said, feeling a gangrene eating through his system. Why so soon?

Again the beauty of her hands.

My grandfather is old, she said. He is sad with this sale, but overjoyful with the price. He wants me there. I must go. I shall mix for us a champagne cocktail. You have been so kind. Stay with me for dinner, please. I feel you are lonely?

Champagne cocktails, orchids, hamburgers on silver, a wonderful Cheval Blanc, and he felt no surprise to see her, naked, in the doorway, another "La Primavera" but of her own time, and of an alabaster beauty long past any words.

Of the night hours, little memory except wonder, and newer experience, unknown before, whispers, those hands, a tongue, a Canova torso, and next morning, a kiss at Kennedy, and a blear fog of loneliness turning back for the city. My dolling—my tender one—you are so kind. *Querido!* A curious word. From her mouth, a benediction.

In the office, Bilara brought coffee and the mail, and that look, and he asked her what was wrong.

She phoney as a three-dollar diamond, Bilara said, pouring. I'm glad she's gone.

Tell me your reason.

It's not a reason. I feel it down *here*. Way *you* look at a canvas, and you *know*. That's all I have to do. And *I* know. She just don't have no signature. She Times Square sidewalk. Before they cleaned up.

Ah, now, Bilara.

It's all right. It's all right. You asked.

Why not say it before?

Mr. Paul, there's a big sale going through. I know the size. I worked here long enough to know I just couldn't work anyplace else. That's the gospel truth. So I kept my big mouth shut. Else I could lose what I have. I wouldn't trade what I'm doing here for any wife of Solomon. If you told me to go, I don't believe I could live.

Purest, shaken passion in the voice, and he stood, and went to her, but she turned only slightly from the touch of his hand on her back, and he raised it as if burned.

Bilara, he said, into her nape. You think I want to come here and see somebody else with the mail, drink somebody else's coffee? Think anybody else can take care of things the way you do? Think so? Bilara, let me tell you *now*. I *don't*. And remember this. I never quarrel with anybody's cold opinion if I know them to be honest. That's what you are. Honest. And listen to me. We're colleagues. You work for me, but we work together. If you feel that sort of radar thing, you ought to tell me. Will you?

She nodded, and the cold air brought in the first clients

of the day, and she went to her desk, and watching her
walk, he felt, without being able to find any good reason,
that some sort of milestone had been passed. He never
forgot that slightest turn of the shoulder to fend unwanted
touch. He compared it in flash of thought with the Contessa, whitely, unasked, naked, in the doorway.

He considered that the Hill's main building should be on
the shade side of the Plaza, a block of masonry in solid
stone, no decoration, with all the windows out of the sun,
and this side, only slits, with bronze grilles deflecting sunlight upwards on the ceilings inside, and a double bronze
door at the southern end, always in shadow. He had to find
somebody capable of moulding and casting in bronze, because the pedestal for the marble Aphrodite, and her fountain, must be of one style and metal to match the doors.

He always had that feeling, as if an ESP center worked
inside his head, that something, somewhere, was wrong, but
never certain where. Walking across the park in the mornings, and going on through to Fifth Avenue, and turning
right, he never forgot the midges that seemed to get less,
and then none, and he knew that somewhere, something
was out of tune. So far as he was concerned everything went
well. Melsom came in a few times a month, nearly always
with excellent profit, and only the best of the market, names
at the top, no disagreeable doubts, and with each sale confidence firmed, because the works took proper place, were
demonstrably themselves, without argument or any breath
of misgiving.

But still Bilara went in the back room when Melsom came
in, and sent Sam with the drinks or the coffee.

Madrid on the line, Mr. Paul, she said, that morning,

in some curious sort of mumble, running the words into each other as if she were pushing them out against her will. It's that Melsom guy. It's urgent.

He remembered talking with what could have been a climbing rat in the stomach, but Melsom's excitement convinced, and he felt he had been unjust for too long.

Two wonderful Goyas, a Velázquez, and a small Titian from a private collector, Melsom bellowed. All papers in order, inspected, packed, and ready for flight.

In the next room, on the other line, Bilara took shorthand notes of the details, and while he listened, three names presented themselves as buyers. Melsom said he had a possible further deal in Paris, but a cable to Miguel de Llano at the Bank of Spain, Madrid, would put the consignment on its way, with insurance from the time it left the vaults till arrival in Customs at Kennedy.

Mr. Paul, Bilara said. Won't this kind of a deal want clearance from the arts committee? He don't mention it. Did I ought to call Mr. Martinez at the Embassy?

Ah, now, Bilara. Please. That's booting a beehive. If the papers are in order, and the Bank of Spain's in on the deal, why start looking for bugs? Once they're here, we're set. Rest is their responsibility. Not so?

You know best, Mr. Paul.

You don't like it?

No, *sir*.

Tell me why?

It's all down *here*. I don't *know* why. Just I don't like who's in it.

Mr. Melsom? He's done a lot for the gallery.

Yeah? I wonder why. Doing fine without him.

That was true. Not long after, he met Walter Sedrow, owner of a print shop in San Francisco, and over a drink in

the King Cole bar, he said that Melsom had asked for a catalog and photographs of the Breughels.

Oh yes, Walter said, and put down his glass. Know anything about him?

Only that he writes here and there. Knows a lot of people.
Most, I'd say, of the private collectors.

Walter looked across at the regal King Cole panels, nodding, an owl in transparent horn-rims.

Ever find out who they are? he asked.

I know most of them.

Reputable?

Certainly. Why?

Well, now, look. I don't want to say too much. But I'm a
Blantyre boy, too. It's why I'm talking to you. Except he
put me in prints, God love his memory.

I'll drink to that.

So-oooo? Remember his way? So-oooo? I had a funny
kind of a run-around. A collection of Currier and Ives prints.
Complete. Mint. Signed. Originals. Well. As you know,
that's once in a lifetime, and I sold to a top collector I'd
known the past twenty years. The price? Jesus, it'd break
Mr. Blantyre's heart. Even then. Anyway, the years pass.
I get an offer from Paris, it's the same set. So I phone the
man I sold it to, and he tells me he sold it years ago at a
pretty nice profit. He gives me the name and address of an
attorney in Quebec, so I call him. Sure, he arranged the sale,
but he can't name his client. Unethical. So-oooo? I had business in London, and I flew on to Paris. It was the same
set, in the same condition, mint. And worth five times as
much. I put in a couple of calls over here, and made a beautiful deal. But the teller's stamp wasn't dry on that check,
and the buyer gets a call from this guy Melsom offering to
buy at twice the price. *Twice*. How *about* that?

Sale's private? How could he know?

I never even called my office. How *could* he know?

Who was the buyer?

Don't jump the gun, son. So the set gets sold again. Behind the scenes I get the bank to give me details of the buyer's check. It's through an industrial complex right here in New York. Owned by a Japanese electronics outfit on Taiwan. You couldn't unknit that, bankwise, in two lifetimes. I figured some Japanese wanted Currier and Ives with his saki, and forgot it, till just over a year ago. Then some guy phones me from Honolulu, and says he has a set of Currier and Ives. Cut a long story, it's the same set. Plus two hundred-and-a-few-more lovely silks and prints, Tao-Chi, all that. I mean, just glorious. I called in a Chinese colleague. I have to learn, too. *He* said it's plain theft. I said, Hell you mean? He says, It's a steal. So I said, From who? He says the big collections got robbed in the time of the Japanese occupation of China. It's just beginning to surface. No doubt about the worth of these. Just gold. But if they got stolen, they got a curse on them. I wouldn't touch them, he says. Well, I can't afford to run a business that way. I sold, no pangs, everybody happy. And one morning, Melsom shows up. He wants info for an article on the Tao-Chi stuff. I said, Who told you? And he said, Well. You know. I go to a lot of parties. Word gets around. Anyway, I saw no harm in it. Lots of people like to see their names in art mags. I phoned around, got him appointments. Suddenly, my lawyer phones. He always draws the contracts when it's necessary. He says, What's this I hear, somebody called Melsom bought most of the items in two-eight-three—that's the bill of sale to me—and I don't get a piece? I said, This is the first I know. So I did some phoning. It's a fact. Melsom bought through an attorney in

Portland. Pretty near twice the price. Does he have that kind of money?

He could be a front, he said, feeling an almost steam-heat cold all the way down, sweating and freezing together.

Let me give you a tip, Walter said. Any enquiry about money winds up in Switzerland. That's where you bog down. Who's behind him? Whoever it is, they're making a nice piece of kale. We don't mention the mafiosi, do we?

I see no reason why we have to.

No? Listen. How do you provide somebody with a bundle? Suppose one of my *capitanos* needs cash. Lots of it. I come in here. I buy a few of these. I give them to my capitano, he sells back to you or somebody else, and *he's* got the bundle. Above board. Honest transaction. Art? Great business.

You have some nasty questions to answer.

Think they're not available? Think these deals are off the cuff? Study a little, son. Study a little. You're on the broiler.

I'm happy enough to say I'm not. Melsom's no more than a go-between.

Go-between is so goddam right. With his kind of right-on tech', who wouldn't want to be? He *knows* everybody. Right out of the public eye? How? How did he get that kind of connection? I've been in this business pretty near forty years. I was trained by the best man in the profession, but I still don't have that kind of a finger. Do you?

No.

How about another drink?

I'm miserable enough.

You said it for *me*.

Did you sell the Currier and Ives?

Sure. And all the other stuff. It's why I'm here. Some of

the prints went to Paris and London. Rome, Athens, a few.
Most went to Osaka. They'll be back, baby. When somebody else wants a bundle, they'll be back. That's fifteen-
twenty-thirty percent for us? Or whoever. Only good thing
about it. What do you *know* about Melsom?

Too little. Unfortunately.

I believe you have the answer. Who's behind him?

I resent you should ask. I should have asked a long time
ago. I don't know. The deals come out of what? Oblivion?

There's got to be a hell of a lot of money in oblivion.

I'm glad we talked.

I'm a Blantyre boy. Listen. What's he doing, operating
out of Madrid?

You probably have the answer. I have enough to think
about.

Madrid was not the only center of sale. Places in France,
Belgium, Holland, Luxembourg, Switzerland, Lebanon,
Denmark, and Norway went in the books on Melsom's introduction, and in every case, a sale, no fuss, all well, commissions high, life normal except lonely, and even Bilara
seemed in better mood. But he never heard from La Contessa, and both his letters went unanswered. He often
wondered, and thought of her, until she became something
like remembered poetry in a lost book, and Effie sent
around her best girls now and again, and he got by, if
living had something scraggy about it, a stench of stale
meat just beyond a sniff, the morning's coffee grounds remembered, an odor of the unbathed, and long-cooked cabbage in forgotten soup kitchens.

He stood at the top of the path from the Plaza-to-be,
winding between olives, pine, azalea, and rhododendron,
down to the road, in mind's eye seeing new, blue tarmac

coming up to the space for the car park, and a broad stone stairway curving the rest of the way. No cars, buses, or trucks in the center. That was a rule. No noise, no smells. All chimneys properly designed, especially the restaurant's. No smoke. No coal, no wood. Electrical power from a duplicate unit, so that if one broke down, the other would function immediately.

How? Arye Aron, the co-architect asked him. Mind telling me? If main power breaks down, where's the power coming *from*?

Store it, of course.

Going to cost money, Arye said, tipping a green pencil, point to eraser, point to eraser.

Stop fooling with that thing, he said. Plan as I tell you. When's the maquette going to be ready?

We have a team of girls working on it. They're pretty good. Probably ready this coming week.

Look, Arye. I don't want to throw you and Miko out. But I *do* want to hear some bells ringing. I'm getting sick and tired of nothing. This is months going by, and what?

He knew he was being unjust—even cruel—from the lowering sorrow in Arye's eyes, the distant access of pain in that so-sensitive face, the nervous hands, uneasy moves of the body.

Don't give up, Arye, he said, and dropped a hand on the shoulder. Everything takes time. Everything isn't patient. Only we—only us—the humans, we have to be patient. Nothing else has it. Only we have patience. And hope. Who else prays?

Arye looked up with those eyes, lost pools, blue.

You believe, Mr. Denis? *You* pray?

Why else am I here? What *keeps* me here? I have a prayer. Of course. I have a dream. I need help. Where do

I get it? From people like you? *You* give help? Even to yourselves? You need more help than anybody. So where should *I* look? Help is *where* you pray. You have to wait till it's ready.

But waiting tore at the days, and patience seemed to stamp its feet, and yet a morning came when parcels delivery brought the maquette, a wonderful architect's model, and for the first time he saw the dream in miniature, not in a succession of maps and blueprints, but solidly in one place, where he could imagine himself an inch high, looking up at a marvel of buildings, all of them the white flowers of his mind grown in the fertile imagination of others, and now, perched on and around the hill as he had dreamed.

A team of good-looking girls put the segments together, and a few took palettes and paint boxes outside to copy the area's colors, and others planted sponge-rubber trees, so that by lunchtime he saw the entire scheme as it might look at the end of a telescope, and he felt as an emperor.

Give these girls a month's pay extra, he told Arye. It's a great job. When do we start construction?

Arye laughed outright up at the temporary roof, for once sounding human, carefree.

You're impatient, he said, and nodded at the girls. *They* can tell you what we've been through. I'd say, if Miko can get the permits signed today or tomorrow, we'll be stockpiling material by the weekend. It's all ready. But they won't shift a truck till the paper's right.

Nearly a year? What the hell do they do? Hibernate?

You're lucky. Only reason you're getting it this soon is the place itself. No good for agriculture or housing or anything else. Except this idea. Which we all like. We got real fond of it. Seems a good place to tell you a few of the girls want to join. Ora, Tikva, and Shulamit'd like to weave tapestry. Laila and Miriam have the secret for dyes. Or Laila's father has. Genia and Moura want to design jewelry. Not that wire-hippie stuff. Lots of them want to quit and live here.

Great. But they know they'll have to compete? I want only the best, or most promising. And only one of a kind, or a partnership. Weavers, or glass-blowers, or metal-workers—whatever—no more than one workshop for each. They'll all have to pass my test.

They've been told. Miko and I'd like a drawing office here. Down the hill. North light.

All right with me. Pick your own location. Let's see a model.

It's there. On the maquette. We build among all the rock. Except for the windows, I doubt you'd pick it out. The water-board inspector said there won't be any trouble about the swimming pools. We can recycle the water. We made a bet we'd never get this far in the time, if you must know. I lost.

Goddam bureaucrats. Never saw them worse than here. What is it, in us? Always screaming about liberty, democracy. Put us behind a desk, we're all czars.

But he had a sense that the idea moved, at last. The dream was becoming real. Turning off the main path, he walked along a track through what he intended would be one of the gardens, and at the end, stood at the wreck of a stone parapet, looking down at two teams of Arab laborers, working toward each other, clearing brush and piling stone, marvelling again that enemies at open war could be got to work, not as prisoners, but as free men sweating a good day of eight hours, and no complaint.

The fragrance of Toni's grilled lamb wafted down from the flat space behind the tents at the end of the Plaza, and he climbed the rocks to reach it, enjoying the colors in dozens of different sorts of wildflowers, making up his mind that they, too, all of them, would have an important part in the new garden among their friends, the guardian rocks.

Toni, the Yiddisher gaucho from Azul, south of Buenos Aires, had been a real find on that first day, even before the main path was cleared. He spoke Yiddish, but little Hebrew, a few words of English, and torrential Castellano, and everybody copied that last, sky-enfolding gesture of despair when he knew the Word was not in him. He worked for years in kibbutzim, and on farms, always moving on, looking for a place that only he could fill, as butcher, grill cook, driver of any machine, and mighty horseman, but everywhere had something wrong. Nobody wanted a grill cook except in the towns, but he liked the stars and quiet. Dietary laws prevented the grilling of many meats unless the blood was out. But this, in his belief, was sacrilege, and he refused to eat, and so starved, holding that cheese, eggs, yoghurt, chicken, turkey, staples of Israeli diet, were for invalids and women, and might have gone back to Argentina, except that he met Arye and got a job as construction-gang cook. Building workers were more lax in religious matters, for the most part, and he knew butchers and farmers, most Druse or Bedouin, ready to sell cuts of meat or animals, and so the Orthodox brought their own food, or quit, and the secular were given meals of crisp bread, perfectly grilled meat, and dry red wine, everybody glossy, and in return, Arye said, he and Miko had the best construction team in the land.

Climbing, thinking, he had a pleasant feeling of being with intelligent people of good heart and mind, young, alight with dreams viable as his own, wonderfully in love with the many decencies of working in harmony of spirit with their brothers and sisters, for the moment content with little, but in constant reach for richest harvest, now, or when reward was due.

Still the thoughts niggled, so many midges, and clout though he might, they were always there, and he knew he must face that onset, break through, cleanse his mind, as the shrink said, Once you can get it straight, see it for what it is, call it what you want, serious misjudgment, connivance at fraud, anything better or worse, but give yourself a straight answer. Basically you're ashamed, but you don't want to admit it. You won't accept the responsibility of telling yourself, point-blank, that you alone were responsible. Nothing to do with Nelda or anyone else. You cower behind wretched excuses. Why?

Why did you leave New York?

He looked about, in agony, and all that had been so peaceful and friendly before seemed black with threat and ugly in menace, and he put fingers in his ears, and lurched up the path toward the smell of grilling meat, and girls' voices, and Toni's song with the horsehide drum, and surcease, in companionship and the nearness of cleanly bodies, innocence, beauty, the creative, and, please God, the undefiled.

Yes.

Above all.

The undefiled.

Three huge bowls, three yard-wide circles, on the curving stone stair going down to the dye lab, one marine blue, one cornflower, and one violet, above a lower stair, with the same size bowls of primrose yellow, a brilliant Jaffa orange, and a pink, and down below, a bright scarlet, a deep rose red, and a wonderful turquoise, and he stepped between them, following Miriam, leading him down to the looms on the ground floor between round copper lakes of every color, little dishes of in-between colors, all the trials, the plates of experiments in many greens, and hanks of yarn drying in sunshine, dripping tones of mauve.

You have some beautiful colors, he said. Is this Laila or you?

Laila's father was chief laboratorian with the Polski aniline dye corporation, outside Lodz, Miriam said. He'll be back from his other job this afternoon. Her mother's cooking for us. That saves us a pair of hands. But we didn't get too much done. If you don't think we're doing enough, or not showing results, you could tell us to go. That's a worry.

I'll hold you to my heart, he said. You're doing fine. Anything you want?

We haven't enough lights inside. We'd like lots more lamps. Then we can see.

You'll have them. Today. I like to know people are working right.

Mr. Paul, you don't know. It's so right I think I'm dreaming.

What sort of other job does Laila's father have?

Well, Mr. Paul. We're not making anything here, yet. These powders take time. They cost money we don't have. So he had to take a job. He clerks in a supermarket. Six in the morning till two. Then he starts work here.

I wish he'd come to me first. Or Laila. Or you.

We decided we had enough from you. Credit for rent. And the other things. We don't like to think we're begging.

I'll be goddamned if you are. Tell her father to see me in the office. This afternoon. You've given me a lump in the throat. Shalom.

He went through the little door to the main byway, glad not to be drawn into the please-sit-down-and-eat he knew so well, that time-waster, making him late for the next call, to the left, and Boaz, the sculptor, looking at a slab of rough stone.

I don't know what it is, Mr. Denis, he said, that warm, sore-throat morning. Probably granite. Who cares? I'll cut. I'll hammer. I just want to see what I want. From my own hands and arms. I don't want a machine cutting for me. I want to see what comes out of *me*.

He wondered if any artist ever knew what might come out, in surprise remembering Bilara saying, Yeah. I often thought about that. Just what *does* make it? That's what I'd like to know. What makes *him* a painter, and this guy not? What's between them? This one'll talk paint till the orchards grow candles. But he can't produce. This one don't have the words. He brings in the work. Leaves 'em. But he don't talk. And you don't have to know. He's *good*. He's going to sell.

Artists are modest, Bilara. They know how far they can go. Without help, it's not far. Mr. Blantyre told you. Told me. It's a quality of love, either in the eyes, or the voice, or a little help from the cashbox. You have it. They know it.

I'll help, Mr. Paul. But they sure get the feelings all creased up. I don't know. I don't know what goes. Wish I did.

Well, all right. Tell me.

Why don't we have black painters? Or sculptors?

Oh, but we have. Certainly we have.

When was the last one *we* sold?

They get bought up by their own people, I suppose.

Well. I get around pretty much. I never saw one good one. I sure seen some messes, though.

What brings this up?

Schoolfriend of mine called me. Younger brother wants

to be a painter. Like, well, he's trying, and I said, What's he trying? and she says, Well, he paints nights, and he don't want a regular job. He wants to be a painter. I told her, Either he *is* now, or he's never going to be, and she says, That's the easy out. Why don't you come around and see them? So I dragged all the way over, past Lenox, and it was like I say. It's terrible for a grown-up to kid around. I had to say it. *I* couldn't help. Either *there*, or here. I'd never want you to hear what they called me. I thought I was going to get beat up.

It's difficult. I've never been faced with it.

We don't have black collectors?

We may have. But we may not know them. There *are* other galleries.

I think we have something missing someplace. Isn't a no-privilege situation. The whites come off of farms and out of back alleys. *They* make it. Why can't *we?* Something missing. The hands. The head. Color, maybe we have.

There's also the eye. If they don't have that, color won't do them any good.

And they up to here with *hate*. You should have heard those two. You'd never think it, looking at them. We kind of talked and teased around real nice over the coffee, then they showed me the stuff. You think I was straight Wallace.

Reminds me. How about a little straight coffee?

Coming up, Mr. Paul. Black.

He was a little ashamed that the black artist had never set a trip-wire in his mind.

But it's ridiculous, he heard Mr. Blantyre saying. Art is everywhere. It's part of your job to *look* for it. That means finding the artist. Introducing him. He can't hold a knife and work? Teach him. His talent's his grace. The rest is only salad-dressing. And bargaining.

He called Sam Ravicz, an art supplier and picture framer up on 111th, and talked a little about business, and asked him if black painters ever came in for canvas or paints.

Oh, sure. I wouldn't exactly say I get trampled underfoot. But I get them.

Any of them any good?

Nu. Look. There's no school. No place for them to train. Two guys and a gal, I have some work of theirs in the window right now. Ten dollars, up. If they don't sell inside a month, I buy. I have a nice selection. Nothing to shake the Metropolitan. But remember Van Gogh's sugar bags? How did *he* look, then?

Think you *have* a Van Gogh?

Well. I buy because I like. And I think I know enough to take a chance. Ten dollars, what do I lose? Know something? Word slides around here. I get a lot of black custom. I don't hurt.

Sam, you tell those three I'd like to see them here any Saturday morning, bus fare paid, lunch, perhaps a sale. Any of our people show promise?

Promise, sure. They don't get in the window. But Mr. Denis, I have a gal, works in ceramics. Her designs have a lot of Rouault and Chagall, know what I mean? She *could* break out. I believe she'd interest you. Name's Rivka Shulman. I'd say twenty-two, -three? She's worth a blink, I'd say.

Send her along. Anytime you're around, come on in. Why not bring your selection?

Saturday morning became known as Bilara's hour.

She took them in the back room for coffee, and looked at the work hung on the line, correctly, as any other artist's work was shown, and sometimes she called him, oftener not, but she always bought something, and if she liked it, she bought for a hundred-dollar bill, and if he felt it was worth more, the artist got the rest by Western Union. But that only happened twice, and each time he thought she seemed to glow from inside, a big, kindly lamp looking around for something to shine on.

But that was as far as it got. She sent five of them to a training school twice a week, and four lasted three weeks, and the other went on for the course, but Tullio, the drawing-master, said that was only because of the nude models in the last weeks. The work was negligible.

What's the matter with them? he asked.

They don't want to learn. From us. If you could find some African, you might do better. Whitey boss, they don't like. Anyway, what's the rush?

Rush? I'd just like to find a few black artists, that's all.

Go to Africa. Don't worry about here.

Why not?

When did a revolutionary period ever produce an artist? Which one? How many years later? You have to have pa-trons for artists. What we have is investors. They follow the fashion. What else?

Is this a revolutionary period? What revolution?

Without a guillotine, or a tumbril, or anybody to knit while the heads roll away? Certainly. Revo*lu*tionary. Inci-dentally, *we* have to start getting careful. They'll soon be wearing swastikas.

Ah, now, Tullio. For God's sake.

Look, Mr. Denis. Where I am, I hear more. I see more. I saw it happen before. We didn't take notice then? We're not taking any now? We're comfortable? Don't rock the boat? Don't drop the matzos, they get crumbs? Isn't it so?

Tullio, I wish somebody'd drop you. On your head.

Mr. Paul. I heard it *all* before. Shalom.

The quiet voice unsettled him, made him feel as if a lid had been lifted to let in a breath from the open pit he once saw in a photograph of hundreds of dead flung on top of each other.

Bilara said nothing about her protégés. The meetings on Saturday mornings were small, and then of three or four, and two, and on two Saturdays running, only one, a girl, and Bilara said she would like to train her as an assistant. She had a feeling for it, and she knew a lot from books, and going to lectures, but she was no good with a pencil, except in a shorthand notebook, or anything else but a typewriter, and there, she was another Bilara, and he said, Take her on.

Rivka Shulman was something different, small, almost a little girl, long red hair in two plaits with shoelace ties, soap-clean, no make-up, jeans, and sweaters like sacks, raggedy sneakers, nothing original, little of what he considered to be the essential, the individual, in an artist, never one of a crowd, but one alone, on its own. He looked at her designs and found them labored, copies, nothing he could taste. He told Bilara to give her twenty dollars to buy larger sheets, a couple of brushes, some water-colors, and start working.

Know what she *did?* Bilara said, showing a handful of greenish confetti. She tore it up right in front of me, and *threw* it at me. I *like* it. I'm going to tape it, and the bank's going to give me a new one. Do for somebody *need* it.

Sam Ravicz had no address for her, and it had been weeks since she called in there. He thought she lived in New Jersey, and Bilara said, Sorry, Mr. Paul. That was the only address I didn't get. She was kind of shy. She wouldn't give it, and he said, Let's not worry. She'll be back.

Madrid on the line, Mr. Paul, Bilara said, that morning.

That grey morning, that always made him shudder to think about. It's the principal secretary of the Name. She sound like she swallowed acid.

The Name was called that because he had forbidden his correct name to be used in print, correspondence, or any type of memo. He sometimes called at the gallery after hours to see works, or oftener they were delivered to one of his many offices or apartments for approval, and the check always came from the lawyers, De Ruysker, Heddleshaw, Blain and Jahl, on Wall Street. Since Mr. Blantyre's day there had never been a slip, no sediment, in any deal.

Mr. Denis? the rasp said, man or woman he was unable to judge. I'm speaking from Madrid. Your secretary has the facts. Are you able to fly to Madrid today?

I'm in Chicago tonight. San Francisco three days later.

It could be to your advantage if you postponed those visits.

Impossible.

Very well. When could you make an appointment in New York?

In what matter?

In an enquiry affecting De Ruysker, Heddleshaw, Blain and Jahl. I believe you recognize the name?

I do. What does the enquiry pertain to?

I'm not prepared to discuss the matter over the telephone. If you could possibly reach Madrid tomorrow, it would save time and possibly a good deal of trouble.

That's not my way of doing business. I don't deal in trouble. Understand me. My secretary will deal with whatever appointment you care to make. Clear?

Listen, Denis!—another voice—the Name? You better god-*dam*-well get here—

I don't know you, and I don't talk to people I don't know.

He put the receiver down, staring at the Rowlandson.

All he had ever felt in falsity seemed to perch, and chirp obscenities on a fence somewhere in his mind. Some smart son-of-a-bitch had seen through the forgery in that red morocco folio. That was obvious. Somebody—possibly an El Prado curator—or a dealer—might have looked at the El Greco collection, and sniffed the rot. They were no better, and no worse, than any on the walls of all the galleries he knew. They had been through all the tests, whether chemical, in the laboratory, or electronic under the microscope. In those areas he had been thorough. But thorough or not, he had—no denying it—caught the deathbreath of forgery in the first few moments. Why should others be less sensitive than himself? Why should others, knowing as much, or possibly more than himself, accept a lot of high-sounding nonsense that he, by intuition, knew had been basted together in some extremely clever forger's studio? How was he to defend himself?

Mr. Paul, I wish you quit worrying, Bilara said, in the doorway, that late afternoon. You didn't have no lunch. Man can't work, he don't get something in him. Suppose I go along here, fix you a sandwich? Won't be nobody coming in here, this time of night.

I don't want to eat, Bilara. I should never have touched that deal.

Don't know why not, Mr. Paul. I have a file, their acceptances, the lab tests, and the place out there, y'know, they had the eye in all them microscopes, and that other whatchamacall, the carbon something-or-other. They had all the information *you* had. You *had* to take what the experts said. That's all *they* did. *They* bought. They going to bellyache, why don't *you*? Only, louder. They just giving you trouble. Hand it right back. That guy Melsom in this?

Wouldn't surprise me. Somewhere.

You ever want him back in here?

The words barely on the air, and Melsom came in, a shove at the door, holding the handle as if needing the crutch, the stare, a tasting of lips, all against darkening evening. Presage?

Denis, he whispered, looking into the corner, at a flight of Peter Scott ducks. You heard? What went wrong?

I don't know what you're talking about, Melsom. Pull yourself together. Bilara, do we have a drink for the gentleman?

Melsom felt his way to the leather viewer's bench in the middle of the room, and sat, in a bump, let his overcoat and walking-stick fall, and put hands on knees, staring between his feet.

Knew there was something, he whispered. *Knew* it. Going too good. They been to see you?

His manner, speech, was changed. A vulgarian, he heard Mr. Blantyre say. *Never trust them.*

Nobody's been here I didn't expect, apart from the day's chance clientele, he said, easily. Who are *"they"*?

Police.

Why would the police come here?

That deferential smile, but sidelong, impossibly sly, the depths, with a quirk of the mouth, wider one side, showing the rotten teeth. Hallmark.

The deal, *you* know. Like, the Giottos.

I thought it might be the El Greco. I had a call from Madrid. Anything to say?

Melsom stood, looking down at the overcoat and stick, making no move to pick them up.

Do me one favor, he said, going for the door. Don't give anybody my address.

Just a moment, Paul called. Come back here.

But he seemed to jump in the night, and he was bending to get in a taxi, and the door slammed, and the traffic on Fifty-seventh moved in a speeding barrier.

Bilara put the overcoat and walking-stick in the wardrobe, and came back with a drink on a tray.

What's left, out of *that?* he asked her.

She made that curious clicking sound with her lips, that sometimes seemed thick and yet were not.

Trouble, she said.

What sort?

All kinds, especially for him. *You* can answer the questions. *He* can't.

What makes you say that?

I don't see you leaving your good coat nowhere, Mr. Paul. I can still find you right where you belong.

Bilara, I have to tell you. You're a comfort. Would you run just a couple of fingers more of that mothers' ruin into this glass? I'm feeling a little somnolent around the knees.

I'll be here. Any time. And Mr. Paul?

Yes?

I have his address. Phone numbers. All of them. 'Cluding the ones he never gave me. And the ones called *him. All* of them.

How did you get on to *them?*

Mr. Paul, I have friends got friends. They Con Edison, ITT, and such. Operators. Supervisors. Line crews. Give one number, don't take long get two, three. Any time he call, or any time somebody call him, it's in the book. Book don't go noplace, 'cept here. I have numbers long's my arm. All got a name, *add*ress. And, Mr. Paul, the Name, he's there a dozen times. Him, or somebody else. I have the call, who called, the number, time, date. I don't believe you have one drop of sweat anyplace.

Bilara. What in God's own name would I do without you?

No, Mr. Paul. What would *I* do without *you?* Anything be any use? Not to me.

The week away took any surplus fat he ever had. Worry had never been a mental sauna before. But he sweated in sleep and out, and appetite went at any sight of food, and drink of any sort was sip of a dry mouth. But one morning, he sat with a member of the law firm and a couple of others, and he knew that here, on his own ground, he would fight a cold battle, and win as he might.

The lawyer went page by page through the folio, and Bilara brought in photostats from the files, and one of the lawyer's assistants showed photographic close-ups of hands and faces, and Bilara opened albums of other close-ups of more hands and faces.

I see what this is, the young lawyer said. It's a clash of expert opinion. I can't judge. I just don't know enough about it. Fact is, I don't believe we knew you had this kind of arsenal. I believe we're chasing something we won't catch.

The answer's nearly a thousand years buried, he said. But nobody can say they're not the work of Giotto and his school, studio, whatever you want to call it. Let me give you a little tip. The stronghold, the bastion, of Giotto's work are the panels of St. Francis of Assisi. Yes? Or no? Is it? Are you sure?

Why, certainly. Everybody knows that.

Who's *every*body? Going to bring them into court to testify?

I don't know what you mean.

I'll tell you, Paul said. During World War Two, when the sandbags were still around that church in Assisi, the monks were up there on the scaffolding, repainting the frescoes. They're still Giotto's work? Like hell they are. Is the paint, the plaster, the anything, any part of Giotto? Only, and listen to this, *only* the sanctity, the historical hallow of that chapel maintains the dignity of Giotto's original work. The facts deny. I don't know who started this thing, but you can tell whoever sent you here. I have all the hard evidence I require. Let's see the next move. I want to go home.

I have to tell you, Mr. Denis, I don't see any kind of a case here. Do you have any idea who this guy Melsom is?

Beyond the fact he's been extremely useful in the introduction of clients, no. He seems very well connected. But his private life's a blank. I know he writes art reviews. That's about all.

If only that had been so.

A call, a couple of nights later, brought in Bilara to say that the Name would be there at seven-thirty, and be sure Melsom was on hand.

I didn't get the time to say we didn't have his address. That overcoat and stick, it's still in the wardrobe. This kind of weather, he like to catch cold. I *hope*.

The gallery closed at six, and in the next hour and a half he gave the El Greco file a thorough inspection, but without finding anything out of order, and in fact, contrary to that first impression, he felt a certain confidence that all was well.

But the Name's appearance changed that. Two big men came in with him, standing over by the door, at a glance, hoods.

Denis, you couldn't come to Madrid, so I came here, he said, and took the folio out of a black crocodile briefcase. This man Zarapeda? The Spanish police couldn't find him. The address is false. This Contessa whozis is his granddaughter? So am I. The Spanish Embassy here has no knowledge of the covering letter. Forgery. Likewise the Consul-General's. None of these names ever worked for El

Prado. They're not known. Whole thing's a criminal forgery.
I want my money back.

I shall have to consult my own sources. First, Interpol—

The finger pointed behind to the two figures. Their eyes
held animal points of light. Neither moved.

Don't you want them for friends, Denis? They're part of
an outfit specializing in East River ecology. They clean up.
Laughing. Get it?

I don't succumb to threats.

Think you're going to talk your way out of this? Why, you
dirty Jew crook. You yid *bastard*—

You'll regret that—

Like hell—

The door rattled. The bell rang, went on ringing, and
Bilara hurried to turn the key. The two stood aside.

Three policemen came in, and one in plainclothes, all
black.

Hi, Miss Tancy, the plainclothesman said, looked at the
hoods, and slowly pulled aside his jacket to show the badge.
Well. Joe Calvocori and Mario Stozzi. You all set to go back
to Leavenworth? And you—

He looked at the Name.

I'm Sergeant Mackearn. You know me? Miss Tancy. Is
that tape still running?

Yes, *sir*, Sergeant.

Tape's legal evidence these days, Mackearn said, in a
smile of spendid teeth. Did you know? Now. There some
question of fraud here? Want to file charges? We can all
mosey around to the Sixteenth Precinct—

The Name shook his head.

I believe this bastard cheated on me, Officer. I just want
my money back.

You first of all have to talk to Bernard Melsom, he said.

He introduced this deal, and those papers, there. You saw
them. On those you bought. You could talk to him. I'll start
my own investigation first thing tomorrow morning, but tonight I'll warn Interpol—

I'm not interested. All I want's my money.

You bring that collection here. I'll pay you my commission. The rest you get from Melsom. He was paid by your
check. I don't buy. I'm a dealer. As you know.

Yeah. I do. I'm going to smear your name in shit around
every art dump anyplace I can. You won't do a hell of a
lot of business from now on—

The telephone buzzed.

Grateful if only for respite, he picked up the receiver.
Hullo? Paul? Henri Tameur—

Yes, Henri?

Do you have any idea where our friend Melsom is? I've
been waiting for over a week. I phoned around but nobody's
seen hide nor hair. Is he in Europe?

Could be. When you get hold of him, tell him *I* want
to see him. *Ur*gently. What's wrong?

He left a couple of Renoirs, and some other pieces, and
I have buyers stamping. But I'm getting stuck for insurance.
Place two doors down got burgled last night.

It's entirely his responsibility, not yours. Listen a moment.
Are you sure they're genuine?

Genuine? *Gen*uine? Why?

I'm having the goddamnedest trouble with a recent deal
he brought in here. Did he bring in documentation?

Certainly. *All* certified. No doubt about the authority.
Why?

Did you get in touch with the owners? I mean, the people
Melsom got them from?

No.

That's the biggest mistake I ever made. Can you take a tip?

I most certainly can. Oh, my God. Thanks, Paul. See you.

All right, Mackearn said. Everybody ready? Miss Tancy, if you want, I can see you home.

Be happy about it, Sergeant. But I have around thirty minutes more work here.

Take your time. I'll be back here, let's see, right on the half-hour?

The two went out under the policemen's stare, and at the moment he brought out the checkbook, the folio was thrown across the desk.

All of it, or nothing, the Name said, picking up hat and briefcase.

I'll give you my share of it. Remember, your representative gave that check to Melsom. Not to me. *He* paid *me*. *His* signature's on that check. Not mine.

All or none, the Name said, and went out with Mackearn, behind, shutting the door.

Bilara, you called the Sixteenth Precinct?

Yes, Mr. Paul. I thought a cop around the place might calm things up. Sergeant's a friend of my brother's.

Tape was your idea?

I figured we might as well.

You're a great gal. What's this thirty minutes more work you don't have?

Well, sir, I have a lot of Melsom numbers. One of them might turn up the ace.

All the time, every weary moment in the minutes he listened to Bilara dialling, he heard that voice calling him Jew crook. Yid bastard. Dirty Jew crook. Yid bastard. He wondered why nobody ever said, You Catholic crook. You dirty Presbyterian bastard. Nobody he ever heard of said, You dirty *Chris*tian bastard. The words seemed alien to each other. Why, then, did the noble English language lend itself so supinely to You dirty Jew? Why did English-speakers so foul their mouths? Because their minds were foul? Or had they *been* fouled? By what?

Chom Vissel had put himself out of the first clearance squad by refusing to throw rock in piles. Instead, he chose the largest and lined them, and dry-walled, and built beautiful little funny-shaped, many-sided, all-sorts-of-colored piers and pillars exactly suited to the ground, and friendly to the wildflowers. Paul watched him, that morning, bent-backed, standing away to gauge the effect of granite on basalt, burnt brick and a ruin of marble, and when Moshe, in charge of labor, shouted at him, *he* shouted that Chom had a job of his own, and he would be paid by the office, as chief groundsman, from then on.

He never forgot the look in Chom's eyes, a son come home, a baby picked up, a hand taken in trust.

Arye showed him the plan, marked the areas, and Chom worked as an artist, on his own, deaf to everybody except the girls. They told him about love-seats, and his smile, when the meaning got through the bone, was joy to see, and love-seats began to invite under the gnarliest olives, among the pruned rhododendron, and in the sunshade of cut-back azalea.

Wait till this begins to bloom, Tsahali, running the perfumery, said. If we get just a little luck with the rain. The fertilizer'll all be spread at the end of the week. Watch it all grow. Do you suppose Chom could work with us?

No reason why not. Why?

Where he piles and builds, we can prepare and plant. As

it is now, he only piles the rocks. We have to wait for the cleaners. If we had Chom and a few men, we'd have this top level planted in the next couple of weeks. The Plaza, for example. It'll be a month before they get up there. Chom and a few men to help'd have it all clear in a few days. Look beautiful. And I'd have the flowers I want.

Tell Arye.

No, Mr. Paul. He doesn't like suggestions from us. He's a man. Women have their place. They have nothing to say. The men in this country pray to God every morning to give thanks they weren't born women. You didn't know?

No place for women's lib?

She laughed white teeth at the sun, but without much humor, a touch of bravura, sardonic, a trace of hopelessness, pathos.

I'll see Arye. You tell Chom to pick his men. Start now.

But he was surprised at Arye's eruption.

I soon won't have any au*thor*ity around here, he shouted. Nibble here, nibble there. Who's going to take any notice of me when they can cuddle up to you behind my back?

*No*body cuddles. Remember it. They have a lot of good sense. *Use* it.

He told Miko about it that evening in the planning marquee. The permits were signed, and the first trucks were raising dust down on the new road, bringing in cement for the mixers.

I believe everybody has the same problem, Miko said. I don't know any solution. Sure, women have to find a place. But a man doesn't like to think he's working with a lot of woodlice, eating away at his job.

Ah, now, *Mik*o. *Wood*lice? Why, goddammit, I never met a finer lot of girls. Brainy. Eating away *whose* job? Why didn't Arye think of it? Is that what makes him sore? Getting picked off-base? Let me lay it down right now. This is *my* property and my *one* job. The rest of you are assistants. You and Arye are in charge of construction. There, you take control till I don't like what you're doing, and I can't imagine it. Apart from that, I'll use *all* brain, *all* ability as I think fit. Clear? This man-woman nonsense can go. You don't have the labor force to differentiate. You know it? *Live* with it.

He had a disquieting feeling that Miko was right in one sense. Arye's authority had been eaten into. Tsahali was a smart girl. She knew what sort of answer she might get if she asked him direct. Instead, she talked to Arye's boss, hiding the suggestion under cover of a little gush about the future.

Eve's way.

But?

It worked.

He had to take precautions. Others were smart enough to try the same play. He had to be smart on his side, or he could lose a couple of first-class architects and their entire team. For what? A little purely *femme* blandishment?

Under the straining arms and sweat of Arab workmen, that big hand, cut in the shalom salute of the open palm, settled in the middle of the Plaza, and Yehudit climbed up on the thumb to cover the fingertips with the Israeli flag. Boaz chipped splinters out of the headline, blew them away, passed a hand over the surface, dropped the hammer and chisel, and lifted Yehudit down.

I don't want any gold in those letters, he told Arye. When the sun hits, they'll stand out in light and shadow. That's *all*.

Don't we get an English translation? Ruth, the Londoner, called. I can't read Hebrew. If we get a lot of tourists here, how'll they know what it means?

They can ask, Boaz said, flat. Why English? So important? What did the English ever do for us? Except send my mother a couple of years to some island down there in the Indian Ocean? And how many *thou*sands 'others? Internment camps, they called 'em. What's *Eng*lish? My dad spit every time he heard it. I *hate* them.

They had some hard luck, Miko said. They happened to be holding the bag for the United Nations. Lots of Arabs in there. They hate *us*. We can have a board painted. English, French, Italian, Spanish, Portuguese, Russian, Arabic. All right, Mr. Denis?

All right. And, Boaz. Remember. Art and hate don't go well together. You'll never get anything of beauty out of yourself while you hate. You won't be fully in charge of your talent till you scrape off those hate words, and that scaly feeling. Remember? Scales falling from the eyes? It's a fact. Isn't it? It's in the Book.

I don't believe in no book, Mr. Denis. I believe what I *see*. What I *do*. The Book? All right. Some of them go mad over it? All *right*. It's *their* way. I have *mine*. Room for two of us. Just give me rock and a few tools. I'm happy.

You forget who supplies the place, first, and then the rock. A lot of things have to happen before you get them. Thought of it? English-haters. Arab-haters. Book-haters. Why?

There's a call person-to-person coming in from Sharm-el-Sheikh, Mr. Paul, Leah said, down the hollowing corridor. Any time convenient?

Certainly. Two o'clock. I have to watch the bronze cast. Red-letter day. If I'm not around, and it's Yosef, tell him I want the caravan right back here. I'll live in it till the house is ready. Put a call in to New York for nine o'clock. That's three o'clock our time. Switch both calls to the construction shed.

Chom Vissel and his gang were digging at the plugs of hardbaked clay when he got there, and Catan, long blondish hair and beard wisping in breeze, hands in pockets, watched from a platform over the mould, almost dancing with nerves.

I hope we get our own generator working soon, he said. Just had a ten-minute power cut. I hope it didn't murder the stew. Always something wrong in this country. How often you have cuts in the States?

I heard of one along the entire eastern seaboard, he said. I was in it. Hours, no light. No power. New York blacked.

That's East. That's not the States.

Well, now. If you don't like what we have here, you can go. Just get your goddam tools together, and get the hell out. We can do without you. Understand me?

Ah, now. Mr. Paul. Just a moment.

No moments. You finished here. This is strictly pioneer. We don't have any comparisons. Ever hear these girls complain? I want you out by tomorrow morning, nine o'clock latest. Understand?

He went along to the construction shed, down the passage to Miko's office, and walked through the open door to a meeting of half a dozen.

That guy Catan finished here, he told Miko. I want him out by nine tomorrow. See it's done. Load his stuff on the truck, throw it out where he wants. I don't like bellyache. I don't want to be told this isn't the States. It is no place except what it *is*. We are making it. *We* are. Any bellyache is against *us*. *All* of us. I see people working too hard to put up with that sort of cheap nonsense.

Mr. Paul, he's a considerable name, Miko said, on the hurt, defensive side. Perhaps there's a way to smooth a little, well, you know what I mean? Sort of misunderstanding? I brought him here.

Miko, he said, and perched on the drawing-table. I'm not given to misunderstanding when there's the slightest chance of clear meaning. The next item is *this*. When I give an order, it will be obeyed without just-a-moments, or any delays, or chatter of any kind. Or *you* go. Understand? Finally. Ca*tan*, nine in the morning, *out*. Clear?

How about what he's done? Miko asked. I mean, his *work*.

We don't want *it*, or *him*. Load it, and relieve us. Now let's find ourselves an artist. Too many of that type of *kitschnik* running around. But don't invite anyone else till you consult me. I like to see what I'm buying. That kind makes me sick.

And again Bilara stood in the doorway, barely seen in shadow.

Mr. Paul, you want to talk to this woman? Upstate. Near Albany. Keeps a grocery store. Melsom uses her phone. Lives right near. Half a block.

What about it?

Would you talk to her? I switched through.

This is the Reid Gallery. My name's Paul Denis. Who is this?

Mr. Denis? This is Mrs. Reynolds. I was just talking to somebody in your office? I believe I have to call the police. It's about Mr. Melsom.

What seems to be wrong?

Well, sir. He's rented here the past three years. Off and on. We're neighbors, see, and he don't have a phone, so I take messages and he generally comes in around five o'clock, takes the messages and calls around, do the shopping, and the boy takes it up. He hasn't been in for more than a week. I just looked. No light in the house. I don't like it. Why, he could be sick up there.

How do you know he's there?

Oh, why, he wouldn't go without leaving the keys here. It's my house. But the cleaning woman called me this noon. She says it's the third time she couldn't get in this past ten days. You a friend of his?

I am, yes. Why didn't she tell you this before?

She lives way on the other side. Comes in when they take stuff to the market. She cleans three houses. He's always last. I don't like it. Think I call the police?

I believe you should. Just as an act of good neighborliness.

Well, thank *you*, sir. I'll do that.

And anything happens, would you please give me a call? Any time.

I believe you ought to call Sergeant Mackearn, Bilara, he said. Let him get through. Quicker.

Mr. Paul, Bilara said, that late night. You want to talk to Sergeant Mackearn? On the line.

Paul Denis.

Yes, sir, Mr. Denis. Well, sir. We just got a radio report from a police car up at that place. I can't see just where it is. Reception's real bad. Well, sir. Melsom and a woman, case of suicide. Dead about a week. Squad's going up there, now. There was letters. I'll be through tomorrow morning, anyway. Could I talk to Miss Tancy?

But that vigil was nothing compared to the hours of waiting for the first batch of glass from the new furnace built for Yael and Ayelethe. He looked into the seal at a glowing dull red, and there was little to convince that if the batch was right, the new gallery's first blowing-glass was only a couple of weeks away.

All the girls and everyone else danced in there, and the

Arabs outside waited to see what they had been told by Azma'uta was another miracle. She came up from the Druse village and talked to Leah about a job. She spoke English, French, Arabic, and Hebrew, a girl of the best family, educated at Beirut and Cairo, willing to sweep floors as a start, but hoping to learn office management.

Why office management? he asked Leah. Strange?

Women are treated worse than camels, she said. This girl has a good head on her. She doesn't want to marry. She's had a first-class education. She's a Bachelor. That's rare. She knows if she can learn how to handle an office, the accounts, banking, secretarial, she could run her father's business better than *he* can. From running *his* business to somebody else's, that's a simple step. But a business management company in this country's just what they need. She knows it. Ten years, she could be a number one. Mr. Paul, I wish I could take her on. She can deal with a lot of things I can't. I don't have the Arabic. But I'll train her. Only, you'll have to talk to her Daddy.

The glass poured beautifully, from all the seals, down the runnels to the pots, and Yael and Ayelethe put the blow-rods in, and made all sorts of little shapes, and gave them to the girls, and the Arabs, and Toni called them to the grill, and Ayelethe gave him a little horse in golden glass, but with a white mane, socks, and tail, and he looked away from her, saying nothing, holding the horse to his heart. But she got the best cut of the shoulder of lamb, and the only tumbler in the place for her wine.

They had a glass each, Sergeant Mackearn said, that morning. Don't know what was in them, yet. But they both got all twisted up. They like you to go up to identify this man, Melsom. Sometime today?

I couldn't do that, Sergeant. I haven't the nerve. Just have *not*.

Sergeant Mackearn's eyes made somber work of distance.

Mr. Denis, I have to give you the best advice I can. Either go up there, or somebody get here with a warrant. What time convenient for the car?

Trying to close mental eyes and memory together at Melsom's horrid wax caricature, and the woman, taking moments to realize that she once had been La Contessa, though when the small hand showed, finger bloated about the diamond, nothing of Phidias, no grace, or wonder, and in that stink of human rot and disinfectant, no desire, he retched the acid grease of protest into the mask, and the policeman put a strong hand under his arm, or the place could have swung away, a long, long way away.

I believe you better let your lawyer handle this, somebody said. I represent Mrs. Reynolds. There were several letters. Two of them mention you. They are now in court. Ask him to call me. Get things straightened out pretty soon.

If only they could have been.

Bilara let Sergeant Mackearn in that Saturday morning, just after they finished balancing the books.

Mr. Denis, I'm *off* duty, so I can say what I can't when I'm *on*, the sergeant said. I won't sit down, sir, thank you.

But you could drink some coffee with just a lace, Bilara said.

Make that just the lace, and I'm warm, Sergeant Mackearn said. Mr. Denis. The two guys in here the other night? There's others. That buzzard sitting here, he can take his time. We can put a guard on you. Here, where you live, anyplace. For how long? Month? Six months? A year? Two? He can pick it. Only reason I'm talking, Miss Tancy's brother's a buddy of mine back in school. He asked me to. Else I stay out.

You think he'll try?

Sergeant Mackearn took the glass, and raised it.

That's the way we hearing it, he said, and drank, in one, looking at the empty glass. I don't have to tell you. That guy has more power down below than the governor of this state. I say something?

Why don't somebody take the thumb to him? Bilara asked, from the door. Slide him out.

Who got the thumb? Slide, sure. Where? You know anybody know the place he's at? What time? The night he was here, you didn't know he had another carload right outside the door?

Thank you, Sergeant. What's the answer?

Bilara took the glass.

Leave town, the sergeant said, and shook himself further in the overcoat. That's the word. You can't fight him. He's free. Guys working for him? Free. How do you know when he's going to come in? Anyplace. No computer tell you. Look. I'm not worried about *you*. But I got a real headache about Miss Tancy, here. Anything happens to her, what do I say to her brother?

That's the root of your problem, the shrink said, and his voice seemed to hollow down a corridor, just like Leah's. You won't build on bedrock till you can look yourself in the eye. You don't need analysis. You *know* what's wrong. You know ex*actly*. But you refuse to admit it, even to yourself. The two you's are fighting. The awake, the working, the everyday *you* is fighting with another you. And it's a *you* that's nothing like the one people know. Or, let's say, it's the one you'd rather hide. Why? Is it so ugly? Why don't you give yourself a little time to look at it? See how ugly it *is*. Dishonest. When are you going to tell yourself? What's going to *make* you? When will it be that *you*, the you that works, feels, tries, that has to bathe and shave and dress every morning, worry about what sort of tie to wear, what to say to this one or that, the one that has the catalogs in mind, all those names, the responsibility of the gallery, the yes or no of some sale or other, the essential *you*. When are *you* going to burn that other out of the hedge? Look him in the eye, and *burn* him. Why don't you? What's the use of him? Why do you need him? Why does *any*body *need* anybody? Who *is* anybody? We all die. Why aren't we all at peace with ourselves. With *every*body, till then?

Peace. A flight in gentle blue of the mind, careless with music.

Chom Vissel, with bones taken from the grill, regaled the half-dozen stray dogs called to him by hunger, and then by a scratch behind the ears, a murmur of dog-talk, and he lay asleep, in shadow of the shalom hand, and the dogs lay on and around, close to him, asleep, in trust.

Peace.

We don't have it, Miriam said, looking up from the dye vat, a lilac boil with silver bubbles, and sunlight making gold background through black diagonals from the barred window. Peace? What's that, for *us*? My brother and his wife can't get out of Moscow. They applied two years ago. They got thrown out of their positions. He's a professor of physics. She's a chief chemist. No job, no money. And they have to pay thousands of rubles to get a visa? Paying the state for education? What education? Without brains, without study, without dedication, in a place where everybody hates you? *What* education? Who educates, without the positive material? Do you educate a victim? Peace? Who *knows* what it is? They only talk about it.

But Miriam, he said. Don't you have it here?

Here? You mean outside? In Israel?

What's wrong in Israel?

She put up a hand to stop the motor, watched the bubbles smooth to velvet.

What's wrong there's what's wrong in Russia, she said, in sudden, deafening quiet. All those bastards behind the partitions. Behind the desks. Government schmucks. Every shit bastard of them. That's what's wrong. The form-fillers. The rubber-stampers. The come-back-next-weekers. And the week-after-that-ers. How long do you think we waited for a house? House? Two rooms was what we got. My father died in one of them. He wanted to go back to Russia. *Shits*. If this country ever loses a war, it won't be the soldiers' fault. They'll lose in the offices. Among the rubber stamps. The coffee-breakers. In Russian, I know the word. It's the same in English? *Shit*cunt. That's what they are. There isn't one who doesn't stink in its own shit.

Aren't you a little overheated? I mean, your language?

Over-what? What do you know about language? You don't speak Hebrew. You don't speak Arabic. Or Russian. Or Greek. Or Spanish. Or Italian. I *do*. I use the words I choose. My mother was secretary in the Embassy in London. That's why I speak English. She taught me. Don't tell *me* what to say. Next, you'll tell me what to think? Then why did I come here? Why didn't I stay in the Soviet Union? Let me tell you. I had a better life there. *Much* better.

You want to go back?

She shook her head, using a wooden paddle in the dye.

Not now. I'm *here*. It's beautiful. We owe a lot to you. We are so grateful to find this place you made, I don't think we can tell you. You make life so good. Every day is wonderful. But we think of so many in places that are not. In empty streets. A street isn't empty until you have no job, no money, and a cold place to go back to. *If* they let you have a place. If you have no friends, you die. How many have died? How many, *now*, are walking in empty streets? Who helps them? And why not? Because they worship the Lord God? It's a crime? The priests of the Christian churches have nothing to say? What's a Pope?

Miriam, that's going off at a tangent. Our people and our problems have always been essentially *ours*. When did we permit interference?

The snow clouds going over, all light grey, bitter wind cold through cashmere, and Chom Vissel, wrapped in torn blankets, followed by the family of dogs in shelter of his heels, pushing a cartload of chopped brushwood toward the main room for the fireplace, and that voice—Uzzi's?— saying, That old crook. He's selling two loads to our one to the Arabs. This lasts, we won't have any fire. He's making money on our goose-pimples.

Uzzi, he said, You know this for a fact? He's selling to the Arabs?

It's what they say, Mr. Paul.

Who's they?

Well. *You* know. People talking.

Who *were* they?

Ah, Mr. Paul.

Look, Uzzi. You go on out there and take that cart. You deliver that load to the main room, and two more just as full. Meantime, Chom and the dogs are coming in here in the warm. And tomorrow morning, before breakfast, you come to me in the office, and you give me the names of all those accusing Chom of cheating, or stealing. Understood?

Or you can pack yourself off right *now*. If you can't prove what you say about a solid workman like Chom, you get out. We don't want you. Go on. Or I'll have the guards *throw* you out. *Go*.

All the dogs came in on their hinds, dancing in the warm. Chom ran his cap over the window, trying to banish icicles, frowning a smile between one and the other to find out why he was called inside, and somebody else was outside, pushing the cart. Soon, he was outside, with the dogs, giving Uzzi a shove to take him from the shafts, and the brushwood tipped into the big hopper, and Uzzi trotted downhill to his place in the wood-carver's shed.

I don't believe it's Uzzi's fault, Mr. Paul, Leah said. The wood's in three qualities. First is the thick stuff. It cuts easy. For the fireplaces, and Toni's grill. Second quality's for house warming. Third's thin stuff. Twigs. We don't use much of it. The Arabs do. For cooking. If he sells anything, that's what it is.

Don't ask him, ask Azma'uta, he said. She'll know.

Azma'uta did, and she brought the thicknesses to show what went in the fireplaces, and the grill, on the firestones to warm the houses, and in the hearths to cook. But all that Chom got in exchange was aged sheep for feeding the growing family of dogs, and homemade *arack*, the local firewater, to keep him warm, and a couple of blankets, a cognac now and again, and welcome in the village coffee shop to play chess.

It's so much? Leah asked. He's getting a millionaire? Coming out of this best, you ask me, it's the dogs. And we need them. We can get pulled out of bed by the rats, else. You seen them round the grill in the dark? Size of cows.

Uzzi came in before eight, and started apologizing before he shut the door.

All *right,* he said, to shut him up. Now I'll tell you what
we do. You go in charge of the rat squad. That's an important job. You go into Haifa with Yosef. You buy five dozen
rat traps. You put them down, around Toni's place up there,
all around here, anywhere rats might feed, and you bait
them. Catch them alive where you can, and sell them to the
laboratories. You and Chom go fifty-fifty. Understood?

The rat campaign amazed him, everybody. They all saw
rats now and again scamper here and there, one now, one
then. But to see strings of them, poisoned, and caged, live,
by the dozen, daily, brought knowledge that the earth was
alive beneath their feet, and an enemy lived in warrens
rumorous as streets, fecund, and murderous in threat.

Pull out all the stops, he told Leah. Bring in the experts.
Let this boy Uzzi train with them. Put him in charge when
they go.

Suppose he doesn't want? she asked. He thinks he's too
good for what's being done already. He just as soon go back
to his own job.

What, exactly, *is* that? he asked. I thought he was some
kind of a sculptor.

Some kind, very right, Leah said, in a regal bend of the
head. Why, he's even been known to sharpen a chisel now
and again. Then he takes a mallet. Then he puts it down.
Then he goes along to the glass-blowers to give some big
advice. Girls, you understand, don't know too much. Then,
after a couple of coffees and a doughnut or two, he goes to
the weavers. Lots more advice there. Mentions a couple of
books. Authorities, of course. More coffee. Then it's lunch.
After lunch, there's a warm place just beside the furnace
in Ya'acob's place. This takes us to five o'clock. That's coffee-
time up here, and a pleasant discourse on the crime of
Israel's usurpation of Arab lands, and the coming of the

Messiah, our guilt complex, all going on up to Toni's place, thirty minutes to gorge, more coffee in here or whatever he can get somebody to stand him, and home to a nice warm bed. He never went in the Army because he's Orthodox. Now, he's an artist.

How did we get him?

He got here, and put his bag down. Mentioned your name. That's all.

Leah, what *is* Orthodox?

I don't know, Mr. Paul. They're very religious. That's *all* I know.

Make it a rule. Anybody else coming here, they have to report to you. Nobody can live in any building without your express permission, plus the payment of rent, and all dues. Visitors are welcome to stay anywhere below the car park. Nobody further up except renting tenants. You'll want a system of watchmen down there, and you'll have to find a way of feeding them. You'll need bathing facilities. See Miko. We'll need some sort of hostel for visitors. As we grow, we'll have plenty. Lots of young people are on the move. Among them there just *might* be *the* artist we're looking for. I find that an exciting thought. We can't throw away the chance. That's the wonderful way it works. A star shines? Somebody follows it. It's the way it always was. We have to be kind, Leah. We hope people are going to be kind to us, don't we?

Mr. Paul. What did you say about Uzzi?

Out. And listen.

Yes, Mr. Paul?

Don't let anybody push Chom around the place. He's old, and he's hairy and he's all sorts of negatives. Doesn't interest me what he *isn't*. What he is, he's a friend of ours, and if he wasn't here, a lot of things wouldn't get done.

Including feeding the dogs, and *they*'re friends of ours. Where does he sleep?

I'm not sure anybody knows. He's another just put his bag down. Only I don't believe he even had a bag. Just himself, and a dog or two, maybe.

Find out. We don't want him sick.

Mr. Paul, I'm glad this came up. We have more than fifty people working here. We have no ambulance, and no doctor. Shouldn't we have at least a nurse? By the time an ambulance gets here from Haifa or Nazareth, it's going to be a good hour. Or two.

Find one. *Fifty* people? That's wonderful.

They're coming in every day, Mr. Paul. This place was needed.

Running away from things?

No, sir. Running *to*. Lots of people dream of doing their own thing their own way. Where else can they?

Mr. Paul, I don't know who they happen to be, Bilara said, that late afternoon, among the flowered baskets and bouquets of the *vernissage*, the opening night of the exhibition. They just come in here, threw every last one any dam' place, and shut the door. That's *it*. That entire El Greco collection. All here. I got them out in the kitchen for the moment. Back door's on burglar alarm.

You did just right, Bilara. Hope there's a cop or two strolling nearby.

Sure is, Mr. Paul. I believe you could do with a drink.

Once again, you're so goddam right.

The exhibition went on and on, and people talked, and drank, and despite the air-conditioners, the place became blue, and everybody and their shadows talked of Melsom, and the loss, and the this-and-that, but listening to them, he could not forget that he had been the only mourner to follow those two caskets into the crematorium, and Bilara's small bouquet of white roses had been first to shrivel when the doors opened.

He set the smile for everybody. He even tried it with Bilara. But that black stare melted, made it into glass, and it ran, and she took him into the back room, and put him in a chair, gave him a drink, patted the cushion for his head, rested a hand on his shoulder.

Don't get to worry, Mr. Paul, she said, in that little voice. Nobody going to do right in the worry. Just let me get some of these freeloaders the hell out of here. But I have to tell you we got the sold stickers on fifteen, and the rest's going to go the next couple of days. You want to bet?

He marked the time—a little after eleven o'clock—when he finished booking checks and entering the sales register, and while he tapped figures on the tabulator, the bell rang, and Bilara, emptying and stacking ashtrays on the back table, looked at him.

See who it is, he said.

The gate opened, Bilara unlocked the door, and the Name walked in, and a couple of others stayed outside. Bilara shut the door.

I heard about Melsom, he said. I don't want to get in this. Understand? The Grecos got back here? O.K. I don't want to hear about it. Don't want any money. Don't want nothing. Right?

Wrong, he said. They're not my property. I don't want them. Going to cost a fortune in insurance every day they're here.

A fortune? For Chrissakes, they're forgeries.

You'd have to prove it.

The Name stared, the small grey eyes in many-pouch bags. Threat slackened in a sudden ease of shoulders.

Right up till this, I trusted you. Everybody else did.

Bilara, could we please have a drink? And turn the heating up, will you? I'm cold. Now, look. We had too many deals together to want any bad feeling. You have, I'd say, of its kind, the best private collection in this country. Most of it, you bought here. I appreciate it. That being so, am I going to throw a lot of junk at you? What *could* be the most important single item of a fine collection? Do I need that sort of a deal? I *know* who you are. Could I afford it?

Bilara brought in the drinks, and pulled out a chair.

The Name sat down.

Just let me ask you one pertinent question. Who put you up to this forgery story? Who tipped you off?

It was a woman. She called my office.

Bilara, let me have the file. With the new additions. Now, let me ask you question number two. These people in Spain, the ones said the papers were forged, the whole deal was a fraud. Did they make an offer to buy?

The Name nodded, staring, pale grey, sideways, wary.

You mean to tell me that people employed in one of the world's greatest galleries, *know*ing these to be forgeries, made an offer?

They said they wanted to add them to their collection of forgeries.

You mean to tell me they col*lect* forgeries? El Prado? Bilara, let me have the El Prado catalog. Now, this offer. Was it anywhere near what you paid?

Less than five percent.

So *they,* not you, could sell them again for at least ninety-five percent profit?

The Name sipped, as if tasting something new.

Bilara put the file on the desk, and went to the bookshelves for the El Prado catalog.

He took out two prints, holding up one.

Ever met *him?* he asked. It's a morgue photograph.

The Name looked, fumbled for spectacles, put them on, nodded.

Can't remember his name.

Bernard Melsom.

Got it.

He held up the second print.

This the woman?

The Name stared, nodded one downward jerk of the chin.

Right.

She was living with Melsom. Called herself Contessa Something-or-other. She was a Spanish-Moroccan actress called Tita Ciocchi-Gonzales, so the police records show. They seem to have worked together.

I have a question. Who does this all belong to?

Interpol's working on it. Until something else turns up, it's yours. You want to take my advice, you'll take them back. Did you ask at the Spanish Embassy or the Consulate-General if these certificates of theirs are forgeries?

No.

Let me set your mind at rest. They're not. I've checked. Why don't *you?* Call in anyone you want. Bring in every so-called expert. Prove your case. I'll tell you now. You won't. Why? They're not forgeries. Stolen? Perhaps. Anytime in the past couple of hundred years. Doesn't make them less than what they are. Or you could claim from Melsom's estate. He left quite a wad.

No idea where it came from? Who owned them?

They say—I'm spouting gossip—European Mafia Incorporated. You can take it from there. I'm not interested. I just want them out of here. Or would you want me to sell them? For more than you paid. Simple.

You mean you really think they *are* El Grecos?

No question. How *can* there be? *Look* at them. Who the original owner was, is that anything to do with it? Look. They came from the Bank of Spain. Since when do they deal in stolen property? All the Customs certificates in order. Spanish Embassy, Consulate-General, in order. Authentication? Well. You have the originals. Did you go to the Spanish police to check?

I was there on business. Had too much to do.

So the Contessa did the talking?

Her, and a couple of guys.

You were in the galleries? In the curator's office?

No. They came around to the hotel. I had to take their word.

Why?

They had an awful lot of evidence.

He smiled, swung the big leather-bound volume, and opened at the index.

You'll find the Spaniards about as meticulous as anybody else when it comes to a catalog, he said. Just find me, in that, any reference to a collection of forgeries.

I don't read Spanish.

You don't have to. That's an English translation started by Mr. Blantyre, and kept up to date ever since. Find the forgeries. They *have* to be there. Or they don't exist.

I don't want to fool with it.

Right. Save time. Wise move. Know why? Forgeries, they don't collect. Original copies, by the *same* artist, they just possibly might. You'll find them in this section. Not in the main gallery. Any more questions?

The Name stood, buttoned his coat, took his hat off, put it on.

I'll have Brink's collect these tomorrow. Also.

He paused, looking down at the glass.

I said things I shouldn't. I get mad, I say things. I'm sorry. Real sorry. I should have listened. I'm sorry. Didn't mean it. I was wrong. When you have anything else, call the office. Have to forgive me. Good night.

Bilara opened the locks, pushed the button to open the gate, let him out, and turned the keys.

I expected trouble, she said. Mm-hm. Going to call the Sixteenth, there, for a minute. But he finally listened to some sense. Mr. Paul, you sure got all them chickens back in the sheds. Easy's pie. That dirty crook.

He put his head in his arms, pressed about by a corroding sense of misery.

No, Bilara, he coughed. He's an honest man. In his own way. *I'm* the crook. Every word I said I didn't believe. What *he* said was in good faith. He apologized. I *should* have. To *him*. I didn't. *Why?*

Mr. Paul, I believe you had a hard time, these past few days, here, she said, hand on his shoulder. What do you say we share a cab home? You don't want to get mugged. I sure don't.

I'm the crook, Bilara. The carbon-fourteen, and all the other stuff, you think I believe it? That's no more El Greco than I am. Beautiful job of copying? All right. Canvas of that time? Right. Stretchers, woodwork, same period? All right. Paint? For a chemist, easy. So? *I'm* the crook. I *know*. I didn't have the guts to say so. *He* was honest. Oh, Bilara. I wasn't. God*damm*it. I *was*n't. *Why?*

Bilara coming in that morning, with the boy from the delicatessen behind, carrying the basketful of what she called the hog-trough for the evening's opening, put the newspaper on the desk, folded at the Melsom inquest story, and went on to the kitchen.

He saw what she meant. There was no need to say anything.

In his own name, which he had always forbidden to be used, the Name made a headline across the page. Melsom's letters mentioned him twice. Once, as lord of the meat-flies in the underworld, and second, as the man responsible for most of the art robberies and sales of forgeries in the past twenty years.

He felt unable to read, sick in spirit. His own evidence made less than a paragraph.

But he knew what to expect.

I believe you'd better alert the guys in the Precinct, Bilara, he told her, through the door.

Yes, sir, I already did. I called in there.

All evening the place was full, and if he was a sack of nerves, he wore the stuck-on smile, booked a useful first-night crop of sales, talked the usual nonsense, always found someone else to talk to when Melsom's name came up— and it seemed as if nobody had any other topic—and generally ran himself into an ice-cold mire that whisky only just penetrated.

I believe you have to go home early, Mr. Paul, Bilara said, taking another red SOLD sticker from the register. Look kind of 'flamed around the eyes. Can't have you sick. You got two big ones coming up tomorrow.

Have a feeling you'll be taking care of them, Bilara. I'm getting sick of this whole goddam business. If it isn't crooks, it's nitwits. How many real lovers of art do we get in here? Look at *these* bastards. Anything to do with art? Refugees from soap and decent thinking. What the hell am

I *do*ing here? What are *you* doing here? Compared with any of them, you're the goddess of hygiene. What the hell was *her* name?

Well, I *know* my name, Mr. Paul, and I just earned commission on two hundred and twelve thousand-plus dollars, and boy, was I ever glad I'm *me*. Let me fresh that kind of flabby-looking drink. Ten minutes, I grease the steps for this bunch, and you go home. The *back* way.

She must have made it a three-decker paralyser, because he came to, alert, on the settee in the back office, and the Name stood over him, overcoat apart, hands in jacket pockets, looking down.

Wake? The Name said.

Suddenly, and almost as lightning strikes, he had the thought.

Why should this type of louse enter that office without permission, and why should he be on these premises at all? The clock over the door pointed to ten after midnight. A rage consumed, curdled, cooled, froze.

He sat up.

What are you doing *here?*

The Name went up on his toes, came down. The mouth split.

I'm here about the papers, he said, almost a whisper. Newspapers. How much you get paid for the stories? Where else they get them details?

No stories, and no pay, he heard himself say, almost as in a dream. That was a court. United States law, and the police. Two dead people. Lot more to come. There were five letters. They only read two. *Her* letter says a lot about you. You'll read it in the columns. She lived with you before Melsom? How could you come in here and talk about forgery? How could you buy them when you owned them? Tax man going to come looking for you?

The Name bent down, feinted, and punched him beside the head, and the horrid bubbles sang inside the ears, in the nose, and the bone pained, and he was on the floor, looking at red carpet-pile.

You dirty Jew *bas*tard. I was right the first time. They want you on the stand again? You won't be around. How much Melsom pay you? Who else you talk to? Come on, get your goddam—

Hey, you, Bilara said, in the doorway. Leave him alone. Hear me?

The Name looked around in clumsy, thick-handed pretence of big-eyed, open-maw surprise.

Well, if it isn't that big, black, dog-*bitch,* he said. We going to take you along and put you on the table. Get the rags off of you. We finish, then we roast that fat black ass on the stove—

Hell you will, she said, laughing in the little voice, lazy. Ever see my daddy's present? Never will any more. Meet the Lord God. My compliments. The *black, dog, bitch.*

While he ran toward her the shots hit, turned him, and he fell, and still she pulled the trigger until it *clicked!*

That's it, Mr. Paul, she said, lazy as ever, and turned, hearing the front door almost take out the windows in a slam. That's the gentlemen with him. They don't like deadies. Deadies don't have no-o-o money. But cops, that they have.

The doorbell rang, and she came off the wall like a sleepwalker.

I'll get it, she said. Wipe off the blood. Clean towel in the rack.

He heard her slow steps, the unlocking, a quick tread,

and Sergeant Mackearn stood in the doorway, looking at the Name. Slowly, the smile spread to a wide amusement of white teeth.

Mammy, I prayed to you, and baby, you come through, he said softly. Let's see, now. When we getting here, we saw these guys run out and get in the car. Officers I was with, they chased the car, and I come in here. What do I find? A body. Who? I don't know. Don't suppose you do?

Never saw him, Bilara said. Ran in, the other guys come in, lots of shooting, good-bye. What *is* this, Black September?

Give me the gun, Sergeant Mackearn said, and Bilara seemed to bring it out of her skirts. O.K. Now you go wash your hands. Up to the elbows. Got some good, strong dish cleaner there? Use that. Soak them good. Mr. Paul, you didn't see a thing?

I was out, cold.

You have a considerable welt on the side of the head, there. How'd it happen?

The shooting woke me up. I fell off the settee.

Six shots, *all* on target, *any*body wake up. Except the target. I believe we have the story. Only thing is, you *have* to know him. He was in this Melsom case today.

I didn't know him till I woke up. Then he was down there. Quite a shock.

Why would he come in here?

He was mentioned in the inquest. So was I. Melsom did business here. For *him*. Did he have some questions for me? He bought a lot from this gallery. Everything here was above board. In the books. No loose ends.

Oh, sure. Let's see, now. You're cleaning up after the night show. You laying down to have yourself a *re*lax, and this guy comes in here, and before you know what, these other guys bust in, lots of shooting, this guy's stiffed, the other guys make a getaway, and I hope we don't catch up with them. I believe that lets everybody off the hook. Except.

Except what? he asked.

Sergeant Mackearn wrapped the gun and put it in a hip pocket.

Goes in the river, he said. Yeah. Except. Ex*cept* the guys got away. They *know* they didn't do the job. Who did? Mr. Paul. You have to make up your mind. They won't wait too long. I know them. They just bide their time. I like to see you out of this town. Miss Tancy, I don't believe you much better off.

Said they was going to get the rags off of me, Bilara whispered, piling her hair at the back. Put me on the table. When they finish, roast my ass on the stove.

Like they done lots of times. Nobody caught up. Boy, what I just pray to give. Anyway, I get you a cab, I write the depositions, and look, you sign here, my book. Good enough.

Taking a lot of responsibility, here, Sergeant.

Yes, sir. For a hunk of salami. Miss Tancy, you want to call that cab?

Bilara put ice on the bump, and he took a couple of aspirin, and when the cab came he felt almost civilized. Bilara gave Sergeant Mackearn the keys, and he signed for them, and when the squad got there, he took them out to the cab, spoke to the driver, and away they went.

Look, he said, when they were turning out of Fifty-seventh, Why don't you stay with me tonight? We have an armed doorman. I don't believe I could sleep, else. I don't like that piece about the stove.

I don't like any part of the table, and I don't wear rags.

I kind of like the idea. I'll feel a whole lot safer. Do you have a gun there?

Two. Permits for both. This time, if necessary, I do the work.

Suit me.

They were going through the tunnel, and she leaned.

Mr. Paul, you taking his advice? I mean, leaving?

He pulled in the deep breath, that made the head throb again.

Bilara, I'm plain sick of it. I think I have to. I'll always hear that about the stove.

They didn't mean it, Mr. Paul.

No? They get their hands on you? Easy enough. Think *I* rest easy?

You always been good to me, Mr. Paul.

You're good to work with, Bilara.

You know where you might go?

Idea's too new to have any real idea. I'd have to sell the gallery. That's too painful to think about.

She sat straight, and the passing lights scampered in and out of her eyes.

Mr. Paul, that mean I'd have to go? she asked.

Not unless you want, Bilara. While I have a crust, you have more than the half. I don't know where I'd be without you. I certainly don't want to *be* without you. I have to make up my mind. Then you can make up yours.

Sir, Leah said, that grey morning, in almost early spring-time, Azma'uta says they have more than sixty women in the village. They make a wonderful lace. They embroider dresses. But they all go to work in the fruit factories. They earn twice as much money. Or more. Their daughters will never learn. It is pure Arab work. By hand. How shall we have lace? Or embroidery?

I don't want anybody canning fruit who ought to be making lace. How does it compare with what they get on a machine?

Leah made that gesture of the thighs in refusal of the male, gloriously Eve.

Oh, Mr. Paul, she prayed. It's beautiful. It's *ancient*. Part of their bloodstream. And the dresses are marvellous. How can a machine do this?

Pay what they ask. We don't have to make money. We'll find a market. But who does the selling?

Could we open a shop?

I don't want to lose you as secretary.

I thought Azma'uta could take charge. She can work with me in the mornings. She doesn't need such a lot of training. She's got most of it.

Up to you. Anything to keep them out of the factory. That's the reason we're here.

Miko found space for a shop in the angle of the gallery, outside the main door, where the path led out of the Plaza and down to Yael's new pottery, a wonderful place on many levels downhill, panelled in ceramics of all colors, with barrel roofs, in orange, yellow, pale blue, and tanagra. He often went there for the best coffee in the country. Yael and her partners, Hedva and Zorah, called themselves coffee-*nuts*. They got a sack of coffee beans every three months or so from Haifa off a ship from Brazil, roasted and ground and sold packets of it to anyone on the place, though it never tasted the same as theirs, and he asked Yael what the secret was.

You have to *love* coffee, she said. Taking it and making it, what's that? What you get is like a little peck on the cheek instead of a big, beautiful kiss. That's what a cup of coffee *ought* to be. Nose, palate, the rest of you that loves what's good, a trinity, what else? That's what coffee's made for. It's not a drink. It's a libation. Not for the gods. For *us*. All you have to do is take care. Use love. A bottle-opener gets you a drink. Or turn a tap. Twist a spigot. But coffee? Patience. Love. Intelligence. Don't you remember? Where did the intelligence meet? I mean, in civilized times? In the cafés? Of course. Coffee, it's the fragrance of thought. You can't make it without. That wishwash they make in urns? In those percolators, they call them? Bladderfill. Coffee, it's first, *love*. Then patience. And respect.

Well, let me have a big, beautiful kiss, will you? And what do you mean by civilized times? Don't we have any now?

She looked at him with the green eyes, that altered in light and shadow, a luminous green, paler than emeralds, and then dark as amethyst and sometimes, in a splash of light, pink, of startling heat.

Here? and she pointed to the floor. Here, yes. Where else? New York? London? Paris? Rome? Where? I know them all. Socially. In every way. You *will* find certain people. A few. They fight to survive in a horror of the mediocre. What have they? Cinema? Of a vulgarity impossible to consider. Theater? Pitiful. Restaurants? How many? *What* civilization? For how many? And the manner of life? But ri*dic*ulous, of course.

I think you overstate, he said, counting matchsticks. Overemphasize. After all, fifty years ago, sixty, how many working people ever saw the inside of a museum or a gallery? Let us make no mention of the last century. The vast majority *were* slaves of industry. There were still pogroms of our people. You don't want to remember?

And one to end them, a grand finale, how long ago?

Of course. How far did civilization reach down? The wealthy at the top. Tradesmen in the middle. The rest below. Twelve-, fourteen-hour-a-day slaves. For just enough to eat. Where *is* civilization, here? There was law, certainly. The courts and the prisons. Fear of punishment. To keep the wilder spirits in order? But civilization? A few thousand drawing-rooms among tens of millions of kitchens, is that civilization? What *is* civilization? Frock coats and top hats? Would you suspect that among them were demons capable of designing gas ovens to fry their brothers and sisters?

She shook the cropped, chestnut curls, turned down her mouth.

Not what I'm talking about, she said. I mean, *civilization*. When everybody has a chance of having at least a taste of the best life has to offer. Here, for example. We don't ask anyone to *give* us anything. We work for it in a sort of wonderful you-help-me-and-I'll-help-you, let's say, spirit? We don't want *any*thing free. We'll work for it.

You have that privilege. It was prepared for you. Who else is lucky? We're not discussing coffee. You happen to know *which* coffee, and how to make it. Why?

Coffee was in my family. My father was a factor.

You're lucky. How many others are? I'm sorry for myself. *I* didn't know. Unless I'm shown, how could I? So I'm uncivilized?

Oh, now, Mr. Paul. That's running it all the way in with the gravel.

Why?

Well. You're just using words.

What else *is* there to use?

Hedva came up the steps with the coffee, two cups on a

tray, but without saucers, the spoon in a puddle, and sugar in a caked plastic cup.

Anyway, finally, here's the coffee, Yael said.

Drink it yourselves, he said, and stood. You talk about civilization? Look at that tray. What is that slop except a lack of it?

Now, Mr. Paul, Hedva said, open-eyed. You always had it so.

Right. Until I had this civilization spiel just now. We seem to want it badly for others. Not for us? You drink that stuff yourselves. I can make my own.

He walked out, wondering if the show had been put on for him, deliberately, to keep him away in the future.

Doubt it, Leah said, in the office. They like to treat everybody what *they* call the same. It's getting worse. Same standard of treatment for everybody. Nobody gets more than anybody else. You, the head? You should be the least. This isn't Yael, or Hedva. It's Zorah. She's beginning to do the talking. Funny ideas.

Who's she?

I've only met her twice. She's knee-high. But sharpest.

You like her?

No.

Why not?

I prefer boys.

Is that the trouble down there?

Well.

I agree. It's their business. In future, you make the coffee.

I'll bet I make it as good as them.

No bet.

She was right, and he saved money. But he was troubled without knowing why, until the Saturday night monthly meeting, just after a show of hands, which gave Toni the right to build a grill to serve the general public on the slope below the car park, and Dov Lipsky a piece of land, opposite, to open a kosher bar.

One question, here, a croaky woman's voice called, from the back. Where do the Arabs come into this? We're giving their land away as if it belonged to us. Even here, with all the artistic and the other moral claptrap, the crime still goes on?

He stood up.

Identify yourself, he said.

She stood at the back, short, hair in long braids, eyes as two large black holes.

My name's Zorah Graetz, she said, in that strange little croak. I'm not anti-anything. I'm only sick of injustice. *We* never had anything ex*cept* injustice. Why do we allow it when we deal with the Arabs?

Let me straighten you out on this, he said, quietly. It took pretty nearly two years to take this piece of land on lease. Nobody buys land in Israel. This place, this piece of land, of no value to agriculture, or anything else, was leased to me to promote a living area for Israel's artists. There is no Arab owner. Records show that nobody's lived anywhere near here for at least two hundred years. There is no water here. It had to be installed. That's the water you drink. Bathe in. Make coffee with. I spent the money. You do the talking?

No, she almost wailed. It's *not* that. We *know* all you've done. If you hadn't, we couldn't *be* here. But what about the Arabs? They're people, too. Don't they have the right to resent their land taken over, and not a penny in return?

You'd better start reading a little, he said. This was never Arab land. You might just as well say it belonged to the Crusaders. It did. There's evidence, in rock, they built here, and they were here for two hundred years. What's that, in at least three thousand? You look out of your windows on the land of Ephraim to the south, and north to Manasseh, west to Gilead. Where were the Arabs? What *is* an Arab?

Ah, look. Just a moment. That's no sort of argument.

Not? Would you give us your idea of what an Arab *is?* Let me make this plain. I want the common or garden meaning of the word "Arab." You say a man is an Arab. What are you talking about? What *is* the meaning of the word?

Oh, now, come *on.* Everybody *knows* what an Arab is.

Good. Now, would you please tell *me?* Because I don't know. I know what a man of Eretz Israel is. He's mentioned in the most ancient literature. The earliest history we know mentions Israel. As a land, as a people. Does it mention Arabs? Or Americans? Or French? Romans, yes. They haven't been around in something over fifteen hundred years. What's an Arab?

Well. The people here before we came here.

We came *back* here, and I mean *here,* the spot where we're now talking, in nineteen-twelve. No Arabs. We used it for a hot weather camp for the children down in the kibbutz. They brought the water up in carts. Pulled by camels. Lent by the village along here. Any fight between the Arabs and us in that time? Anything heard from Jordan at that time? Saudi Arabia? Lebanon?

I don't know.

They didn't exist.

But they were *here.*

Look at a map. Look at records. Don't talk until you know. Before the British pulled out, what was Egypt? Can you point to frontiers? Who made them?

We'd want an Arab to tell us.

Bring him here. We shall give him warmest welcome.

Why *him*?

He looked across the silent room, flat faces, stone-eyes.

If you can find a woman, he said, and paused. *If* you can. *Please* bring her here. Do they have any spokes*women* in Egypt? Or anywhere else? Could you name one? In any Arab country?

That's demagogy.

What do you mean by that?

Oh, you know the meaning. Too well.

I'm ignorant. Tell me. Tell *us*. What *is* the meaning of demagogy?

It's appealing to the mass, of course.

You mean, I'm appealing to forty or fifty people, here? On their emotions? Yes.

He looked at the flat faces, in rows, so far, so spread, not a smile.

Does anyone here feel I'm trying to talk to emotions? he asked. I'd rather talk to what you *know*.

Ephraim Wirtz, the metallurgist, put up a hand, and stood, grasping the back of the chair in front.

I like to say something, he said. I'm in the United States nearly thirty years. I love it. I never wanted to leave. Except I felt I ought to be *here*. Wife's the same. We never knew what we were coming to. We never *give* a damn. Know what I mean? Just to be *here*. So we got to talking on the plane, see? And this stewardess, hostess, what they call 'em, she tells us about *this* place. So when we get to Lod, we ask. What do you know? I make a call, I say who I am, what I do, so we put all the stuff in a cab, and next thing you know, we're *here*. Next day, I'm working. I never worked like this in my whole life before. Let me ask a question. I'm doing Arabs out of a job?

No record, Leah said. No evidence.

So? If Arabs want to come and work with me, I'll train them. If they have anything to teach me, I'll learn. And I'll pay.

Zorah, you agree? he said.

Ah, it's all what *you* want to do, she croaked, in a higher frog's range. How *can* I produce a gal who got trained? Isn't this the very basis of what I'm saying? The only ones get trained are *men*.

But we were talking about Arabs.

All right, *Ar*abs. *Any*body. Women, they're always down below. Left out. You don't hear about them. How *can* you, if you can't get them *trained?* If they can't *learn?*

Are you talking about Arab women?

Talking about *any* women, us, anybody.

What do you want to do about it? Any ideas?

I have, yes. I believe if we could advertise a school only for women. To train them in anything they wanted to do.

How about men?

They can train for anything they want. Anytime.

Where?

Well. Look around.

All right, he said. I'll make a deal with you. In front of these witnesses. You produce the places where men can be trained, and we'll start a school for women, one for one. Every time a man gets taken on for training, wherever it may be, we'll take on a girl. She can take her pick. We'll pay. Accepted?

You're pretty sure of yourself, the croak said, flipping a braid.

You are the surest. You always have an argument. You never do anything for yourself? Or yourselves? You want somebody to do it for you? A man? Somebody with a troubled conscience? I don't have one. If I find one here, I'll kick him out. I want people here to be men, *and* women. Calm. At peace. Except with work. That's ideas. *They* interfere.

Don't you see that? the shrink said, those long mornings ago. You speak of ideas. Where from?

All right. *You* tell me.

You pay to do the talking. Where *do* ideas come from? Inside your head? Outside? Chain of reference? Inference? *How?* Let's hear it.

Ah, listen. This is a *god*dam-sight harder than any day's work *I* ever did. I go out of here *weak*.

Getting rid of a lot of mental pus. Something's worrying you. What is it?

Why one thing more than another? Lot of things worry me.

One. Above all else. You'd like to hide it. Even from yourself. Give it words.

No.

I can't torture it out of you.

Torture? I have enough.

Why? Is it health?

No. I just had the six months' check. Great.

Is it the police?

Why should it be the police?

Experience. When people have a worry they can't face, it's generally something they've done that might be found out. The last few sessions you've given pointers. I've said nothing till now. Why don't you throw it in the open? Before you give yourself away?

How?

You're hitting the bottle. Something that's never troubled you. What is it? Two bottles a day?

Not *so* much.

It's *too* much. Cut it. Or why waste my time?

Your time? I'm paying for it.

My time is never paid for. I accept a fee for trying to be of use. I could be doing someone else some good. You think I enjoy listening to a lot of mumble from a soak?

A *what?*

Look at yourself. When did you change your linen last? Growing a beard? It's fashionable. Shoes don't *have* to be shined. Rub with a towel? Isn't there anybody at home to tell you this?

No. No, goddammit. There isn't. Ah, Christ help me.

Curious.

Mh?

I say, it's curious. Why should you appeal to someone outside your own religion?

Religion? I don't have one.

Then why appeal to Christ?

Ah. Figure' speech.

Is it?

You see, Mr. Denis, the monk, calling himself Brother Canopus, said, crawling his fingers on the table, it's a matter of great urgency, first. And second, you'll understand, of exceptional secrecy. You know we've had a grievous time these years. Fees having to go up, schools almost out of poor parents' reach, and Congress unwilling to help. I say no more. That's the size of it. Well, now. We've a small store of things of value down in St. Cleophas. Church of the school. Haven't been looked at since the great riots of eighteen-sixty-something. Everybody thought the world was coming to an end. All the church treasures were taken down and put in the vaults. Well, those that we have were never taken out. Nobody knows they're there. They're in no in-

ventory. We've already made exhaustive investigation.
What we'd like to do is sell them to anybody interested,
privately. We want no publicity.

Why did you come to me?

Well, Mr. Jonathan Cole told us. You were the most reputable dealer of them all, he said, and you work without
publicity and minimum fuss.

That was good of him.

Ah, he's a splendid man. A great help to the parish. He
said we'd need documents and permits. Well, there aren't
many. But what there are, I think you'll find in order.

The paper, in a narrow, shrivelled leather pouch, certified a Cranach, a Vasari, and five sketches by Botticelli.
Doubt, which had accompanied both the monks from the
door, grew as some ugly creeper. But their faces were serene. Small men, in threadbare habits, sandals. Nothing
out of harmony. If they turned about, they could never
have been recognized by any feature.

How much are you asking?

Every cent we can get, Brother Canopus said, eagerly.
We've more than a hundred and thirty pupils, to start with.
Why should they have to go without, and these things have
never been out of their cases since the day they were nailed
in?

What does St. Patrick's think about this?

I was waiting for the question. You're a careful one.
We were told of it. Come down with me to the episcopal
office. You'll meet the bishop. And there'll be further business. We need money. We've got to have money. But we
don't want people saying we're selling the sticks. We're *not*.
We're selling things we've never used for a hundred years,
and not likely to use for the *next* hundred. Then, why keep
them? There's many a faithful son or daughter wanting a
fine piece of holy art on the walls. A blessing for the house,

no less. Will you sell for us? Jonathan told us how much you charge, and so forth. Would you be seeing what you can do?

Where can I see these pieces?

We'll have them here this evening at five-thirty. We'll then arrange a time to go down to the office tomorrow morning. When sales result, you could pay the check in there.

Bilara watched them go. Her smile brightened all the other side of Fifty-seventh Street, and everywhere beyond, and filled in all the cracks past Columbus Circle, and even to the Pole.

I swear I never saw two smaller-bigger *bums* all the time I been here, she said. The phonies get in here sometimes, boy, they just *bush* league. Want me to call Father Brant?

Of course. Bilara, in your own way, you're pretty smart.

Don't have to be smart to smell that kind of stuff. You going through with this?

Matter of duty. Call Father Brant.

But cropped-white-haired Father Brant frowned a little behind the steel spectacles without seeming in the least surprised.

I've heard it's being done, he said. I've heard—I've only heard—a lot of things are being sold. Including the churches themselves. The property. We're in a bad way. We need the cash. You can't feed, or school, a child on art. If you don't feed him, *and* school him, he'll have no appreciation of art or anything else. Would you care to stroll down to Fifty-first? Let's find out.

A lot of building was going on, with buckets, and ladders, cement in troughs, cheery whistles, and the young priest in the outer office listened, smiled, nodded, and took Father Brant to the office beyond.

That's right, he said, holding a long envelope, coming out

in a hurry, picking a way around sacks, planks, and workmen. Perfectly all right. They both were in here not ten minutes ago. I have a letter. I think you're perfectly safe in the sale. At least, here's as far as you can go. There's nothing beyond, except Rome.

Then I'll arrange the sale.

He knew where to place the items, and they went in one lot at a blistering price, true, but had they been auctioned, it might have been so much more. As it was, everybody seemed satisfied, and he rearranged the pictures in the client's drawing-room, with the Cranach in place of honor, a beauty, and his client gave him a kiss on the cheek.

It was *so* good of you to think of me, she said. I'm *so* happy. Never *been* so happy. I feel as if the Savior's hand were on my head.

But, he wondered, how could people *think* like that?

They don't *think*, Bilara said. Start thinking, you go for gone. You *feel*. That's the way it is for the Lord. He said, Suffer the little children to come unto me. All ye that are weary. Who else said it? Anybody? Well, that's *why*. Nobody else got the words. You *feel*.

She's right, Father Brant said, that afternoon. I've been so low, I could toss aside everything. Walk out. Get a job. Anything. *Anything*, not to hear people call me father. It's such an undeserved piece of scabrous nonsense. But, of course, it fits into the general pattern of ignorance. Father equals God. But you see, it started with the monks. They were brothers of an order. They called themselves in those days Frater. Or *Frère*. *Frère* this. *Frère* that, meaning brother. But in time it was written with a capital F and a small r. And the illiterate English read it as short for Father. So the nonsense goes on. You sold those works?

Yes.

Satisfied?

No.

Why?

I don't understand why the Church authorities would want to part with them. They're priceless. Ten years, they're worth at least twice as much.

Ten years, where are those children?

May be right.

Where am I wrong? There's a picture, or whatever, down in the dark for how many years? For what reason? Hang on to them? But children have mouths. They have to learn. It takes cash. What do *we* do? Fold the hands? Stand by? Oh, when I was a young man, I could fight through a legion of the devil's own, and come out the other side, refreshed and triumphant, not a mark on me. Now? I'm weary. I am. The muscle doesn't hold. And the foolishness of pictures? Compared with the want of a child? Satan must be tickled silly. You can hear him roistering, there.

You believe in Satan?

The tired eyes turned grey upon him, and terror leaned in a corner.

I have all the evidence I'll ever need, the priest said. If you need me, just call.

The worn heels went over the doorstep, and Bilara locked and bolted.

Well? he said. What's the verdict?

I don't believe nobody put the finger on *you*, she said. Took all the *pre*-cautions. All them papers in order. I still don't like any *part* of it.

I don't. But I have the Bishop's letter. Well, hell. What else *can* you do? Give the sale to somebody else?

Wish we did. Messing around with work been done for the Lord? Been in the house of the Lord? Asking for trouble.

I can't believe that way.

Hope nothing don't happen, that's all.

He never forgot the turn of her eyes toward him when Father Brant came in with Inspector Hanrahan, that Friday evening.

It's something so serious I had to go and see my friend, the Inspector, here, Father Brant said. You know each other? Good. Now look. I was at the parochial meeting this afternoon. I happened to mention to the Bishop the sale of the Cranach, and whatever. I *never* saw a man so *out*raged. Expect a visit. He's never given permission, of course. He never would.

I have his letter. Among other things. All sworn by the public notary.

Who were the two who offered these works? the Inspector asked.

They were introduced by a client. As Father Brant will tell you, we—the two of us—went down to the cathedral offices. Everything seemed in order.

Let me tell you about *that*, Father Brant said, and nodded at the Inspector. We just came away from there. There's no office there. There never was.

But we *went* there. You went inside. You brought out the letter.

I did. I was deceived. That was no office. That young man was nobody known on the staff. Those rooms have never been offices. The building going on was to enlarge rooms on the upper floors, and those two offices have been knocked into one for another purpose. The Inspector and myself were just there. I'm a terribly confused soul. I feel I've misled you. I do. I'm in pain about it. But worse than that. You see. There's no St. Cleophas Church, or school, *any*where. There's no record of a Cranach or any of the other things. Everything's too carefully registered for any mistake. Now, what *is* it your client's got? If it *is* a Cranach, then it came from somewhere else. Is it not a terrible thought?

He could smell the arid waste of the ossuary, that place of bones and finished life.

I'll call her, he said. I'll be in touch with Interpol.

I can help, there, the Inspector said. This is a con-job. I believe I know who those two "monks" happened to be.

Whoever they were, they had the right stuff, he said. And they were smart. None of those items were on any of the lists of stolen works. So far as I'm concerned, what I sold were exactly as stated. But I'm getting in touch with the client. If she doesn't want them, who gets them? Who repays her money?

I believe it's turned my head, Father Brant said, and stood, and the grey eyes were exactly the grey of the whiskers prickling his cheeks. I'll hear the Bishop's rage till my last breath. An *angry* man. And then we found it was all for nothing. No church called that. I should have known. No works of those names. No office down there. I feel I passed through some awful dream. We suffer terror for thieves and liars. *They* should do the suffering. They never do. *That's* what's wrong. They *never* do.

But the client listened, straightened her back, and smiled, equable, calm as the mass of white lilac behind her chair.

No, Mr. Denis, she said. I'm used to risks. I love them just the way they are, and I can't tell you how much they've been admired. I don't care where the accusations come from. I'm ready to meet them, and I'll back you all the way to the post. Count on *me*.

He walked out on Sixty-sixth happy as he had ever been,

and after the stroll to the gallery, Bilara looked at him, pointing a thumb between her breasts, meaning behind.

An old priest sat in the office, and spectacles flashed his smile.

I want to say only two words, he said, and stood, straightening the broad maroon sash about his waist. I've heard the story. I'm not likely to forget it. Now, then. If it worked once, will it not work again? Because next time, it might *really* be property. We never know when we're to be attacked. Would you do me the privilege of calling me direct? Any hour of the day or night. Any smallest whisper I'll appreciate. We've such a lot of art. It's a dead weight of sheer worry. I don't know how we support it.

Without the Church, there wouldn't have been many artists, he said. Or many of anything. If there's ever anything I can do, just let me know. And if those two ever try it again, I don't want to see them get away.

You've no idea where the Cranach might have come from? The Vasari? I'm terribly afraid they're from robberies in Italy.

Or other places in Europe. Middle East. Many places are pilfered we never hear about. We always do a careful check. That's routine. This might be from one of the South American countries. Who reports in the event of earthquakes? Looting? Robberies? Churches? Monasteries? Private homes? How long does it take to get in print?

The sash gleamed silkily under the Bishop's probing fingers.

I'll leave you, he said, looking away, tired. I believe we're all in peril. Evil's everywhere. And it's well-paid. Goodness rarely is. It's one of our great shortcomings. People see the other side getting fat, and slipping off with it. Then? What do they think? They're human. Good's *no* good. It's smarter to be a thief. And don't you think that's a splendid thing to be saying, this year of so little grace at all?

He seemed to wake up in those days to a curious sense of living in some faint aroma of loss, a feeling of error, a cloture somewhere in the senses, perhaps, that began keeping him awake, an elusive notion that evaded however hard he tried to think about it. But that morning, whether by intuition or some impulse almost as tenuous, he dressed over pajamas, and took a cab to the gallery in French-blue dawn, something he had never done, and forgot the alarm was on, and had a police car there before he opened the door.

He put the pot on for coffee, and sat in Mr. Blantyre's chair, looking at the gallery, at the rows of pictures, thinking of racks in the strongroom, those in the bank, and all the endless others known through the years stacked in his mind.

He tried to imagine what Mr. Blantyre might say, and almost heard that gentle voice whisper, You're being a damn fool. Go on home, and get back in bed, *do*. Get a*long* with you, now.

But the coffee was black under rising steam, and while he poured, he heard the Bishop, saw him standing in the doorway, seemed to see Bilara's smile, and the elusive almost came in grasp, and in a moment fell to nothing, the same sense of want, regret, loss.

He wondered what he supposed himself to be doing.

He put the coffee aside, and deliberately, for no good reason, went on a tour of the gallery's exposition, standing in front of each canvas, examining the grouping, placing, color, texture, light, and, in general, using the tools of experience. The pictures covered a period of about six hundred years, from a small Ghirlandaio, a marvel of greens, to a pair of apples, a charm in reds and yellows, by De Chirico.

He dropped on the viewer's bench, sitting there, turning to look at canvas after canvas, most with fifty years, a man's life, between, and what he sought, suddenly, in extraordinary light, was there in each, and glowing, and he *knew*, and there lay a quiet peace of enjoyment, and a deep bed of satisfaction.

In that quick moment he knew the very spirit of Mr. Blantyre.

Everything roundabout lay in wondrous order.

He *knew*.

He locked up, and walked along to Park Avenue, on down, to Grand Central, seeing the tall green walls of glass giving back beauty to the sun, blessing the architects for vision, and down to Sol Levin's place, a printer's shop very much out of the ordinary. He had fonts brought from Eastern Europe, and his classic Roman left all the others with their serifs down, and none carried such a range of paper.

But when he finished writing, Sol looked at him over the spectacles, and read again, making shapes with his mouth, and looked up.

You don't *mean* this, Mr. Paul? he said. You want I should set this?

Just the way it is. I want to see a pull. Let me have it either some time today or tomorrow. I'll let you know around ten o'clock exactly how many.

Black and white?

Plain black and white. The way the best of us always communicated.

Could I ask? You going to retire?

No, Sol. I don't feel any need to retire. I'm going to sell out and start over. From scratch.

Sol took off the eyeshade. His eyes were still puffy with

sleep, and pebble lenses removed made them smaller, more watery, more sadly aware.

You feel it, too? he asked.

Feel what?

Well. Y'know. The general. Well. Let's see. There's a kind of . . . Look. Were you in Poland? Or Germany? Latvia? Lithuania, maybe? You don't know? Sniffing the air? You don't find it here? I *do*.

Nothing of that, Sol. My feeling is to get away. *Away.* I'm thinking of anyplace. Clean. Air. Space. Wherever it is. The clean winds of the earth. Let them blow the sweet air of the Lord God down these two nostrils, and then, any time after, let me die.

Sol put his face in his hands, rested the elbows on the counter.

I wish you let me know this idea, Mr. Paul, he said. Know something? I feel a whole lot better, a man like you makes up his mind. You think there's a chance, I'll go along. I have friends, they feel the same. But all we got, it's a business, so-so. But it's a living. Could we do half, even less, we'll go. Could it be. Just talking off the top of my head. Israel?

Sol, why don't you bring your friends to the gallery this Shabbat? Let's see how far we get. A master-printer like you falls straight into my plan. Transport of machinery and all that, nothing to it. I take responsibility. Your friends, professionals? The same. Get in touch.

But you see, nothing takes the place, Tovah said, down in the atelier, among the hanging rolls of textiles around the walls, with a powdery-blue view of the sea from the long window. People have to dress, and then people advertise they make clothes. But they aren't more than coverings. Uniforms. It's the cave people and the skins all over again. They all look the same. They *want* to look the same?

Why not? They live the same dreary life. They wear the same horrible nonsense. They recognize one another. They lie down and gnaw their bones.

What's the prize-winning answer?

Goes too high for me. Clothing has to be cheap for the majority. It has to last. It has to have certain style. Color. So? How far do you have to go before you're up with Lanvin or Pucci? Somewhere down below, you have a mass market. That's the one you tap. The rest? Forget it. And that's *just* where you lose it.

Lose what?

Chen.

Meaning?

It's what we call the womens army, here, *chen.* It's *c-h.* That's a scrape in the throat. And then e-n. *Ch*-en. All girls of eighteen serve the country. They drill, they exercise. Nothing to do with men. Men don't interfere. But the girls learn to walk. Exercise. They have a style to *be.*

You think it's good?

It's *mar*vellous. Look at the girls in uniform. Look at them when they're out. They've achieved *chen.* They deserve the honor. They are part of an ongoing *chen.* I find it beautiful. They also shoot as marksmen. They have unarmed combat. They are very dangerous if they are attacked. They are strong girls.

Good. Glad I'm not there. But what about this *chen?*

Menahem, the carpenter, planing the long cutting-table under the window, pushed back the paper box-cap, bringing memories of *Alice in Wonderland,* and wiped sweat.

It's true, he said. I got two daughters. One just finishing. But they both got it.

Got what? he asked.

Chen.

But what *is* it?

Well, Tovah said, pinching her neck, looking out of the doorway at clematis, white stars in sun. I believe grace is the nearest we'll get to it in English.

Grace?

We don't want an army of hoydens. Our girls will be first, lovers. Then, mothers. But always lovers. For this, *chen*. There is no substitute. Tenderness, yes. Many things. But grace, it's the most important. Even a clumsy girl can have a certain grace. Makes her more lovable.

The morning visits and the talks with so many different people he liked more and more. He felt himself growing with the place. Every day the walls were higher, roads were longer, and better still, the house on top of the hill grew toward the second storey, and the garden broadened, and flagstone paths and terraces reached around the top of the slopes, and he could walk to three of Chom's love seats, each looking west, toward Mediterranean blue, and the peace of Jezreel's green-and-gold plain to the north and east, depending how he wanted to sit.

Here was the calm he had always needed, here the air he had never more than imagined. But the air was real, and so was the calm, the one breathed, the other listened to, and yet, breathing or listening, he was restless. A lot of people worked on all levels of that hill, and he worked for them, and with them, but he was restless, and he knew the cause, and turned away, and pretended to belittle or ignore, well aware that apprehension was chief cause, or to use its correct name, fear.

Fear.

Mr. Paul, Bilara said, that noon. Mr. Jonathan brought in three pictures this morning. Paper's in the file on your desk. He's been everywhere in the world, he says. But he don't look good. He said he just wants the money. I called the lawyers. They said they'll check. I asked him about them monks. He don't know any. Nothing to do with a church the past forty years.

Doesn't surprise me. What are the pictures?

Renoir, Boudin, Léger. All good. Mr. Holtzer was in. He saw them. He said he'll go to one-forty. You don't look so happy. Coffee? Or a drink? How's the Luberman deal?

Drink, please. I don't like what's going on, there. All right on the surface. In fact, very healthy. But there's something about the people. So damn smarmy. Nobody looks you in the eye. After all, they're trustees, not employees.

I *seen* trustees.

Thing is, Bilara, I'm nervous. Y'know? About the things happened before. It seems to me I'm getting suspicious without cause. I begin to judge without the evidence. I believe my intuition's on the fritz. Getting a glitch here and there. No reason. It's a wonderful collection. Always has been. Some ways, better than the Metropolitan. If they want to sell for cash to buy better examples, why not? The Luberman–Hertz Gallery's a landmark whichever way you look. Now's the time. But why the insistence on no publicity? They'd get a better deal if they'd auction. Everybody properly represented. But, no. No, *sir*. I couldn't convince them. What do I do? Put it round the trade?

I believe you owe it to yourself. Trade'll find out. Then what?

I'm the dog.

You' nobody's dog.

Bilara, I'd like *you* to go around there. Take that file. Check the numbers, the registers, dates, certificates, get into it all the way. Then come on back here and tell me what *you* think. We may have been just a mite careless in other deals. I don't know of one. But this one, we put up all the roadblocks. We get the answer, or else.

But that evening, when the gallery shut, and Bilara made the coffee, and they looked over all the notes, they found nothing to worry about. Everything was in order, it all tallied, the lawyers both sides were in agreement, the checks were in the bank, and it all added up to a deal of classic order.

Except.

Away at the side, and barely mentioned, a smaller gallery of reputation, the Wintle, not in the city, had acquired excellent examples of Vlaminck, Chagall, Bonnard, Mondrian, and Bacon for far less than their market value, in exchange for a Cézanne sketch, and a Manet cartoon, both fitting into the Luberman–Hertz progress-in-time exhibit, showing the artists from studenthood to maturity and on to mastery. But this exchange, part of an important overall rearrangement of the Luberman–Hertz, and much to the advantage of the Wintle, surprisingly, went unpublicized.

In the ensuing weeks, other deals became known, and an angry trade began to rumble. Apparently, all the deals favored the smaller galleries, whether financially or in realms of art, always to the detriment of the Luberman–Hertz, and doubts became questions, and then the reporters began calling, and the worries began.

Walter Sedrow called that night from San Francisco, and after they put a deal for a series of Dürer prints out of the way, he asked about David Coningsby, and if he were still a client of the gallery.

Certainly is. He just bought a Renoir.

By any chance, did it come from the Luberman?

No. Why should it?

I believe you have to be real careful over there. This
is the third deal I've heard about this past week. From the
Luberman. I mean, transferred to other galleries on exchange, and held awhile, and sold at a nice, fat profit.
Who's sharing the odds?

An unhappy question?

You have to ask why he buys one from you, and one from
Jim Glasberg, out here, and where Jim got *his* from. I was
down at the house this afternoon. I saw them. Both good.
Was your price near two-five?

More. Much more. Twice that. Plus. Why would Jim settle for half?

I wonder why? I leave the question with you. Funny
thing. I thought of Mr. Blantyre. I'll call Jim. One thing
makes me curious. Doesn't *he* know the market?

That was another sleepless night. The deal for the
Renoir was entirely legal, all papers in order, but something,
somewhere, was wrong. Jim was a smart operator. Why
would he accept fifty percent of the market price?

He turned away in disgust from the intuitional answer.

Fake.

But that was impossible, from the Luberman?

Well, a copy. From the Renoir atelier. When the painter
was crippled with arthritis and his students helped. But it
would have to be sold as a copy. Jim was strict as that. He
had the reputation. But was any copy worth anything near
a hundred and fifty thousand? And would the Luberman
own a copy?

So many questions, a horror of midges back again, no
rest, no balm.

Of one matter he was certain. The painting he sold was
a genuine Renoir, and on that rock, he slept.

Call from Mr. Sedrow while you were out, Bilara said,

that afternoon. He says Mr. Glasberg had no comment, and he couldn't talk to Mr. Coningsby. He said, impasse. What's *that?*

Means you're stuck, he said. Forget it.

The paving of the Plaza had almost reached the asphalt path leading down on the far side, and the main gallery wanted glass in the windows, the bronze doors, and furniture, and there were only seven more workshops for rent.

The idea, the Hill, was ready for business.

But still no telephone, and no goading, or letters, or calls at the local office made any difference.

Let it take its time, Miko said, sadly. Everything's ready. But those bastards won't move till *they're* ready. A little cash under the table might do it.

No. That's the answer.

Miko shrugged.

That's the answer, he said. Six months. A year, maybe? Some people waited a couple of years. Nothing in sight.

I'll use a megaphone, first. How about those radio two-way jobs?

Miko went to Tel Aviv to see what he could find, and came back with three, and they worked from the office in the gallery to the main entrance, and up to the last place on the hill, Moura's, the jewelry workshop, and next door, Tsahali's perfumery. She was last, out on the point, where sea breeze took away the fumes, and sometimes drifted a perfumed veil over the Plaza, and too often tickled errant desire on the road up to the car park, though that, usefully, led to sales among the tourists steadily coming up, finding the place.

There again, others were jealous.

Don't be stupid, he told them. Stock a line of her bottles.

Sell them on commission. Give her some of the stuff *you* make. Let *her* make some money. Hell's the matter with you? We all work together here. You want to hog the lot?

How does she take some of the stuff *I* make? Moshe Carmel, the metal sculptor, shouted, from the back. My stuff weighs a couple of tons.

Make it a couple of pounds. Sell more. Who wants a heap of junk?

I don't make junk, goddammit.

What I've seen *is* junk. You want to leave, you have permission. See Leah. Get your money back. We don't need you. Understood?

You're getting a name, Arye said, that morning. Tossing people out didn't even get a chance to get their laundry done. They're afraid to come up.

All right with me. I want the confident. Not just talkers. People sure of themselves. The artists. The others, the try-to-be's, the would-be's-if-they-could, the hangers-on, pretenders, *no*. Keep them out. This isn't the place.

Just what *is* this place?

Go down to Ephraim Wirtz. He's casting a bronze plaque for the main gate. It'll tell you just what this place *is*. In ten languages.

Why didn't *I* know this? It's *my* design—

It's my *place*. Why don't you walk about and find out what's going on?

I resign. I believe Miko will. You won't talk to us like that.

Good. Your money's in the bank. Shalom.

You'll have no workmen here.

Great. Your kind we don't want.

There was never any need to worry. Chom Vissel, and Toni, down at the grill, found all the workmen they needed, and surprisingly, did a far better job. Windows were put in the main gallery, the work gang pulled up the bronze doors on rollers, Leah at long last got the carpets and furniture out of the crates for the offices, and to cap it, the telephones went in on Thursday morning, and that evening he was able to call Bilara in New York, though, while he waited for the lineman to connect, he thought of another Thursday that went into Friday, and could have gone as far as the graveyard.

Leah's offhand attitude to the upsurge in work underway surprised him, and he came back from the window and asked her again, but she had to run down to the cashier's office to pay out. Azma'uta, at the desk in the corner, looked at him with the dark eyes that said much, and little, and smiled from far away, and then she picked up the books and went down to pay her girls.

He was left there, feeling curiously alone, wondering if he had any friends, asking himself if he made a mistake to go there, if he should take the Mandelbaum offer, make a big profit, and quit, leaving someone else with the worry, and a ready-made housing estate for summer visitors.

The idea savored of midge-flight, though it was certainly a business proposition, and in the highest bracket, and in a way, tempting.

But the wonder of the view from the window had more to say, and loud in his mind, heard, he imagined, in his heart.

Perhaps some ancestor of his father or mother had once stood here, lived out the years in this place, might have left their bones among the tombs found by the clearing squads. He felt certain excitement in the thought.

Yet, living seemed to be in fragments, not as in the old days. No more the comfortable New York apartment, soft light on silver and crystal in the drawing-room, and the walls of masters, the Da Vinci, and Urbino, among their magnificent brethren, and the leather-comfort of the study, the fire, and the walls of books. No longer the pleasure of the walk across Central Park and down to Fifty-seventh, a glance at the newspapers, a skimming of the art reviews, latest sales reports, and then Bilara with coffee and the mail. Year after year, with few breaks, and then the sheer luxury of going back to what he loved, that seemed to love *him*.

Now, for one or other reason, the mind swung between memory and what was, now and then, a tearing apart, destructive, not the quiet of other days, or the calm summary of fact, but a frenetic muddle of names, times, dates, that brought him to realize how much he had depended on Bilara. And the only place to go back to, these nights, was the one-room caravan.

Perhaps Sam Ravicz broke the chain when he came in just before noon, carrying a large green baize folio tied in a bow with black tapes. The way they hung reminded him of a funeral armband. He stood in the background, waiting until the client had been shown to the door, and on a nod, followed to the office. He looked as if he might have had a drink or two or three to give him that calm face.

Mr. Paul, I been breaking my head about this, he said, and let the folio rest against his knee. You know I been doing special jobs for most of the galleries all the time I'm in business? So I get to know the painters. Schools. Periods. All like that. This come in day before yesterday. Rush job. I had it before. Somebody must have forgot.

Let's see it. What, forgot?

Sam undid the bow, and drew out a fine example of Caravaggio, and went across to put it on the easel.

Every time I frame one of the greats, I put my little mark on the back. If I don't tell you where it is, you won't find it. My way of shaking hands with the painter. He's been dead three, four hundred years? He's still giving Sam Ravicz a nice piece of business? I framed *him* eleven years ago.

Well?

Sam held out his hands, hunched his shoulders, looked up under his brows.

So where's my mark?

Eleven years, the mark could have faded, he said, walking across to the picture.

Not *my* mark, Mr. Paul.

He went over to the desk drawer and chose a magnifier out of the rack, took a loupe from his pocket, and went back to the picture. The magnifier brought astonishment, the loupe confirmed, and he looked up, at Sam's nodding head.

That frame, probably fourteen–fifteen century. Come in two five-foot battens, broke off of something else. Why?

Fear of asking a question had never before worried him.

All right, he said. I know the original of this is in the Luberman. Who's this for?

The Luberman, Sam said, through the window. That's why I'm here. That picture don't have my mark. It *was* my frame. Still good. Why go to the expense? Strip a good frame, and then have a frame of this? Ask me, the batten's worth more. That's why I came to you. I don't want no trouble.

It took a little time to think, but then he agreed with himself, wishing he had a witness.

Sam, if you'll leave it here today, I believe you're in the clear. Come in any time in the morning. I'll have a few of the dealers see it. This is pretty damn serious. Happen to have any pieces of that batten left?

In that plastic wrap in the outer pocket, Mr. Paul. Shalom.
Shalom.

Strange word.

Ageless.

As crime is ageless.

He called Berthold Gluck at the Chalmerston Gallery, not
exactly a friend, or even acquaintance, but certainly a stare-
glare competitor over the years, yet a man he respected,
first for knowledge, second for reputation, third as forth-
right critic of museum sales without benefit of publicity. His
wife said he would be back at nine o'clock from Chicago,
and he asked him to call the gallery any time after.

He had a lamb chop at the St. Regis, and got back just
when Gluck's car drove up, saved any awkwardness by a
friendly nod, silence on the way in, and he switched on
the lights flooding the easel, not a word, simply a look.

Gluck let his overcoat fall, threw his hat in the chair,
and, hands behind, walked over to bend forward, turning
his head to see the brushflow, taking out a loupe that made
a sound going into the eye-space, pulling out a key chain
with a small flashlight, holding the white circle on faces,
small details, and stood straight, slowly, clasping his hands.

He dropped the flashlight in his pocket, put the loupe
away, and turned.

The broad head was combed smooth, white. The eyes
were almost the same color. The nose might have been
Assurbanipal's, lips a line, chin blunt challenge.

All right, he said, in the small voice. I believe I know
what's coming. This is supposed to be a Caravaggio? The
one in the Luberman? What's it doing here?

Sam Ravicz framed it eleven years ago. He had it back for
reframing. The frame batten's fourteenth century. It was
supplied. The odds and ends are in that baize folio.

It's a wonderful copy.

Being charitable.

Let's hear it.

You tell *me*.

A fake? Why?

Where's the original?

Should be at the Luberman.

Why's it going there?

This? To the *Luber*man?

Sam's taking it there tomorrow. Getting his money. For framing it.

Gluck's face seemed to withdraw to a narrower space. His eyes were hidden.

Wouldn't want to tell anybody what I'm thinking, he said, mild. Any ideas?

Why don't we both go there tomorrow, different times, and see if it *is* there? If it's not, we both ask. Somebody has to tell us. Or if not?

I'll be there around eleven, Gluck said, and picked up his overcoat. Glad you called me. Had a feeling. This backs it up. I believe we have a job.

If they're selling copies, never mind originals, I'd say we have. We can go out of business. They have the originals, and a school of copyists, let's say. What's to prevent selling a copy as good as that for the original's price? It doesn't want too many scruples. It doesn't need *us*.

Wait a minute, here.

Why? Would you put down a hundred thousand, cash, and challenge anybody to prove that's not a Caravaggio? You know it's not? Why? What gives you the right to say so? You own a gallery. You have an axe to grind. Lets *you* out. *I* own one. Lets *me* out. Why *isn't* that a Caravaggio? All the tests say it *is*.

That's a dish of squash.

Read what's certified on the back. Now go as far as the Supreme Court. I say we're at the mercy of a lot of interested money. We're being infected by the copyist. Can't make a living as a creative painter? Fine. Why not copy? Great control, draughtsmanship, color. Any amount of canvas available of pretty well any period. Scrape the paint off. Mix it in the lab. Chemists'll produce anything. Put it through any test, carbon-fourteen, all that. Make no difference. You have a painting, by so-and-so, of that period, attested by these certificates, signed by these authorities. Who's going to argue?

We're going to be agents for a bunch of fakers?

It's what some of us are in danger of being right now. Even, remember, Picasso can't tell what's his, and what's a copy. And how many others? Dead, among the tombstone dates?

How about lunch tomorrow? One o'clock? Versailles?

Remembering the cigar the waiter offered, seeing patterns in the smoke, greyish ghosts wisping to nothing in air-conditioned, sauce-scented air from the chafing-dish on the next table, wondering what to say, how to say it, or if he should say anything.

Behind grey whorls, Gluck's eyes staring, paler than the cloud, touched with amber from the table lamp, pellet-hard unblinking, rimmed by squeezed lids.

Talk to that fat guy up there? he asked, in the mild voice. He nodded.

Tell you it was none of your business? He nodded.

Did he tell you he never heard of Sam Ravicz? He nodded.

Gluck's fist opened to rap short nails on the table.

I believe we have to call a meeting—tonight—of the association. No word outside. Put the case. Agreed?

He nodded.

You're not saying a hell of a lot?

I'll tell you. I used to think I was in an honorable profession. Old Mr. Blantyre once said to me, Never forget you are the safeguard both for your client's money, and more importantly, for the artist. If you do anything to forfeit that trust, go on out and sell a tray of pins and elastic. It's about all you're going to be good for. Be *sure*. You don't belong in this profession. You have no right to have any share in a world where men suffer to learn, suffer to express ideas, suffer to overcome their own ills and the appalling ignorance and forgetfulness of the world outside. It's a magic place, a royal place, and the shill and the huckster have no part. Keep faith with your professional ethic. That's what he said. It's what I always tried to *do*. Know something? Those days, I didn't know what an ethic was. I had to go around to the Mercantile Library and find out.

Gluck took out a pen to sign the check, waving him off.

Instructive lunch, and I enjoyed it. Meet at my place tonight, nine-thirty? No word anywhere. We have to get a thorough, well-based campaign going. Gather the information, choose the proper time, and knock the hell out of them. But we have to have a team of top lawyers. Let's not forget there's such a thing as libel suits. But I'm not going to have the good name of my gallery ruined by a bunch of time-serving swingers. Hips. The wide-tie guys. Like that bastard this morning? None of your business? Got a little news for *him*.

Strolling up the top pathway, almost staired in stone blocks, all the brushwood cleared, trees breaking foliage,

most in bud, planted bulbs coming up in green spikes everywhere, he had a feeling it might be time to open the gallery.
Just open the doors, and see how long it took to find the
first client. Visitors now and again came up as far as Toni's
grill, and after lunch climbed to the Plaza, looked around
at stones and rubble, and walked down again, perhaps brow-
beaten by silence and a sense of age.

The workshops were not ready to open for lack of stock,
and anyway, he wanted an outright show by everybody, so
that any visitor, buying or not, would find pleasure simply
in looking at items not to be bought anywhere else. That was
the main idea. One of each he made the invariable rule,
never a copy, except in the perfumery, though even there,
all the flasks were different, made by Ayelethe and Hedva
from every sort of glass, but only from the lees of the pour,
because with the main run they made flower vases, light
fixtures in chunky crystal, surgical glass and laboratory
shapes, and, even without visitors, they did well, far more
than paying their way.

Tovah had already made a name with a ten-day exhibition in Rome of colored textiles, wools, and cashmeres from
the looms below the Plaza, and almost next door, Zipporah
cut the simple dresses and ensembles, and the team of seamstresses put them together, one of each, but only one, and
day by day, the wardrobe racks filled the long room lit by
the Mediterranean's blue, and even, perhaps, by the hope,
or the prayer in the singing needles, most Russian and
Iraqi, few words of Hebrew among them, little more to sus-
tain than Zipporah's hand on the shoulder, a reassuring
shake of affection and perhaps a sense of being at last among
their own, in a land of their own, safe, protected, at peace.

From the beginning he had a working agreement with
the Absorption Ministry, through Yehudit, to send all the

needlewomen, whether seamstresses, embroideresses, or those expert in knitwear, crochet, or petit point, direct to the Hill for immediate employment. Four large marquees and a dozen tents lodged them for the moment, but housing was being built. The difficulty lay in husbands and children, though most of the husbands took whatever job was offered, and the children went either to the kindergarten, or to the small school started by Hannah, a footloose American stroller, one among the many, brought up to the Plaza by Yehudit, shown the older children, starting a game in dumb show, and staying on to take charge.

Misfit husbands, engineers of all kinds, clerks of works, buyers of various lines for wholesale and other markets, window dressers, bookbinders, scholars, plumbers, and a dozen other activities, were all in the keeping of Yehudit, and she did a great job, a triumph of diplomacy, although, since she spoke Russian, half the job was done because everybody understood, and trusted her. Diplomacy, certainly, because all of them had a definite idea of status. Any notion that Marxist or Soviet philosophy permitted all to regard themselves as equals was shown to be absurd in squabbles for precedence, devil take the hindmost, I-want-this-and-that, I-want-to-live-where-I-like, I-don't-give-a-damn-for-the-next.

Don't worry, Yehudit said, tiredly. They're our own people. The Chosen? They have it built in. We're better than anybody else. And I'm better than you. You have to tread on them. With a smile.

I know just how they feel, he said. Careful where you put your feet. Remember, they're *home*.

He wished *he* were, back in New York, at the apartment. But it was sold, everything moved out, with some part of himself he never wanted for any moment to remember.

It seemed impossible, but so was the gallery, again, with so much of himself, gone.

Gone.

And Mr. Blantyre accused. Ac*cused*.

He looked down the length of the Plaza, past the two rows of olives, twisted as if they had to suffer to be fruitful, almost seeing a pattern of his thoughts, and the rose bushes beginning to root, trying to assess what had happened, striving to see what more he might have done.

You ask the questions, the shrink said. You know the answers. Why bother *me?* Why not look yourself in the face and say it in words? You know them. You come here to *say* them. Why *don't* you? What stops you?

He knew. Bilara knew. The others knew.

It did him no good, standing in evening light, nowhere to go except the caravan, knowing anything, knowing nothing.

The whole place was his, but it meant so little. He could have walked away from it. But there was a lot to do, many to help, a word to be kept, and if he ran away once, he swore, in stone, he never would again.

Absconded. That was the word.

Left it to Bilara, and Sergeant Mackearn, and Inspector Hanrahan, and Berthold Gluck, and Lucien Weil, the lawyer, in ascending order.

But he ran first, and sold out after.

Say it, the shrink said. Don't just think it. Get a hold of yourself. *Say* it.

But it made no difference if he said it, or not. Everything was gone. Life was something else. Everything was different. Even the girls. There was no Effie, with a call service, or if he felt like a drink, the apartment on Park, with all the babes standing around in nothing much, your choice, drinks on the house. Until you got the check. Then, it seemed, the house was on you.

That night, Bilara put the books and the cashbox in the safe, and while she shut the door, the telephone rang, and she reached.

Reid Gallery? Right. I'm sorry. We closed. Open Monday, ten A.M.

A man's voice sounded like filtered chicken cackle. She looked around, covered the mouthpiece.

Somebody talking about the Name, she said, smiling her own especial non-smile. Says he's going to be here in fifteen minutes with the collection. Wants you to buy them all back.

Tell him it's no problem. You go on home. Call in at the Sixteenth. A sniff of the blue won't do any harm.

You sure about this, Mr. Paul?

I'm sure. That collection's good as they come. Let me handle it.

Bilara wasted more time getting into a hat and coat, and turning faucets in the girls' room, and just as she reached the door, the buzzer cut her Good Night, and she opened it, and a man came in, followed by a line of others carrying pictures underarm and dangling from their hands.

Evening, the first man said. I'm from the family. We just like you to buy these back, see? He bought 'em off of you.

Wait a minute. Get this straight. I don't "buy" anything. The owner of these was a client of mine. All right. I know what they're worth. Find the right buyer, I know what I can get for them. Take time, that's all.

Men were still coming in, lining pictures face to the wall all round the room.

That's the lot, the last man said. Thirty-two, right?

Right. All I want now's a receipt for thirty-two pictures,

and I'll be around tomorrow and find out when we collect, see?

When did you people stop using your brains? Or did you ever have one?

The man stared, sideways. He was the bar-pallor type, black hair greased down, talcum like leper's ash on a shadow-shaved jowl.

Look, he said, in a couple of paces forward. We don't want no trouble, see?

You look. Do you have any idea what these are worth? It takes time to find a buyer.

How long?

Maybe a month. Maybe more.

Listen. That's too long, see?

Then take them away.

They stay right here, and I collect from you. Get it?

Almost without a sound, Inspector Hanrahan and two plainclothesmen came in, and Bilara stood in shadow.

The Inspector smiled, head down, pulling off his gloves.

We-he-*hell,* my old friend, Gino Va*nuz*zi, he said. How've you been keeping? Got a little business going?

Ask *him,* Vanuzzi said. I'm just representing a party.

Repre*sent*ing? *Well.* What are you waiting for?

I want a receipt.

You get no receipt from me. The Inspector can count these canvases. He has witnesses. I take no responsibility of any kind. You left them here without permission or agreement. I want, first of all, a document, drawn by a lawyer, assuring me that you have a legal right to sell this property.

The widow told me to.

Good. Then it shouldn't be all that difficult. But I can't do any business until I have that document on my desk, naming the pictures, the date of purchase, and the amount

paid. Then I'll let you know when they're sold, and the
widow can come here and collect the cash, or else her attorney can save her the effort.

Listen. You pay *me*.

Unless you have the requisite power-of-attorney, not one
cent.

O.K. Gino, the Inspector said, in harshest good humor.
Thirty-two, right? We're witnesses. Let's go. And listen. I
know the widow. I'll call her. Make you feel better? Mr.
Denis, you want these pictures left here? Because there's a
law of trespass. I can take them along. He has to go to the
Sixteenth Precinct and provide the proof he's legal owner,
or has the owner's permission.

I wish you'd do that. Puts the responsibility where it belongs.

The Inspector waved to the plainclothesmen.

O.K., you guys. Take all of these out to the car. You have
a piece of chalk, we could number 'em, maybe?

Bilara went over to her desk.

Right here, she said. I also got labels, put the names on.

But the first canvas he turned about should have been
one of the Modigliani, and was not, and walking slowly
along the line, he picked out the other, and neither was that.

Inspector, I call this an act of God you and these officers
are witnesses. These two are fakes. They are *not* the original
paintings I sold.

The Inspector sat against the desk, smiling.

Better take a seat, Gino. This is going to take some little
time.

Look, I only know what they give me.

Right. They all here, right? So you sit there, be a good
boy. *Right?*

One by one, while Bilara wrote the labels, and the Inspector initialled in chalk, he lifted the pictures into the light, and one by one he judged them to be fakes, and at the end, he called Berthold Gluck and asked him to come over.

Bilara and the plainclothesmen were still labelling when he got there, with Joe Rabin and Henny Fuld, and again, one by one the pictures went on the easel, and the three looked at them with loupe and magnifier, and at the end, Bilara brought in a tray of drinks.

I've seen some good fakes, Gluck said, in the mild voice. These top anything I *ever* saw. Somebody has to have one hell of a payroll.

There's a more serious aspect, he said. All these had originals. Those are what I sold. I have the records and color prints. These are sent back to me for sale? Fakes?

False pretences, Henny Fuld said, pouring a drink. Joe? Ice?

Two, please, Rabin said. What you need here's a lawyer, fast.

I like to ask a question, Hanrahan said. What's the total value of the originals?

Gluck's eyes went to the light, suddenly no longer small, but flashing an extraordinary pale glint of mind, and swivelled, chin up, to meet his stare.

I'd say somewhere between three million-three-quarters and four million, he said, and Gluck nodded, sharp, taking a drink from Fuld.

Nice piece of change, Hanrahan said, smiling at Vanuzzi. What's these fakes worth?

Each? Depending on the buyer, maybe a thousand, on up. Or down.

Any reputable dealer would have to tell a client it's a copy, Gluck said. Take the price from there.

O.K., Vanuzzi, Hanrahan said, pulling the gloves on. You're coming with me, *with* the fakes. I'm booking you as the owner pro tem, see? Get a lawyer, come in when you like. I'll get on to the widow, find out what *she* knows. Be in touch tomorrow, Mr. Denis. 'Night, gentlemen.

Listen, Vanuzzi said. I thought this was strictly a delivery, pick-up job.

Right, Hanrahan said, with a hand on his arm. So what else? You deliver, I pick up, right? Boy, you're sure headed for the stars. They hand-picked you. Mugging, the first time. Pushing, the second. Now it's false *pre*tences on Fifty-seventh? What's wrong? Y'ambitious?

You can't book me.

Who wants to? I'm taking you in for being in possession of thirty-two pieces of junk, right? What's wrong with that? How many guys got to be millionaires out of junk?

Bilara shut the outer door, and the steel blinds rattled.

Lucien Weil won't be long, Gluck said, over at the tray. We had this fake problem all along. Now, it's no problem. It's a goddam epidemic. Where are those originals? They have to be found, first.

Let me make a suggestion, he said. Bilara, anything against working a couple more hours?

Not a thing, Mr. Paul. I'm right here.

He turned to them.

Can you get your secretaries in? Or one or two? We could send a night letter to all members of the association, naming the items, warning there may be other fakes in the pipe-line.

Now, there's a goddam good idea, Gluck said. Let me have that phone.

Three more lines in here, Bilara said, and switched her office light on.

When you have a spare moment, call the St. Regis for a dozen hamburgers and the fixings, he said. Three bottles of claret. When they're ready, call you, take a cab. And look, seared outside, rare *in*side, and really toast those buns.

He felt he knew Esau's feelings when he sold his birthright for a mess of rich, good-smelling pottage. He could have sold anything for a real hamburger, a juicy steak.

The country, the place, the people, all wonderful, but the food was bland, tasteless, *noth*ing to eat. Eggs, cheese, cucumbers, tomatoes, olives, all right. But the mouth craved.

Appetite. Taste.

Taste?

Not the taste of all those years ago, when the pioneers thanked God for what they could get. Another day brought other mouths, another palate. Toni's grill was a blessing. But without it, living ran away in a munch. But day after day, it was the same munch. For one reason or another, year in and out, so many seemed to munch their lives away, and prefer it, grow, proliferate.

But looking down that long, empty Plaza fairway, he rejected it, threw it off. There had to be food he could eat and enjoy. The religious stuff was for others. They certainly did not belong on the Hill. Toni was a good start, but crude, even pre-medieval. There had to be another style.

You want the Rabbi up here? Leah asked, that morning. Like to meet you.

If anyone else wants to meet him, fine. Not for me. Any other religion, the same. I don't want to meet *any* of them. Hear me? No religion. It's not a business I understand.

Strolling through the portico of the *soukh* on the other side of the Plaza, he looked at the shut gates, listening to radios, the thumping noise of TV sets behind them, one, other, or both, murdering the night's silence.

All right, he told Leah, that morning. I've seen TV aerials going up here. I want all of them down. At the end of the day, I don't want to see an aerial. There will never be another. Understood? We don't live on that kind of food.

A lot of them won't like it, Leah said. It's lonely up here. They like to be in touch.

They don't belong here.

What *does* belong here?

Artists.

She laughed. Her mouth opened. He heard the noise in her throat. Ah-*hagh!*

Artists? she chided. *Artists?* What's your idea of an artist? That was a question.

Look, the shrink said. What do you suppose yourself to *be?* Tell me. Come on. Pretend this or that. But who *are* you? What do you pretend to *be?* What, exactly, *is* your idea? Why are you living? Why do you *want* to live? What do *you* call living? What sort of answer do you have?

But there never were any answers, and he resented all the questioning, feeling as though a hot spike had been driven through his head, and that was the end of the shrink, then and there, but not the end of the questions. And only the start of the midge-cloud of half-formed queries, more thought-patterns than what could be put in words, plagueing him whenever he tried to think about them, giving up, locking the outer door, sliding the blinds.

He held, wholeheartedly, to the wish that he had studied more philosophy, or psychology. The books he bought to tell him were all in sentences he could read time and again without understanding what they were meant to give, sending him to sleep, or, awake, provoking other questions, none of them in words, more in guise of feeling, but without shape.

He had that odd notion, walking around the first exhibition on the Hill, not for the public, but solely for the artists in residence.

Not bad, but not what I want, he said, at the meeting, later.

What *do* you want? Mordechai, the leather-worker called, from the back.

I believe I can tell you. It's what the older men, the masters, had to say, but they were above communication. People are different today. They went to school. And all *you* do, it's simple, it's *look*. Looking, either you know, or you *don't*. You get burnt, or you don't. It's not an ex*ist*ence. It's not a living. It's not commercial. It's *be*-ing. Being is what you're selling. The greatest gave of themselves. It was *one*, in grace. *One*, in grace is all you get. That's the one you pay for. There *are* no more.

So why can't we do the same? Mordechai called, among a lot of girls. But not the one-of-each nonsense. This is a different kind of a world. You have to grow. Get the idea right.

You haven't got it, he said. You never will. You can move out. I don't want you here.

Mordechai threw the girls aside, and stood, beard, mustache bristling.

Listen, we can take this place over, he shouted. We don't need you.

Take it over, he said. Anytime you like. No trouble. Just pay my price, that's all. Then you can run it *your* way. While I'm here, it's *my* way. Now, you get the hell out, no later than tomorrow morning. Chom Vissel will be at your place to move you at six o'clock. Got it? You and your goddam skins.

That night, Leah came to the caravan and said she had the worst kind of message. Many of the tenants were thinking of moving out. His methods made them feel insecure. They were going to the Ministry to protest.

Sit down and have a drink, and let's see you smile, he said, and cleared a chair of clothing. Now, let's have this straight. I want you to go to those people and tell them they are at perfect liberty to go wherever they please. I'll provide free transport. I don't even want to know their names. While I finance this place, I'll run it as I think.

They think you're too autocratic. Sort of dictator. One of them said, Next thing, gas ovens.

Whoever said that, I want them out tomorrow morning. I make you responsible.

I doubt if we can do that. There's a lot of stuff, first of all. Second, they have rights.

You didn't read the fine print. Tell Chom he'll need a dozen more men.

You wouldn't want to alter your mind?

He gave her the drink.

Leah, if ever you say anything like that to me again, pack up. Understand? I have a right hand. You'll soon meet her. But I don't want a left hand that doesn't grasp. Doesn't do its job. Doubts. It's because you doubt yourself—more than anyone—you can't paint. Get one idea in mind. This is a place for artists. People of vision. Of the image. They have *no* doubts. They gamble their time on this earth. Not for money. Not for anything except to see their particular dream come to life. That's the reward. That's what I'm here for. I have a dream all my own.

Well, I understand that. I just thought I ought to. Uh, well. Sort of act. Uh, peacemaking?

It's *not* peacemaking. It's confusing an issue. If you look back, you'll agree that the people I threw out haven't been artists. They were taking advantage of commercial possibilities. This guy tonight. Mordechai? Pretends to be a tailor in pelts? One of a kind? He knew the rules. So he sends two hundred cutouts to Haifa yesterday to be stitched by cheap labor over there? Doesn't even use our local girls? *Out.*

Going to lose your pottery-workers. No more ceramics.

You deserve that drink. Another trio with mercantile ideas. And besides, I don't like their general attitude. If you're going to live and work in this country, *and* make a nice profit, then be loyal. It's the least to ask.

They're very democratic.

They don't know the meaning of the word.

I've heard it around. I mean, the word. What *is* the meaning?

He looked at her. A smart girl, New Yorker, well-schooled, three languages, all this, pretty legs, and all that.

You never heard of *demos? Kratia?* Greek? *Demos,* people. *Kratia,* the art or science of rule. But when the words came into use, Greece was being run by slaves. The only people were the wealthy. The aristo. It's come to have another meaning? The *real* meaning is just behind you. You tell those pottery people to be out of here tomorrow morning. That's final. And tell Chom.

He'll love it. Doesn't like them.

Decent instinct. No wonder the dogs love him.

But then, some sort of instinct warned, that morning, when Berthold Gluck and Lucien Weil, the lawyer, came in, trying to look like all the other people in there, until he finished a deal for a collection of Islamic eighth- and ninth-century miniatures, a dozen fly-leaves, and a painting on silk from Tabriz of the fourteenth century. Bilara handled the details, and he followed Gluck and Lucien Weil into the office.

You ever meet Marvin Feld? Gluck asked. Has places in Nebraska, Kansas, all in there.

I heard the name.

He just called me. That's why I brought Lucien along. He's got both the Modigliani originals for sale. Wanted to know if I was interested. Where are the fakes?

The widow claimed them. I've heard nothing since.

So what's the position?

I believe she has to be informed of this. By a lawyer. She signed for thirty-two paintings of uncertain authorship, and of no ascertained value.

Smart. What happens if those guys come back?

I'll talk to the Inspector.

Gluck looked at the cognac through window-light.

You *could* be dead. I believe you have to be awful risk-conscious. How did those Modigliani get out there?

We could ask.

I can do better, Lucien Weil said. I have small-town firms I do business with as legal representatives or attorneys all over. Those places, they know pretty well when you change your shirt. I could ask for information. On behalf of clients ready to buy, of course.

No more about this bunch of copyists? Gluck said, always the mild voice. Forgers, fakers, crooks, *and* so on. No ideas where, or who? This has to be a sizeable job. Top men. How many are there? I'd say, damn few. Who are they? And where?

The Inspector's working on it.

Gluck scratched the enormous forehead, looking down.

So they drop him a grand. What's he ever going to tell *you*? Or any other cop. They just sold a whole culch of heroin back on the street. A guy gets twenty years for bringing it in. So the cops sell it? Pretty soon, all you have to do to get a fix is talk to a cop. You want a joint? Ask the guy on traffic duty. But apart from the Modigliani pair, we have thirty other originals floating around. And how many more copies? Who's buying them?

Not if they listen to me.

How do you *know* an original? Weil asked. Here's a perfect copy. There's the original. How do you pick it out?

Thirty–forty years experience, first, he said, and Gluck shut his eyes in a sharp nod. Then, a knowledge of the painter's style of working. But what the hell, your word's as good as mine. A copy, these days, is a work of art. It *has* to be. But that's what *we*'re here for. To stop the spurious from invading the decency of creative art. The creative artist has his price. The copyist takes what he can get.

What interests me is how these people got into it, Weil said. The last people in the world I'd think of. I mean, Mafia. *If* it's that.

Easy enough, Gluck said. Have you looked at the yearly total of art sales? It's money. Money's what interests. So they invest. Then? They find the copyists. Simple? I agree with Paul. A decency has to be preserved. Question is, how?

I'll call this woman, Weil said. Am I representing you, or Mr. Denis here, or both?

Represent the association, Gluck said. We all have an equal interest in this. If it takes a hold, I can see us closing down. Won't be needed.

Anything new on the Luberman front?

Most of the board's touring Europe or South America. Till the heat's off. A little thought to leave with you. The Giotto collection you sold? I have them for sale. They're beautiful. But if they're by Giotto, I made my own head.

Probably parts of a large canvas. Wartime casualty? You're safe enough.

Safe as the people who buy these fakes?

The Giottos have a lot more back-up.

On paper. I can't find out how they got here.

Nazi submarine? Or one of our bombers coming back here? We weren't all that blameless, you know. In any case, prove they're not Giotto. I went right through it. I have all the files here.

I believe you're going to need them. The Church finally decided they're stolen from some place in Italy. So you'll have a visit. Like I had. This morning.

Play pat-hands?

Get the spikes in your shoes. I'm *tell*ing you.

Summer became hot, and desert wind blew to dry up the sweat, but in shadow the skin ran, and shirts became sops in moments. Girls wore bikinis to work, most visitors did, and men wore shorts, sometimes a shirt outside, or a singlet, or the buff. He found it funny to leave the caravan to do a day's work in a shirt, shorts, and sandals. That freedom in clothing seemed to lead to a freedom in all else, though if he heard the hints, he took little advantage. From the start he made it a rule that romance on the Hill was not for him, first because he had to give orders, and second, they earned their daily bread through him. Instead, he made no secret of inviting visiting girls to the caravan. Many were happy to have a few days of baths and a comfortable bed, meals at Toni's grill, or at Dov's bar, or cooking a simple dish in the caravan's little kitchen. None of them stayed in memory. After a few days he forgot them, and they, he supposed, forgot him sooner.

The male–female link surprised him more and more. Whether as youth or young man, or until he had been married for perhaps ten years or more, women had been closed off, treated as creatures of any other world except his own. The romantic idea of women had always been a bane. But it was imposed by the norms of courtesy, the choice of reading, and his father's insistence that women must be treated differently, kept at arm's length, and on certain days, when they were unclean, avoided. The unclean part he never understood until Mitch Ganz, a medical student, told him, in bitter contempt.

You are the unclean, Mitch said, eyebrows up, looking one-eyed at the neck of the beer bottle. Your sort make me puke. I suppose you and your precious father pray thanks every morning that you weren't born women? Like the rest of them?

I don't. I don't pray at all. I don't know about *him*.

I'm going to send you a little book. You mean you've lived to be twenty-what? And you still don't know what goes on with your sister? What sort of friend are you? What type of ideas? You're not even a decent savage. You'll get the book. That's all. Sorry I ever even *talk*ed to you.

He never forgot that searing voice, and never heard any tone to match, until Bilara came to tell him the Bishop Petretti Eldonado would like to discuss a matter of mutual interest, and came in, below Bilara's shoulder, clipped white hair, skull-cap, thin, bony face and hands, and the hardest brown eyes he ever saw, that never looked anywhere else except at him, even while he showed the dossier, item by item, starting with the original canvas, that must have been almost as big as the Assisi frescoes, taken from a church near Potenza by retreating German troops, all detailed, in a report of many pages.

He listened, let it run, and opened his own files, bringing in Melsom, a suicide, and the paramour, and the Spanish count, his castle, title, family, lineage, all recorded, and false.

When the Spanish police got that far, we gave it to Interpol, he said. That's as far as *we* got.

It is the property of the Church. It is of no interest?

Far to the contrary. If you can establish a claim that a lawyer could argue in court, then you have a chance. But it's a long time since Goering lifted those train- and truckloads into Germany. Many claims aren't settled even now. With this one, a buyer paid in a straight deal against these documents. They're supported by the Spanish Embassy. You may say they were forged. You'll have to prove it. Second, you'll have to prove that those are Giotto portraits. Far more difficult.

Difficult? There was only *one* Giotto.

We won't argue. But are the frescoes in the church at Assisi his original work?

But of course.

You'd better enquire. You'll find they were overpainted by the monks around the end of World War Two. Not for the first time, possibly?

The Bishop got up, and made no doubt of bad temper in pushing files and papers into the briefcase.

Mother Church is so helpless, he said. We are crucified between thieves. It has always been, from the beginning. Surrounded by liars. But when we find our very substance taken from us, we must say so. These works of the ages are from the sons of our family. Messer Giotto was of the earliest. Why should you be permitted to trade in our blood? You make money on our suffering?

The moment you have any real evidence, come and see

me, he said. Or see a lawyer. All you have at this moment
is talk. Doesn't go any place.

But naturally not. There has been talk for almost two
thousand years. It covers what is thought. *You* people, and
what you think, for example.

Would you care to explain that?

The Bishop snapped the clasp of the briefcase, and stood.

I explain nothing, he said. I have no reason to explain.
You and those who trade with you, why should you explain?
You make the money. On everything that is stolen. Money
is your god.

That's not quite true.

Partly true? After all, you are a Jew.

It means something to you?

A Jew is a Jew.

True. Bilara, show this man out.

Yes, *sir*. This way.

You will regret this lack of co-operation. This rudeness.

I regret I even allowed you in here. Next time, make it a
letter. I'll burn it.

The Bishop looked back in the doorway.

If it is of interest, *sir*, I see in you precisely the qualities
that crucified the prince of love, he said, loudly, turning
heads. I shake off the dust.

Both feet trod hard.

You raised more than you shook, he said. Why not spread
the Word instead of dust?

But the silhouette flapped skirts halfway down the room,
toward Bilara holding the door open.

I do not wish your help, the Bishop said, in the same
loud voice.

You don't get none, Bilara said, giving him those eyes.
Just letting out kind of a nasty smell, that's all.

The Bishop looked up at her.

You are a Christian? he asked, high-pitched, and it sounded *chreees*tian.

First Baptist, Birming*ham*, and that's in Alabama, she said, in the small play of hips. Have a proposition, maybe?

The Bishop threw up a hand in an Ah! of disgust, went down two steps in a pace, gone, and Bilara shut the door.

How do these guys get the jobs? she said. Wouldn't rate janitor back home.

Takes all kinds, he said. Did you see any of the prints he pulled out, here?

Saw a couple of the El Grecos. Didn't the big ones look like Titian?

And a Breughel. Now take a look at our file on the famous thirty-two. Don't they appear? Get Mr. Berthold Gluck. He'll be interested.

Leah came in that morning with a long document in Hebrew, and a face almost as long.

The people you tossed out, she said. They've made common cause. They're suing you for breach of contract, restraint of trade, and a lot of other things.

Don't bother me with it. Call Mr. What's-his-name. Ginzfeld, Bauer, Rosen, and Cohn. It's almost poetry.

This isn't, Leah said, holding up the paper. I did three years of law. Enough to know you have trouble.

Let it come, he said. Nobody has leave to bother me. I'm on my own hill.

Here's somebody wants to join you. Emmanuel Yigal, and his wife and daughter. He's sort of a painter in metals. She's a sculptress, and the daughter's a coppersmith.

Sounds good. Did they read the fine print?

He's a lawyer. He says.

Let's see them.

Emmanuel Yigal wore shorts and a lot of curly grey hair on his chest, a beard, mustache, and a Ben Gurion mop. His wife, tall, stringy, with grey hair in a knot, a short dress of blue towelling, and the eyes of a frightened mare, stared here, there, twisting her hands, caked with what looked like cement, making a rasping sound that put his teeth on edge.

But the daughter, in a yellow bikini, tall, blond hair below her knees, looked at him from the shadowy half-smile-kiss-my-teats eyes of a harem broad, unmistakable as one of Effie's.

He could have said No, so easily, then, before any word was said, but he felt her eyes on him, a cloak of many touchings, a promise, in abandon, a stripping of all innocence, if, that is, any was there, and in those moments, he had room to doubt.

I'm Manny Yigal, Mr. Denis, he said, holding out a hand that felt like a dried, pulpy fish. The wife, Binnie, and the daughter, Ora. I'm a maker of any kind of ikons. In precious metals. Binnie's a sculptress. Also in metals. Ora's just starting. Makes rubbings in copper. We're just looking for a place to settle. We got kind of tired, looking. We're sick of this world. We took a look at this place, and we said, This is *right*. We're away from it.

Tired of it?

Just plain tired. There's no place they'll let you live any more if you don't live like everybody else. We don't want to. We want to live like *we* want to, work like *we* want to, and just enjoy *what's* here *while* we're here.

You're striking a chord. All right, Leah. Read over the contract. Show them the temporary quarters, and let me know.

Well, thank *you*, Mr. Denis, Yigal said, and his wife

stared smiling mare's eyes sideways, and Ora looked down the Plaza, mouth open, showing lower teeth, but he knew she looked at him from her ears.

He seemed to see, almost feel, Nelda's raised knee, and he felt the hot lunge of danger, warned in so many words, and careless, except to put a hand on those—almost—exposed cheeks, fat with want, or pulsing in wantonness, and he cared, at that moment, nothing.

He knew she would come back to the caravan.

In Leah's eyes, he saw that she knew. The mare looked yearningly at pasture.

Her father appeared not to care, or else to open himself —some odd knot in his stare?—a degree of sly awareness which made all possible.

Almost six foot of sixteen-year-old bait was on offer.

It was known.

Horribly. The air, the place, the ground underfoot pulsed. All seemed rooted, stretching down, and he felt that if he moved, something might break.

But the father moved, and the mare-eyed mother, and in a little pause, the daughter, and suddenly he was alone with Leah.

Believe we're going to be so-rrr-y, she half-sang. I took advantage. I told them it's a month's trial, both sides. Only because they're supposed to be artists. They have a truck-load of easels and things. Looks quite mad.

Good. Let's say they're screwballs. What else?

I was on the phone to the last place they were at. They got thrown out. I forget the word in English. In Hebrew it's awful. Bad conduct. They all sleep in the same bed.

Why don't people mind their own business?

Appears the daughter's everybody's. Including the fa-ther's. The mother's some kind of a half-wit. They start big projects, get the money, and never finish anything. Been all round the country leaving glunk. Statues, memorials, that kind of job.

Couldn't do worse than some I've seen.

But they collect and don't deliver.

You told him we don't finance?

That came first. Second, a month's rent, down. He said tomorrow.

Till noon. Then he pays, or out.

Leah smiled for the first time.

So they don't move out of the temporary quarters?

Until they pay, no. And listen, Leah. You have your instructions, and behind your desk, you're the boss. If you have any doubts, call me. I'll never go against your decision. All right?

Leah got up, smoothed her skirt, touched her hair. She seemed to have grown.

Thank you, Mr. Paul. Because I was going to throw this in. Everybody treated me like the doormat. You didn't say anything so they just went along. Most of them owe rent. Light. Water. Word got round. You're an Amerikansky millionaire, so they make a beeline. Something for nothing. Does that stop?

It stopped. Spread the word. Get the payments in. Or get Chom busy. And, Leah. This is no utopia. It's a business. We're not built yet. We're just running-in. Now get it foursquare on the ground. I'm going to start using my office from next Sunday morning. The entire Plaza and this caravan are out of bounds for everybody except you, and people I invite. Let's stick to that.

But he knew that night, with starshine whitening the net over the doorway, that Ora kept the open-mouthed promise, and without putting on the light, she found the bed, and sat, and he heard the rasp of the zip, and she stood, blocking light, and felt for the sheet, pulled it away, and got in, cool, beside him, lying on her back, throwing the hair over his face, sighing long, once, hands behind her neck.

But the hair held the smell of dust, tobacco. Unwashed. The leg against him felt sticky.

Well, come on, *do* something, she whispered. Listen, I tell you what. I'll come here every night. I don't *like* to sleep down there. I rather come here. You listening?

Listening.

So?

So?

I'm here.

So?

Silence swelled as a balloon. Darkness pressed.

Listen, I can be real nice to you, she whispered. Whenever you want. Just, well, my Dad, he likes this place. So while we're here, I'm *here*. You see?

I see. Is this your Dad's idea?

Mommy's.

She sent you here?

Well. They both did, I guess.

Your father *knows* you're here?

Oh, sure.

How old are you?

What's *that* got to *do* with it?

The pettish tone, almost infantile hysteric, gave gross reminder that he lay with a minor, and well on the way to being a slob.

Get dressed and go. Don't come back.

Hell I won't. Listen. You want me to go down on you?

I want you to dress and go down that hill. *Now.*

The scuffle outside the door and the whispers, in moments became a voice and dog noises, and he laughed.

Is that you, Chom?

Yes, *sir*, Mr. Paul, Chom said, quietly. Thought you might be looking for a little company.

Accompany this young lady down to her family. She isn't allowed up here from now on.

Wait till I tell my Dad, she said, flinging the sheets over him, standing, feeling for the dress. I tell you who's going down that hill. In a goddam box. It's just like he said. That old bastard, we'll just cut him to size. We'll plug his asshole. We're here for keeps. I'll *get* you, mister. The whole secrets of shit on *you*.

That sort of fright he had known only once before. It was familiar. Neckhair ice-cold. A strange undesire to move. He knew in blaze of red that the girl was unbalanced, one of a clan.

He kept still. She whispered while she dressed. He heard no clear word. He saw the toss of long blond hair when she pulled, tore at the curtain, and went out to a sudden howl of dogs, and Chom's voice calling them down, and she, screaming, running.

He got up, put on the light, and took a cigaret, poured a scotch, and shrugged to think of sleepless hours, but weak with gratitude that she was gone, without harm, or knowledge, or any adventure beyond the touch of that gummy, unbathed body.

Dogs howling, and faint shouting came from below, but he sat to read, hearing, but uncaring.

I don't for the life of me understand a word of it, Father Brant said, in the gallery that evening. I've enquired everywhere. I can find no bishop of the name. Nobody with the right to investigate *any* of this. *Any* of it. This has gone to Rome and back. *They* don't know. I can't help. I wish I could. What did the fellow think he was doing?

Might be a good way to find out where the originals *and* the forgeries were?

How would that come about?

A mixture of authority, bullying, and insult. After all, the Church is a power. We all try to help. But I think he overplayed his hand. You feel he was an impostor?

I'm sure of it. Nothing's known of him here.

Well, now. Let's look at it, head-on. The widow of my client—of many years—took back thirty-two forgeries. But I sold him the originals. That's sixty-four, all told. If you matched one for one, you'd be making nothing more than a wild guess which was original, and which fake. And you *could* be wrong. The total value, if each was accounted an original, sold without publicity, as most of them are, would be around three to four million dollars, or much more.

Then why would such a fellow not keep himself quiet?

To find out where things are? We'd be the first to know. Whatever's sold, anywhere, we know. I think the woman's husband died without leaving much of a record. His collection was copied, and I suppose he intended to sell them. It's simple enough. After all, those thirty-two copies are going to bring in two million dollars, more or less. He could do that every two or three years.

But supposing somebody recognizes his own picture in somebody else's house?

Fine. It's known that most of the masters painted one or more of the same subject. There are small differences. Especially when they had apprentices. We know most. But not all. Why shouldn't a new canvas turn up? Who's going to argue? Old "experts" are dying out. Who are the new?

Father Brant brushed cigaret ash from grey flannel trousers, standing, looking about for his hat.

I'd like to help, he said. The Church first, of course. I don't know *who* this fellow can be. Can't think. You've no idea where the originals are?

Two of them, yes. The rest, no.

We go round and round. You can go mad.

That's right. It's a lot of money.

Can you not trace it through the bank?

Look. If I want to buy a canvas for, let's say, a hundred thousand, I put a hundred thousand in some bank or other, plus ten dollars. I give you a check for a hundred thousand, and I ask for special clearance. It's cleared. You have the cash. I have the canvas, and a ten dollar credit in the bank. Trace what?

Well. Your own personal details.

You don't think I do that myself, do you? I employ somebody. Now find *me*.

Father Brant threw up his arms.

Beyond me, he said, in despair. I don't know what it's all coming to. But not a single thing I'd want anything to do with, at all. I wonder what's behind it? I mean, the purpose. Why try to drive people mad? To exercise the spirit, and make them strong? I don't believe it. I visit three mental institutions a week. When I come out, d'you know, I'm ripe to go in myself. How long before I won't?

That rainy night, with gusts spraying the windows, Berthold Gluck reamed him with those pellet-hard silver-paper eyes.

Ever find these preacher guys working with each other? he asked, suddenly.

Why?

Just that. This guy Brant. Did you find out about him?

No.

Never looked up the record? Easy enough. And this

bishop? You just let people come in here, tell you anything they want? That bishop's part of an arts commission. He's real. I have that in a report. This guy Brant, nobody knows about him. He might be a monk from some place upstate. No record. Ever hear of the schlepper? Or the guy with the red herring?

So how far are we?

We're flagged as the principal dealers. One or two more. The fakes have come through us. Where did *we* get them from?

I never sold a fake in my life.

Thirty-two of them went out of here.

Not on sale. They went to the Precinct.

You already sold them. That's the gossip. How many sales did you make since the end of World War Two? Can you justify them as original?

I have the record.

What's it worth?

What are you getting at?

Gluck stood up and buttoned the raincoat.

At a rough estimate there might be as much as eight to ten million dollars worth of fake art spread around, he said, in the mild voice. We all know something's been going on at the Luberman. We still have to hear. And while I'm talking, we know a whole lot more are ready for sale. Privately. Or being exchanged. Without notice. Or coming off the easel. How many a day? Who's putting them out? Where?

Do you have any kind of an answer?

Gluck nodded, tipped cigar ash, touched a loose piece of leaf.

We had a talk at home last night. I haven't been well. Not sleeping. No appetite. So Hilde says, Why not quit?

Quit while we still have a few years we can both enjoy?
We have a pretty nice place in Florida. Fishing, I like. You
know? I always wanted to die in harness. Now, no. I can
be part of a scandal anytime. The trade isn't what it was.
I'll sell. Would you want first offer? Take the stock, sell on
normal percentage, and remit my share every three months?

He took it without a pause. The gallery would become,
overnight, the largest in the country, with all the benefits,
financial not least. Gluck's two older people, the bookkeeper
and storeman were pensioned, and he took on the secretary to help Bilara, but on the second day, she went out
to lunch and never came back.

Might be sick, he said. Give her over the weekend. Then
get somebody you can train.

I don't believe she liked working with color.

I *do*. So match the color.

He never forgot the slide of her eyes, to him, to window-
light, back to him, and a turn away, no word.

Is this Mr. Denis? the voice said, down the line, with
traffic noise behind. I like to speak to Mr. Paul Denis, please.

Speaking. Isn't that Sam Ravicz?

Oh, why it sure is, Mr. Paul. Look. I don't want to take
your time. You remember the last lot of canvases I framed
for you—the recessed—the usual—we had a talk about copyists? And the Luberman job?

I do, yes.

Well, funny things been happening. See, I sell the usual
Windsor and Newton, the Grumbacher, the acrylics, all that.
But only top quality. Well, this morning I got an order for
two thousand dollars, cash, and another order for five times
that. And the guy said to keep on ordering. *Cash.*

Seen him before?

Oh, sure. Often. He's been in and out. Tube of this, couple

of that. But now he's buying boxes. I asked if he was setting up a store, sort of kidding, and he said, Why would I buy retail? Just let's have the paints. No receipt. No *receipt?* I thought I'd give you a call.

That was thoughtful. I have a lot more work for you. Do you happen to know where this man takes the paints?

Well, it just so happens I do. My boy helped carry the stuff to the cab. Cabbie's a friend of mine. I have the address. It's out there near the Amboys. Kind of a fixed-up old warehouse.

Could you get a hold of him, take me there?

Sure.

Ten-thirty, tomorrow morning, here. There and back. Twice his fare.

He'll want to marry you. Mr. Paul. Uh. Could I go along?

Glad to have you.

He looked up at Bilara.

I think you ought to tell Sergeant Mackearn about this. He might have a buddy or two over there. They *could* be needed. But not a word to Inspector Hanrahan.

Don't trust him?

Let's say he has *his* way. I prefer Sergeant Mackearn's.

The sky was a blue of Worcester porcelain, the sun bleached, heat made a shirt smell scorched, and Leah came through the netting in shorts and a bra, and put the files on the desk.

There's a sergeant of Police down there, she said, bundling her hair. I believe he'd like a word.

About what?

Molesting a minor.

He leaned in the chair, laughing, and after a couple of

seconds' innocent-eyed stare, she put her head back and ah-hah'd! at the roof.

Is this that little piggi-wig?

Who else?

Get Chom Vissel.

He's talking to him, now. So are others. Toni, for one. She had a free hand.

Poor little soul. Where's Daddy in this?

Back of it.

That's horrible.

Didn't you know there *are ho*rrible people? People who *use* others? Even their own family? Their own kind?

Leah, tell that cop to come on up. Not in that get-up.

She looked down, put thumbs under bra-straps, settled the shorts.

You don't like it?

Too much. I didn't take enough notice of you.

It'll keep. This policeman speaks English.

A rarity. Get a glass case.

How many policemen outside Israel speak Hebrew?

You made a point, he said. Get going.

But the policeman seemed to change his mind after talking to Chom, and Toni, and a few others, and jeeped off. Anyway, he disappointed everybody by walking up the hill toward the house, and sitting on the edge of the half-built patio, and looking at the sea in gold-and-rose, and pale blue, and dark blue, and then the stars glinted, and still he sat there.

Mr. Paul? Leah's voice lay soft on the evening. Mr. Paul?

Yes, Leah?

You need any help?

I was just enjoying the sunset. Anything wrong?

Nothing at all. Not a thing. New York's calling in a little while. I put the call through to the office.

Good. Now you come to the caravan, and let's have a drink.

I'd enjoy that.

Any more about those funny people?

With the daughter? We have all the guards on alert. But it's difficult. *They* say. That caravan's so terribly open. Couldn't we have a team of dogs up here?

Chom seems to do fine.

Ah, but they'd carry the burglar's lunch. We want a team of police dogs. Nobody'd move too far, here.

If you know someone, get in touch.

They walked down the almost finished path, found hard stones, and went over the Plaza's blocks toward the light of the caravan.

You don't feel lonely here, Mr. Paul?

The voice touched.

Do you?

Often. Especially at night. I mean, now.

You're not comfortable?

Alone? Up here?

You were never married?

No. I'm the ugly one.

Ugly?

Yes.

I'm on the wrong side of the fence.

The dogs' muzzles came first, eyes flashing, then the *ulululu,* and Chom shouting, below.

Mr. Paul, you have New York down in the office. Holding.

Stay here, he told Leah. Pour yourself a drink. Make yourself at home.

He followed Chom and the tribe of dogs, down the winding path to the office.

Bilara's voice held the warmth of a smile. She detailed sales, bank deposits, callers, petty cash, read the few letters and took dictation.

Mr. Paul. If the offers hold, I'm going to be sitting back looking at bare walls pretty soon. That when I go on to page one of the directive?

Warn Mr. Weil's office you're ready to cut the utilities. Get your letter, and go to the Israeli Consulate for your visa. Just follow the instructions in the directive. Then you'll be here. And believe me, I need you.

Going to be so good to see *you*. How about Kumeli? Pay her off?

Appeal—supplication?—in that voice?

Would you want to bring her?

Oh, Mr. Paul. If only I could. She's just great. She's smart.

All right. Tell her she gets the same contract you do. Same sliding scale. Living and lodging free. But ask Mr. Weil to point out it's for training, and when we're ready, we have the option on her services.

She don't even want to *know* about staying here. She got the teeth to go.

That's the wrap-up. Call me Friday?

Sure will, Mr. Paul.

Any news of Mr. Gluck?

I talked with Mrs. Gluck. He's very pleased with the sales. Most days he's out fishing.

I ought to be. Good night, Bilara. Be good.

Mr. Paul, I'm so good, the light just shine all round. I'm getting kind of fried on the edges. Good night.

Chom stood among the sit of his friends outside, and Bilara seemed alive in the light of his smile, and the smiling troop of dogs. In the loll and quiver of glistening tongues, he wondered why he always thought of Bilara, and smiling.

That last time in the office he told her nothing, and she knew nothing, he was sure, and yet she seemed to know, and the smile held temblor, and he put a hand on her arm, but this time she stayed without a move, and he said nothing, and went.

Those bare walls of the gallery were in mind, remembering the warehouse studio, and counting the painters and all the other people on the two floors, some in small boarded-off rooms, others in the long L-shapes, but thirty-odd painters, at least, all working from postcards under thick lenses, or pages cut from magazines, and many with the original on a stand beside them.

He had the dreadful, cold feeling that Berthold Gluck had been right.

And lucky.

Most of the copies on the easels were good, some, almost finished, resplendently so. Others were new "works" in the style of the master. One, a Van Gogh, looked as though the artist had just left the room, but the painter, a little man in a green smock, looked at them over his glasses, and went on knifing a vermilion in white.

You two looking for somebody? a loud and not so pleasant voice said, from the stairhead, above.

We certainly are, Sam said. The guy who bought the paints from my store yesterday? I like to talk to him a minute, O.K.?

What about? the man had a necktie around a fat waist, a singlet, beard, and a bald head. How did you get in here?

Through the door, Sam said, in a whisper of wonder. You think we used dynamite? Look, this guy said, Keep on ordering, see? So he pays me cash. But I don't have that kind of credit. So I go to my friend here, and he'll stake me. All I want to know, now, is when do you want it, what do you want, and the quantity. Then I'd like a fifty percent down payment, and I'll find the rest. But cash on the nail, like before. Asking too much? He said you'd been needing maybe ten thousand dollars' worth or more. Kind of hard to believe.

The man slopped down creaky stairs in sandals hanging from a loop on the big toe.

How did you find this place? he asked, looking from one to the other.

The boy helped carry the boxes out to the cab? He heard the address.

Ah, Jesus, the man said, and held his face. Goddammit. O.K. You the owner, this store down there, Ravicz?

That's me.

Well, now you're here, might's well talk business. Look, we can buy all these paints, materials, a whole lot cheaper. We'd like to make a deal with you.

Just a moment, Sam said. The price you pay don't come near the normal retail price. I already made that deal, see? What do you want to do? Shave off the hair?

We can buy cheaper.

So? O.K. Buy. But you won't get the best. From me, yes. Tell me somebody else. I been in this business too long. What do you have here? An art school?

Call it that. Look, Mr. Ravicz. We'll meet your price. But you need a big stock. What's your friend do?

He's in insurance.

The black eyes rolled to his, and away.

What sort?

Any sort, Sam said. Y'know? What comes along.

What's this place going to cost me?

I could send a valuer, he said. I'll have the answer, maybe, the end of the month. What do you give the value of the stock?

Depends on the valuer. Let him give you the answer. I'll tell you if he's wrong.

You have one big problem. Fire hazard. This place can blow like a box of matches. I think you'll be lucky.

Lucky?

To get a policy. It'll be a hell of a premium. And you'll need dozens of fire extinguishers before they'll even discuss it. You allow them to smoke?

Listen, artists get nervous. They have to.

I'll send a valuer. But don't be disappointed.

You're a hell of a salesman.

Right. I know what'll pass. As it stands, this *won't*.

What do you suppose the premium might be?

I'd have to know the value of the stock. The building's worth maybe forty–fifty thousand?

Not far off. Let's say the stock's worth half a million?

You don't base premiums on let's-say. You want hard-nose value, item by item.

Well, get the guy out here. And look, these paints. We use a lot. We'll deal through you. But just don't pass the word. We don't want too many people out here. It's not for sightseers. Know what I mean?

How about the money? Sam said. Let's stick to business.

Just keep up the stock. A soothing voice, flat of the hands. Between here and a few other places, we use up a whole lot. What he bought yesterday's about a ten-day average. It could go up. Just go down these stairs, turn left, left again, doorway ahead takes you round the front. But *shut* that door, will you?

Sam led the way, and the door-slam could have eased every plank in the entire frame.

Insurance, he wants? he said, in a laugh. Boy, what a burn-baby *that* could be. Hear what he said about a few other places? A few? Like this? They got an assembly line, here. Wonder how many of them they're copying got stolen?

You saw them?

Sure. Renoir, Matisse. Van Gogh. All there. And the older. Couple I didn't know. Flemish school. Guy painting in that little box in the corner, eating the sandwich? Wasn't that a Rembrandt he was copying off of the horse? How do they do it?

Let's see if my insurance assessor can find out.

What company's he coming from?

Sixteenth Precinct. New York's finest.

But the best ideas can hit the unseen rock, and Sergeant Mackearn's shaken black head said it all, and the sad eyes seemed to roll in a reef of mourner's surf.

You got to show the evidence for any kind of a warrant, Mr. Denis. You don't have it? And besides, you'd have to go along, or another expert. Somebody knows something. You could give the job to an agency. They probably get to know a few of the painters. Where they hang out. Over a drink. There's ways of getting to them. It just takes time.

Listen, Paul, Gluck said, over the telephone. Just plain leave it alone. I had time to really study this whole thing. It's going to turn into a dirty business. Nothing you can do to stop it. Too many smart guys chasing the easy dollar. Paul, look, you're still a youngster. Still plenty of time to do something else. Why *don't* you?

Well, in the first place, there's nothing else I *want* to do. Second, I like what I'm doing. And third, I'd really like to put a few in the cage.

No, Paul. Too many copyists. Too many coming along. Too many happy to pay for the copy. How do you prove they're doing wrong? Listen. They have this Xerox, this copying machine. How many books are getting copied? Who says a word? We don't have any morals, or ethics, or principles any more. And *those* three you used to need for *that* business. Not any more. Know something? I'm glad I'm *out*.

There seemed chimeras of loneliness in climbing that hill, an affliction of memories, pressing, crowding, almost as animals in frothing howl, but silent.

Leah was not quite a mistake, but certainly an error, small to begin, but swelling with the weeks, and again he had to remember his father, those years ago, speaking with the back of his hand to his head and every three words pushing out the hollowed palm as if getting rid of limpet sprites.

Don't fool with a *good* girl, know what I mean? They *got* one, they want it, but they know it's wrong, see? So they give it, and they don't. They figure they're doing you a favor, and you have to pay back one way or another. This is the inside-out whore. She'll needle. She'll count on your good nature. Kind of man you are. But she's taking the prick, and wanting it, and when she's got it, she makes *you* pay. Their guilt, well, it's what we say, their sin, they heap it up on you. So you *owe* them something. Keep away from it. Pay for it. Find a *shiksa*. But keep off of the kosher. They'll make your life a goddam misery. And let me tell you. It's the worst fuck you'll ever have. It's like taking somebody for something to eat, and they sick up in the middle. Re*mem*ber me.

He did, and Leah fitted, tight, in the mould. Nothing

wrong. Everything very tender. Until he was in. But then, either she stopped herself from coming, or made him come first, and pretended he was cheating, and began the sobs. This can go on for so long, but one night he told her, No more, and she looked at him, and knew, and ran. That was the night of attempted suicide, and the agony of waiting for the ambulance, and again Chom was savior, warning in time by smelling the escaping gas, calling the firemen, and putting in a new valve, showing the faulty, turning an attempt into an accident.

Each day he went to see her, always surprised by her beauty, and that Saturday afternoon a young man got up from her bedside, and she said they would be married.

I'm happy for you, he said. You won't be coming back?

Oh *no*. We're going to Beersheba. When I leave here.

Anything I can do?

We'd like our own house. Could you help us at the bank?

He looked at her eyes, saw the smile, that held the friable crust of warning, intimidation, the small calculation of possible harm, and stood, held out his hand.

Call on me, he said. Give my name. Be happy. That's all that matters. Anything you want?

She shook her head.

Shalom.

Peace, where he never expected it. Leah left a note which could have given him many an anxious hour. But again, Chom took it out of his pocket on the afternoon of the third day, long after police, firemen, and insurance assessor had gone.

Chom's wages went up, and he and the dogs went into a new, comfortable house at the side of the car park, and the note went in float of strips in the middle of Toni's grill.

He put Yehudit Kaminsky in her place, and found the

day going better, and a tighter hold on everything. He was always surprised at the extraordinary versatility of the European, especially the Mittel-European, and those from Byelorussia, particularly in languages. Yehudit, young thirties, a child of the death camps, spoke eight languages, and excellent English.

How did you do it? he asked her. I'm stuck with one.

We studied. We had nothing else, those years.

But you were little children.

Best time. Then you grow up. You go to school. Comes easy. May I have some answers? This rent file. There are more than twenty people not paying rent. Power. Water. I sent Chom to collect. They threw things at him. This is the place. They're all in the same complex. Looks like they put their heads together.

He looked at the maquette. The building spread along the south side, just below the store sheds.

These are all employees of the self-employed?

They're the helpers. Trainees. They *call* themselves. They think they have the right to free quarters. Who told them so? Any rate, they refuse to pay.

Get friend Chom up here. My Boy Scout days are back again.

Chom listened, and smiled around at the heavens, putting a forefinger to his lips, testing direction of the breeze.

About an hour later, thick black smoke rolled across the southern slope. A couple of cans of ammonia helped a fire in a heap of old tires. All the buildings along the winding path emptied of coughing, weeping shadows. He caught a gust, and hurried back. The fire was found, but defied any effort to prevent smoke, and the fire pump had gone into Nazareth for repair. When the fire burned out in dark of evening, the group left Toni's grill and went downhill to sleep, but just before midnight, the smoke rolled again, and again the coughers and cursers wept up the hill and slept about fires in the car park.

Half a dozen blear-eyed long-hairs made a delegation to Yehudit, and she talked to them from the first-floor window of the main building.

Before midday, Chom collected the rents, and the water, gas, and light bills, and Yehudit got them all together, and he went down there. They were a little crowd, a few girls with leather bandeaus, creased Arab gowns, and the long-hair whiskered men, sullen, pathetic.

Anybody here doesn't understand English? he called, and knew his mistake. Sorry. I speak English. Do all of you understand?

Hesitant hands went up, but very few, and he looked around at Yehudit.

Please translate, he said, and turned to them. First, I'm told many of you are from Russia. You've been used to big daddy taking care of you? Not here. Two. This is a business, not a charity. You either *give* something, or you *get* nothing. Remember the Book? By the sweat of thy brow, thou shalt earn thy daily bread. If you've all forgotten it, or you never heard it, here is where you remember. Or learn, and practice. In this country, we thrive on sweat. Not somebody else's. Yours. Mine. *Ours*. Never forget it. Or if you do, clear out. That's all.

You are not an *art*ist, a young man called, standing on an earth-heap at the back. You are only another American capita*list*. How do you have the right to own here?

I bought the lease. I pay the builders. I *own* nothing. I rent. And I run it *my* way. And if you don't pay what you owe, and don't behave yourselves as *I* want, go somewhere else. What kind of artists *are* you, anyway? You got in here by saying the magic word. I've never seen your work.

We never saw any work of *yours?* a girl said.

Look around you. Look at the buildings. These paths you walk along. Those apartments you're so anxious not to leave. All the trees and gardens. All the half-built houses? *That's* my work. I dreamed it. I found it. I bought it. And I'm building it. Now go to work. Mrs. Kaminsky, I'll give them time. At the end of next week I want to see an exhibition of *their* work. Set the time and date, please.

He left her translating in Russian, and went down to his office, happy to get into the chair, put his hands on the desk, and relish the quiet.

He had time to wonder if he was being fair to the youngsters, or what he, at their age, or a few years younger, might have done if luck had not sent him to Mr. Cernovitch with a parcel from Mrs. Dentz, the laundress, and if Joe, the oldest son, had not asked him to take a package of stationery to the Reid Gallery for ten cents, and if Mr. Stern, Mr. Blantyre's manager, had not asked him to take a picture up to East Sixty-eighth Street, and if the maid had not refused to sign the receipt, and if he had not brought the picture back to the Reid Gallery, while Mr. Blantyre was sitting at the desk.

All right, son, he said. I'd like you to take it back after I've made a call. Suppose you let me see how you handle a carpet beater. That's if you want a steady job?

It took him no time to learn how to use the Hoover, or clean the windows from the inside, or polish the brass, or dust the canvases with the feather brush—gently!—or make coffee the way Mr. Blantyre liked, or deliver pictures in any weather, and all the time he watched, and listened, and remembered, and as the pictures came in, he heard what

Mr. Stern or Mr. Blantyre said about them, and read the pieces in the catalogs, and more in the library, and when Mr. Stern left, and a cleaning woman came in, he became the junior.

But that was luck. Without a parcel of washing, a willingness to use a carpet sweeper and clean windows, deliver pictures and make coffee, he would never have sat there. There was hard work, and long hours, and study in between, very well. But it started with luck.

What sort of luck had the boys and girls down below?

If he had been told to show his work at the age of fourteen, what could he have done? Or at fifteen, or at any age, up until the moment?

Apart from that, at any age would he have come to Israel? At all times, through childhood, there had been talk, and plenty of it, about the Promised Land, and Next Year, Jerusalem, and Eretz Israel. His father had always shrugged, and rubbed an eye, and his mother sniffed, that sniff which spoke its own language, needed no explanation. He, certainly, had no desire. He liked his life. He was too young for the Second World War, and eyesight with a little *protekzia* from Dr. Einhorn, the optometrist, got him out of the Korean spot, and he was too old for Vietnam.

Mrs. Kaminsky, I'm being unfair, he told her. Too hard. Nobody did that to me at their age. What do you suggest?

Leave it where it is, she said, and surprised him. Don't blow hot and cold. They know what they have to do. Let's see it. Why don't you call me Yehudit? I haven't been Mrs. Kaminsky for seven years. I don't like the name. It's a passport moniker. I never liked *him*.

Why *do* we marry?

She held out her arms.

I wanted to get away from my family. I got away. Then

I got away from *him*. Now I'm free. Myself. Never knew the meaning of happy till now. It's why I sympathize with those boys and girls. For the first time, they're happy. Doing what *they* want to do. The way *they* want. After all, are you the *only* one with a dream? Aren't there any more of us?

He thought of that package of laundry from Mrs. Dentz. Not everybody had a Mr. Blantyre at the end, or a carpet to sweep, or a window to clean. But they all had the guts to hitchhike halfway over the world to arrive at the Hill. That he built it, apparently, for them, could make him, in their lives, another Mr. Blantyre. He liked the notion. He almost saw the pince-nez glitter in a smile, and heard the gentle voice, All right, son. You're doing fine.

He wished, suddenly, that he were their age, able to do as they were doing, light-hearted, without responsibility.

Fantasies, the shrink said. You grew up in that gallery. Your mental growth was in other men's lives and work. You dreamed out of train and plane windows. London, Paris, Madrid, wherever, what were they? Shopping sprees? Business? Time to grow? Absorb? Lunches, dinners? Chewing your way through time? Without the gallery, what would you be? Grocery clerk? What?

That question he was never able to answer.

You sometimes sound just a mite tough, son, Mr. Blantyre said, not long before he died. Always watch yourself. Listen to your voice. How you say something. I've meant to say this before. You're not in any neighborhood. No back fences here. Always have a lot of respect for what's around you. All these people worked in creative silence. You just share it. If you follow the same line of thought, you can't go wrong. Quietness has nothing to do with servility. Gentleness is strength, always. I'm not beating your head with a lot of platitudes. I don't have any pulpit here. If you want

to know, I had about the same background you have. So-
ooo? I just had to learn. I hope you do. You'll have no
trouble.

He knew Father Brant from those days. He was of the
Blantyre period, and for that reason, passed as a friend,
either collecting for a charity, or having art objects valued,
and sometimes bringing in costly items to sell. Mr. Blantyre never questioned, deals were made, and so it went on.

Until Berthold Gluck spoke about the record.

Father Brant was unknown anywhere, Bilara found out
in days of enquiry.

I don't get it, she said. Guy's been coming in here years.
Ever since I been here. Before. Always the big religious
stuff. Throw a slew of Bibles at you. And who *is* he?

He'd better not come in here again.

Henri Tameur called in that evening.

Boy, it's a boiler, he said, and took off his jacket, looking
at the highball. You have the right idea. I just trod on a foot
of my tongue.

Bilara, a little first aid, here.

Yes, *sir*.

Paul, I had a visit from Jonathan Cole this afternoon. He
wanted to sell the three he offered you, and three more.
You weren't going to buy them, were you?

Not on your life. They're not his. They're some rela-
tive's. I found out from the lawyers.

They're fakes.

Not the ones I saw.

The ones I have at my place are. I asked him why he
didn't bring them here. He said you cheated him on some
deal. Etruscan art, was it?

Correct. But he wasn't cheated. Normal commission,
insurance, and transport. The collector's in Florida.

Well. It's a pretty sad story. The poor guy was high when he came in. I told him I didn't want to handle the deal. He just hit the roof, and next thing you know, he's having a heart attack. Thank you, Bilara. I really need this.

He toasted, and drank.

Called the ambulance, took him down to New York General. Casualty. He's real sick. In oxygen when I left. I still have the canvases. Want to identify them?

Don't want a thing to do with it.

Wish I didn't. These religious guys, you never know.

He looked up at Bilara, and she looked down at him, and they laughed together.

Re*ligious? Jonathan?*

He had the beads in his hands, Henri said, and drank, rattling ice. Why the laugh?

Bilara, you want to mind the store? I want to see my client, *Mis*ter Jonathan Cole. The re*lig*ious one.

But one glance at the face under the mask in the casualty ward, and he tip-toed away.

That's not Jonathan Cole, he said. That's somebody called Brant.

That's something you have to take up with Registry, the intern said. They'll want to know who to bill. So far, it's the Tameur Gallery.

The hell it is, Henri said. The bum comes in my place, and dies, and puts the bite on me? My *ass*.

The call came at just after two o'clock in the morning. Mr. Jonathan Cole was pronounced dead, and did he know any next of kin, and he said they could have all the information in the files at the office, but only tomorrow.

Bilara called the numbers she had, and the third said Mr. Jonathan was out on Long Island, and they would inform him.

Ever feel you were playing touch football with *Alice in Wonderland?* he asked Bilara. You ever read the book?

No, sir, Mr. Paul. I never did. But I'd say there's one hell of a big *loa* beating his bones around here.

What's a *loa?*

Well. It's one of them things, y'know, they come at you out the dark and nip your heels, and holler, and get you hopping around screeching, boy, you fit to be tied. Why, hell, I don't even want to go home.

Come stay with me. Want your own room again?

She looked at him, and away.

I don't believe you want any kind of trouble, Mr. Paul. I like my own room, and thank you. But I make supper. Just got time for Zabar's. Why don't you get a housekeeper? Some gal *know* something?

Ah, Bilara. What the *hell.*

That empty place. Urbino's *cavalliero* seemed to look at him each time the light was switched on with even more contempt for the base-born, a supercilious lift of brow and lip that made him want to take off a shoe and throw it.

But always try to recall that you're responding to a characteristic that's been put in all of us for many generations by the Torah, Meir Gershon said. The idea of picking up a stone to throw at something you don't like? That's where it comes from. When you catch yourself thinking that way, stop it. You should have grown out of it. The life here, in this country should have taught you. Where do you pick up a stone in New York? They don't have that kind of a street. So accustom your thinking. Don't throw stones. Use ideas instead. Stone hurts. Ideas *work.*

What you require is a course of study with Meir Gershon, Mr. Blantyre said, that Saturday morning. He's one of the *real* scholars. I've told him about you. What you need's an opening of the mind. The sort you'd get at a university. You haven't the time. If you want to try with Meir, I'll fix it.

Every morning for one hour, six days a week, and on Sunday afternoons, for two and three hours, he went around to the apartment on West Fifty-first, and Mrs. Gershon brought in a tray of coffee and breads, and all kinds of cakes, and he started learning from the time of David, on up, through Persia, and Greece and all over Europe, and then America, and back to Europe, and North Africa, each week a list of questions to answer, and if he got a mark of Very Good, Mr. Blantyre gave him an extra dollar.

Those three years put more into his ken than all the years before, and most of those since, but the great lesson he learned was that filling his mind with detail of the past left no room for what was new, and useful.

As long as you know the route, Mr. Gershon said. Just get to know the route. The detail, all the minor stuff, it's all in the library. Look it up. Get it fresh, and right. Never depend on your memory. You *can* be wrong.

Until that rainy Thursday morning, and the snow melting, and all the people on the stairs up to the Gershon apartment, and the ambulance, and going back to the Reid Gallery, and Mr. Blantyre putting hat and coat on, and telling him to take care of everything, and coming back to say that the lessons were over, and for God's sake let me get my feet to the heater.

But anything he knew came from Mr. Gershon or Mr. Blantyre, and from then on, he read for himself, either from books lent by Mr. Blantyre, or taken from the library, six at a time, often two days a week, and later, buying them and loading the shelves, and then, with greatest pride, buying in lots, his own library.

That's the way of it, Mr. Blantyre said. Omnivorous. But weren't we all?

But you're not now? he asked.

No. Not now. You get to a pitch when you've had enough of the main dish, then you sit back and enjoy a wonderful dessert. The wine's in the memories. That's where I am, now. It's a most pleasant feeling, I must say.

That most pleasant feeling he understood only when the roof went on the house, and the team of men pounding the mix that splashed them in small white stars, and cogged medallions, sang the songs of a thousand years, and drank white wine, and waved the branches of white flowers, and the lore, and the music of North Africa's scattered Judeans came back to bless the air where others of their kind had lived, and had sung, as free, and as apparently carefree, so many generations before.

Carefree.

The word, the concept, held the bitter seed of doubt, mistrust, worry.

The land was beset by four others nearby, with a dozen more behind, and the people lived in constant odds of one hundred to one in bodies, and in terms of billions financially.

Sitting in that comfortable office up on the hill, there was ample time to think about the problem, listen to the news from a dozen radio stations, form an opinion tonight, and change it tomorrow. There seemed three main schools with a voice in government, or near the top, and several others outside. The majority said, Hang on to everything until the other side agrees to sit down and talk. The second said, Hang on to what we need, and give back the rest. The third said, Give it all back and let us have peace in our time. The others rang the changes in between.

But they all said, Jerusalem is *ours*, no pricksongs about it.

He agreed, as much because after three wars, they had won the city in battle, as for the prophetic dictum known to him from childhood. Next year, Jerusalem, was always drunk over the winecups, whether as toast, or prayer, or promise, and although his upbringing had been irreligious in the widest sense, yet, he still retained enough in the blood to be at one with his people, wherever they might come from, or whichever language they spoke. His parents had come from Tunisia. They sometimes spoke French together, but never Hebrew or Yiddish, and once settled in the United States, they learned English and cut all ties except the few, at Passover, and the Feast of Tents, and of Lights, and always the Day of Atonement, but he was never taken to a synagogue, and knew the People of Israel only from Bible lessons in the Christian school, and he first heard of the Talmud when he was a young man, but it meant less than the next film, and he still remembered his surprise when Laszlo, the gallery's restorer, told him that Torah was the Old Testament of the Christians.

Don't get into it, Laszlo said. You could go nuts the way they talk. You got the root in here, you got a good life, more you should want? For*get* it.

I think that's bad, Mr. Blantyre said. You lose a lot of your birthright. And it's rich. I have no room to talk. I haven't been inside a church for longer than you've been born. But I had the basics drummed into me, and I never forgot.

Do you believe in God, Mr. Blantyre?

First, define your terms, that gentle voice had said, more of a father than his own. If you mean the day-to-day meaning of the dear old lad sitting up there and quacking, then *no*. If you have an idea in mind of a wondrous intelligence, something mighty, and marvellous, quite beyond our poor human minds, the spirit, as we know it, shining in every creative idiot, all our painters, and sculptors, and mathematicians, and all the rest, then, yes. I wholeheartedly agree. Yes. I've seen enough in my own time. I believe in *that* God, implicitly.

But why do you say idiot?

What else are we? Seventy years, limit. A few years more. Many, less. What *is* this to challenge with? What *are* we except idiots of time? We dare doubt? With what right? These men you're selling are going to live on for many years, for generations. Many hundreds of years, perhaps. Even the cheapest of them. With a simple creation of the vital mind and the less-than-clumsy hand, they insist they are the sons of that intelligence greater than themselves. The one that *doesn't* die. It passes on through time, blesses heads, causes to effloresce. Always in grace. Look for grace. That's the hallmark. No grace, no art. There is no art without grace. *Make* yourself see it.

But it took time.

Grace was what?

You have a whole bunch of people suing you, Yehudit said, showing a rustle of paper. They all want something like two hundred and fifty dollars. They say they were employed and you dismissed them for no reason.

I didn't employ. I didn't dismiss. Give it to the lawyers. Don't bother me.

But that's not all. Remember the daddy of piggi-wig? He wants damages for the statue you ordered.

What statue?

To all the stray dogs. That's what this paper says.

Spike his guns. Ask him to submit drawings. I'm not a mind-reader. I like to see what I'm buying. He's a crook.

Has to be proved, doesn't it? I believe you. But remember, this is Histadrut. That's all the trade unions. I don't think we have a chance.

Let Mr. Ginzfeld look at it.

But Mr. Ginzfeld put a thumb over the left eyebrow and the third finger over the right, turned the pages one by one, slowly, so slowly, shaking his head, a portrait of doubt, sorrow, defeat.

Not a chance, he said, matter-of-fact-it's-all-over. You have forty-odd witnesses against you. You fired them without good reason.

It was a very good reason.

Not according to our labor laws. And this won't go before a court. It'll be a kind of a master. He'll give a verdict as *he* sees it. It'll be against you. Every week that passes adds ten percent. My advice, pay up. If he sets the hearing date in a month's time, it already cost you forty percent more. You can't win.

But I *didn't* employ them, goddammit.

You haven't a document to prove it. And all these witnesses against you? Pay.

Look. They were on my private property. They never received a cent from my office. They were never employed.

They were here for three months. You made no objection. They were paid.

By my tenants.

This is treated as a property. Each tenant is your agent. What they do is with your permission. What they say is what you have said. You have no paper. It's word-of-mouth. How many witnesses against one?

But I *have* witnesses.

I'm trying to give you the best kind of advice. If you want to take this further, you can call your witnesses. I hope you have more than forty-odd. I hope they're all loyal. To you. Even so, it can still cost you five and ten times as much, and a lot of time wasted. Take the advice. Pay.

Those bums?

I'm thinking of time going by in presenting a case. Transport of witnesses. Personal expenses. Lawyers' fees. I'll see if their lawyers'll compromise. But don't lose yourself a lot of money being stubborn. Here, there's no question of law. It's a matter of labor regulations. It's modelled on Nazi lines. What sent them to the gas ovens, that's what they brought here. *I* have the say. *You* have nothing to say. And there isn't a court you can go to. There's no justice. It's their say-so. I'll see what I can do.

And the statue I didn't order?

You're on harder ground. Ask for the sketches.

And a clay model.

Not until you make a payment. That's pretty near a commission.

You see his lawyer, and ask for a sketch. I never asked for a statue. I don't *want* a statue. In any case, he makes ikons.

Ginzfeld took off the spectacles, laughing.

The amusement's strictly from pity, he said. You try to do them a favor, you get a boot in the groin? From now on, you need an agreement for everybody on this place. Down to the cleaners. Remember, they can take you in front of these Histadrut bastards, and you don't have a chance. Any whore can take you.

Draw the papers. Twelve years I employed people in New York. I never signed a paper. *They* never did. I have to come here to find out my own people are liars, crooks, no-goods?

Some. Always you find some. Don't lose heart. I'll fix it. Nobody else is going to take you for a *grush* if I can help it.

But why wasn't I warned about this before?

Ginzfeld opened his hands.

Who could see it? he asked the ceiling. Artists you supposed to have here? Artists, people, they suffer? Suffer what? Too many, they got born out their mother's assholes. So what are they, the rest of their lives? You can't smell 'em? No olfactory backlash? It's not why you need a lawyer? To pick the peeled nuts out of the shit? What do *you* think the law is?

I never thought much about it. Protection? Justice?

Where's the protection? What *is* justice?

Mr. Paul, I got the weekend off, Sergeant Mackearn said, that Saturday noon. Taking the wife and kids out to Jones Beach. Wife's ma got a place behind the south end, there. Soul food. Love it. Mr. Paul, you going someplace this weekend?

No. I have a lot of work here. Why?

What I hear, I wish you stay home.

I can do that. But why?

What I hear.

That's all?

That's all. See y'all Monday. Miss Tancy, have a nice weekend.

Sure will. Enjoy them chitterlings. Boy, I *wish*.

When she shut the door and ran down the steel blinds, he felt better, but for some immediate reason, as if he were in a deep freeze. His legs and arms moved, barely.

What do you think he meant by that? he asked.

I believe he know something, Bilara said, back to him. I believe you have to go on home before dark. Get the latches on. Lock up. Stay right there. Don't answer the doorbell. Take the phone off the hook. Tell the doorman you went to Pennsylvania. Want me to stay there? I rather. You don't have nothing in that icebox. I'm going round the corner. Maybe twenty minutes. Stay here. Don't move.

Her nerves matched his. He saw her trembling, reached out, took the cold hand.

Bilara, don't get worried for me. I'm fine. I'm all right.

We *all* fine. We *all* all right. While we breathing. There's some guys don't want us to. That guy, Mackearn, he know more than he talk. You want to bet you going to find him down there at Jones Beach? Chitterlings or no chitterlings?

So what's the idea of coming in here?

Say the word, no panic.

Quiet warning? About what?

There's people, they after a lot of money. You got it.

But if they knock me off, what do they get?

They get to say what they want. Mr. Paul, stone-dead in the market? Know the song? Nothing to say. They got lawyers. They also got thirty-two originals, and thirty-two copies, plus the rest. All come through this gallery. How much? Just knock off you and me. Burn the files. Slide the thumb. Couple of million? More? Name it?

Bilara. I'm in the wrong business. I like the quiet life.

Yes, *sir*. It *was* the quiet business. It still *is* the quiet business. If *you* keep quiet. Or do as you get told.

Plenty don't get told. Don't have to.

So right. How much they making? Two, three sales a week? Of who? If they lucky. How many get to close up?

I wonder if Mr. Blantyre, listening to us, would understand a word of what we were talking about?

No, Mr. Paul. I don't believe he would. Mr. Blantyre, he was a gentleman. Gentleman, he don't understand this kind of talk.

But I *do?*

Those eyes turned to him, a full half-circle, and smiled.

Yes, *sir.* You *have* to. He didn't. It's just another time. Other kind of people. They used to burn each other. Now they burning themselves. They don't get hurt enough, they got to hurt more. Try to hurt *us.* But we hurt enough. We don't *give* a damn any more.

Terrible thing to say, Bilara.

Sure is. I don't want to see some other poor guy throw a can of gas around, and snap a match. Sitting there, his own ashes? What good's it do? Me, I don't care any more. Let 'em burn. It's not *for* anything. We all got to die. So? Die.

But wait a minute. Shouldn't we *live* for something?

Yes, *sir.* But that's no reason we got to die. Before the right time. We ought to be raising all kinds of hell to get things right. We don't have so *much* time.

What kind of hell?

Mr. Paul, there's only one kind of hell. People don't deserve it, they suffer. But the rest, they better off. Tell me the answer.

Better do some shopping. We have to hole up. Don't forget the smoked salmon.

And lemons. Don't taste the same. I never knew fish taste better with lemons till you told me.

Cuts the fat.

But all the time he wondered when they might come in, or if they would try.

They?

Who?

Nobody knew. Fifty-seventh Street was the same. The walk from the apartment, through Central Park, was the same. The day in the gallery was the same. Everything was the same, the same coffee, same mail, same newspapers, same callers, same deals, different day to day, but the same.

Somebody here, Rivka Shulman, she wants to talk to you, Yehudit said, when he got back from Tel Aviv. She's different.

I like different people. They belong here. Send her in. I know the name.

The red head gleamed gold. She was older, taller, more assured, and she was dressed in plum skirt and navy jersey, white sandals, and she looked herself, ready to work.

Aren't you the wom's lib mycenas who tore up a twenty-dollar bill? he asked, when she sat down. Fifty, this time?

White, regular teeth startled in a laugh. She sat down, looking severe, restrained, even worried, and her fists were clenched, but she suddenly sprawled, beautifully.

Oh, no, she said. That was wrong. But that black woman there said it was no use just copying. I had to come out fighting. Made me so mad. I tried so hard. But I saw what she meant. I changed. I had a talk with my daddy, and he said she was right. So I went to another school, and the principal sent me to a ceramist in Michigan. That's where I heard about this place.

From?

A girl who was here. I don't even know her name. She said you were starting. Well, I always wanted Israel. I dreamed about it. I think that was my mistake. I mean, with the black woman. The sketches were designs for ceramics. I believe I'm a whole lot better. I don't know if I'm making any sense?

Plenty. As it happens there's a vacancy. Living quarters. Workshop. Furnace, everything, ready.

I have my own electric oven and the tools. They'll be in Haifa this week.

You'll need a Customs agent. We'll fix it. Suppose you go with Yehudit, and she'll show you around, read you the fine print and take the first month's rent for the trial period. If we like you, that's it. If we don't, we throw you out. Cuts both ways. Except, you get the rent back. When you're ready, I'd like to see the designs. You know the rule here? One of each, or a signed replica with a strictly limited edition.

That's why I'm here.

On the lines of Sèvres, Worcester, so forth?

On the lines of Rivka Shulamit, Israel. *Nahon?*

Nahon means, You agree? or All right? or, It's set?

Just about that. You don't speak Hebrew?

Sadly I say it. No. And I've gone too far to learn. You do?

All my life.

All of twenty years?

Well. A few more.

Are you Orthodox?

If you mean the two kitchens, the meat and milk non-sense, no. For me, it's all the way out of date. I like steaks, and pork chops, and ham and eggs, and toast and butter, and most of the other things that get the dear rabbis greening. My daddy tries to be. But we're not. He doesn't fight. It's gone too far.

We're a lost cause?

No. Never. We fight the same war every day of our lives. It's right inside, here. I couldn't explain it. But it's there. It's solid. It stays. And I *love* Israel. Let the side-locks and short pants *yeshiva* nuts do *their* thing. I'll do mine. But I don't need a Wall. I like to see it. I'll help keep it there. For us. I'll fight for them. I'll never have less than respect for them. But their life isn't mine. And I'll live *my* life. That's all.

He thought her right. But he never heard it said like that. He wondered what the younger generation had that he never heard of. There had never been any suggestion of two kitchens in his life. It sounded ridiculous. But he had always known that meat and milk were forbidden to be cooked or eaten together, but without taking the smallest notice. It was like knowing that mud would stick to your boots. The pig, and lobster, prawns, shrimp, were unclean, and, too, meat with the blood in it, but he never understood why, and never bothered with it.

Plenty of explanations, Meir Gershon said. None of them in this day make any sense. Remember the pretty little bouquets of flowers on the judge's bench in British courts? You know why? Because in those far-off days, the prisoners stank. You ever smell a man, been in a small cell, doing his business, no bath, months, years? So? When you bring him in court, you give the judge a bunch of sweet-smelling flowers. Hope he can smell through? That's us. The old ones in the desert had a hard time. They made the rules to suit themselves in that day. They were probably right. In *their* time. This time, this sort of life, it's different. You make up *your* mind. Who has anything to say?

Mr. Paul, Bilara said, that Saturday morning, rising tall against window-light. Here's this guy again. I knew we shouldn't have opened. I just *knew*.

Now, Bilara. Which guy you talking about?

He came in, and two others stood outside, with their faces in the turned-up collars of their overcoats.

Time you went home, Bilara. You all locked up? Don't you have something to do?

Yes, sir. My sister, she waiting for me. I got the kids to take to the park. They don't have so much time together. You know how it is when you married. You going to take care of this gentleman?

In the few minutes till we close.

I'm in no hurry, the man said.

Take your time. You have ten minutes.

You think.

That's exactly what *I* think. I'd like you to remember I own the ground you presently walk on. Now get the hell out of here.

The man turned to look at him.

I don't believe you know who you're talking to, he said, over the Saturday midday traffic noise of Fifty-seventh Street. Now, you just sit down, and you do what *I* tell *you*. You listening?

No.

Bilara pulled open the door to slam against the wall.

Have yourself a real nice weekend, Mr. Paul, she said. Lot later than I thought. Hope he's still waiting round there for me.

Round where?

Sixteenth *Pre*cinct. Them lover-button cops, they come off ten minutes ago. They don't hang around. 'Bye now.

The man put a foot out to stop her.

You going nowhere, jig. I'll tell you when, and how. *My* way.

Bilara, did you press that button?

Sure did, Mr. Paul.

So the detail's on its way?

If they aren't, the Mayor ought to stop their money, Bi-

lara said, and looked the man in the eye. Now, *you* get yourself out of here, else I'm going to have to charge you with
offensive behavior.

And I'll beef that up with a couple of charges of my own,
he said. Leave, before the police get here.

From his face, the man might not have heard.

In a sudden move, he turned to the door, and swung it
open.

You order the flowers? he said, in a large yawn, over the
heads of the two below the step, and the further man
nodded. O.K. Guy don't want to hear some advice, what
can you do? Let's go.

He turned about.

Let me wish y'happy journey, he said, in a remote smile
of pity. You got a nice day.

He turned right, one of the men went left, and the other
crossed the street.

Lucky he don't get a ticket for jay-walking, Bilara said.
Mr. Paul, you know something? I don't believe you ought
to go back there today.

Threatened out of my own house?

Least, you get back here Monday.

You could be right. I hardly believe it's me talking.
Phone the building superintendent. Say I won't be home
all next week. Then call the Waldorf. Book me a small suite,
bedroom and drawing room. And for you. Not necessarily
on the same floor. Ten days each. Time for the flowers to
die. Fix a notice to this door. We open Wednesday week.
I'm going out, buy a couple of shirts. Toiletries.

Don't go out, Mr. Paul. Anything you want, you get it
in the hotel. You really think I ought to go with you? I
mean, the hotel?

Bilara, there was a little matter of putting a black ass on

a stove. It's haunted me. As I take care of myself, so I take care of you. Ever thought? You and me out of the way, these files destroyed, they can sell, legitimately, for upwards of four–five million. Anywhere.

We ought to take these files?

He laughed, and she looked for a moment, and doubled from the waist, shaking her head, and the tears filled her eyes, and her laughter vented in a high hee-hee-*ha!*

You think of everything. I'm pretty certain we have to be careful. Yes. Take the files. Just the seven this end. Bilara, I'm going to say it again. To hear myself. I just don't believe this is happening to *me*. Or you. Is this, really, the gallery *we* know?

That's right, Mr. Paul. I'm going to phone around. And we going to get the hell out of here. But *fast*.

In those days the Hill dressed itself in wonderful color, in the gardens, with clusters of flowering shrubs, and small orchards of blossoming cherry, almond, and apple trees, and thousands of Dutch tulips threw out kisses, and the daffodils and narcissus waved in the cool breath of a new spring, and all the vases in the offices bloomed dozens, gathered by Yehudit and Rivka, and the caravan seemed to float, new every day, in a fragrance he had never known, and waking in the palest blue dawn, listening to the birds, and then, as the sun lit the tips of the fingers of the white *Shalom* hand, and the blossoms opened, the scent came on the morning breeze, and half-asleep, he knew himself in the land of his People.

You have the Rabbi Berezhkoy, from Safad, Yehudit said. He's not the big stuff. He's modern. Reform. He wants to know what you're doing for people here.

Me? Helping them live.

Not what he means.

Send him up.

It's such a beautiful place, the Rebbe said. It's a pity there's no synagogue here. No synagogue? Such a place?

You're right. You want to give services here?

When it's built will be time. You don't speak Hebrew? No.

The eyes were grey as the beard, clear as the clouds, and they seemed to smile.

I wondered, he said. A place as big as this, everybody talking, what faith, what religion? Why do you do what you do?

It's what I want, he said.

On what assumption?

My own.

The Rebbe wore a navy blue suit, a grey shirt, a blue tie, and a small grey straw-net hat with a turn-down brim. Through the network he saw the white *yarmulka*. The grey eyes looked over the Mediterranean, calmly, with certain doubt.

Considering where you are, you have the right?

I bought it. I know what I want to do.

Money is enough?

Enough to do what I want. Nobody else wanted to do it.

But money, that's enough?

Money created the country. Take the money away, where's the country? That goes for this year, last year, next year, the next fifty years. How else do you live? If you don't *put* something here, what's here?

There is plenty here, Mr. Denis.

Tell me where, without money?

You make a god of money?

I heard the argument too often. Tell me what can be

done without money? And lots of it. How do you think this place grew? Grows every day. You want to see the accounts?

Thank you. It has no interest. It is a business. There is no faith.

Wrong again. It was built in faith.

Faith?

Look it up. See what it means. I was one against the rocks. I believe I still am. But I'm winning. With money. And, let's say, money is the backbone. But the spirit is faith.

You have no synagogue here.

Nobody's interested in one.

Interest, no interest, there *should* be one.

You're right. There *will* be.

Arye stood outside the caravan that morning like a kicked dog.

Mr. Paul, we were sorry we walked out. Miko's got a job in the Sinai.

It's all right. I want a synagogue here. You know the one at Bar-Am? You looked around at the others? I want a miniature on those lines. Something unique. You have the stonemasons here. You have ceramics. Glass. Metal, any sort. Let's see the designs. That northwest corner of the Plaza. But don't cut down the olives. A place for fifty believers. Enough?

Believers? Fifty? *Here?*

You and your partner are going to design? And you're not believers? You're going to raise something up to the glory of the Lord God, and you don't believe? What kind of place are you going to build?

The pillars, the porticos, the entablatures, the mosaics. I'd prefer to have a ruling by the Rabbinical Court.

Then it's never going to be built. None of *that*. You let me have the blueprints, and start.

Time.

Yes, time.

Only time.

This is the desk, sir, that voice said. You didn't want any messages, or anything. Well, sir, the Commissioner of Police's office wants to talk with you. It's urgent.

Put them on.

That Mr. Paul Denis? The Reid Gallery on Fifty-seventh? And the apartment on West Seventy-second?

Right.

Glad I was able to finally get on to you.

How *did* you find me?

Well, sir. We have a system of hotel registrations. Your apartment got bombed at dead-on three o'clock this afternoon. The gallery bomb went off fifteen minutes later. We had the special squad in both places. Lucky it's Saturday. Nobody around to get hurt. They found the timer in the gallery. It was probably a veteran's job. Military expertise, all right.

What's the damage?

Pretty bad in the apartment, and upstairs. Windows out all over. That gallery, just the window and the door. You want to come to the apartment and see?

No. Call the insurance people. Glosworth, on Madison.

They're there. This happened a couple of hours ago. Took us that to find you.

I don't intend leaving here till Monday. I don't want my whereabouts known.

Were you expecting this? Did you have any warning?

In a way, yes. Suppose you call Sergeant Mackearn, at

the Sixteenth Precinct. He knows a lot more about it. Did the gallery bomb penetrate to the strongroom?

No. Just knocked a few pictures off of the walls. Lots of dust. Nothing much. Insurance people are boarding up. We'll have a guy on duty there round the clock.

Just let the Commissioner know I'm very grateful.

He put the receiver down as if a slab of black stone— he never knew why black—had come down, a monolith without weight, a menhir of the ages, flat across the top of his head.

Bilara, quit reading that mag as if you didn't know what was going on, he said. Go on out and find the first airline office open. Get us two tickets to London. Money's in the satchel. Tonight, or earlier.

She closed the magazine, and put it on the side table, elbow on knee, chin in palm, and the eyes came around, slow, to him.

Mr. Paul, nobody coming after me, she said, smiling. *You* go. Sure. But I have a job. I believe Sergeant Mackearn help me. I *know* he will.

You're in love with him.

She lay back, eyes shut, laughing in her throat, hands open, thin legs apart, helpless in a slight shake of the head.

Anybody else, she said. Not him. Not *me*. My dream man always been on the moon. Now we know they don't even have air. No dream man anyplace. How about the passport?

In the satchel. It's in order. You won't change your mind?

You *have* to have somebody here. They ain't after me.

I'm remembering about the stove.

Well. There's Sam. Kumeli.

Ask Glosworth's office to send an agent. I want you under guard. Ask Sergeant Mackearn to find you a cabbie he can trust. Take you home, bring you to work.

Cost money.

If you're not alive, you can't spend it. That's why I'm ratting out. I believe they'll go on trying till they do. Easy enough. They'll bide their time. Like he said.

The telephone rang. Bilara jumped, nearly six foot of human dynam, took off the receiver, and listened, held her breasts, and deflated in a sighing smile.

Mr. Gluck, she said. All right?

He never forgot how good a friendly voice could sound. Henri Tameur had called to tell him, and his son, the attorney, got the number from the Police Department. No idea who?

Goddam if I know which way we're supposed to be heading, Gluck said, tired. Listen. Let London come later. Go on out to La Guardia. Get yourself a flight to Miami. I'll meet you. We'll do a little baby-sitting. I have my daughter-in-law here. Go fishing tomorrow morning. How are you feeling?

Rotten.

Come on down to the sunshine country. Build sand castles with three beautiful kids. Get your mind off.

That was the wisest move he ever made, flying into sun, blue water beyond the garden wall spread in yellow hibiscus, and meeting Eli Gartry, just back from Israel, and seeing his shaky film of Jerusalem, and Beersheba, and Eilat, and Ophira, and at the end, the Hill.

Took most of two years to get the lease, Eli said. You can't buy anything there. They only lease. Now, I don't want it. I thought I make a summer home there. But the wife died. So why do I want to move? Here, I'm near her. There, where the hell am I? I got what I want. I'm too old to move.

Speaking, let's say, with a great deal of caution, Mr. Gartry, he said. What would you want for the place as it stands?

Gartry hunched silk-shirt shoulders and turned down his mouth.

I already contracted for water, the road, and the other stuff. Most of it's in. I don't know the total. I'll call my office. Isn't a hell of a lot, I'll tell you *that*. Why?

I have a dream, he heard himself say. A white hill. And trees. Gardens. Houses of stone. No two alike. And artists, working as they want to. In any media. One of a kind.

But only *one* painter? Gluck said. What's it cover? How do you decide?

As many as I can find. But only one in any style. No copyists.

I see we learned a lesson?

Lots more to learn. We have factories turning them out.

I never sold one. I threw a few out of my place. So what? People want it, they buy it. But, boy, I'm glad I don't have to sell it. I be sick on the floor. But how do you sell that stuff coming out of Israel? All I ever saw was junk. I'm telling you, *junk*.

Let's find out. Get it, first.

What I've seen, I'm saving money. I'm not in the business. Sell the canvas and the paints, you make a little over the line, maybe? But the product? *Ui*.

Mr. Paul, Sam Ravicz said. We have one hell of a problem with your Urbino. You know what a rag looks like?

Is it much damaged?

*Damag*ed? It's spots of paint all over the floor. Just was blown apart. Right out the frame. I got the two boys picking up with tweezers. Different colors in different plates. I'm putting the main piece on a stretch of canvas. I'll build it up by the cubic centimeter. Y'know? The old way?

Sam, I hope you can bring him back to me. He's an old friend. When I opened the front door, he always looked at me. You know that kind of a friend? For years?

Do my best, Mr. Paul. It's a beautiful picture. We don't have that kind of paint today. They powdered precious stones to get them colors. I don't believe we missed a crumb. I hope.

The small voice, the magnificent promise on little except hope and belief in ability, brought the Hill closer. The dream came alive in the faith of a craftsman.

There was comfort in a thought, off, on the side. If a Sam Ravicz could determine what he would do within his competence, then with the same degree of effort, and an infinitely wider choice, he should be able to do more.

But some bolt struck when he saw the wreck of the gallery. The sign in gold leaf he had always known was gone. In its place, gaping space, no wide window, no door, twisted metal. Rough boards nailed up by Glosworth's carpenters, most of the dust taken out by the cleaners, pictures stacked in the back room, and Mr. Blantyre's big chair, a mass of holes and strips of leather, and the Rowlandson, in crumbs, and the desk all splinters.

He wanted to cry.

Bilara's hand on his shoulder held him.

He sitting there, she whispered. He telling you. Don't let them bastards throw you. Can't do nothing *to* you. I *loved* him. He was the best. I come here skinny. He used to go out and get me a pint of ice cream. I had to sit right there, and put away the last little lick. He said, Bilara, them bones won't hold you. Get some calcium. Wonder what he say, now? *Fight*. Get the calcium. Grow them bones.

Glosworth's people took two days to put in the door and windows, with new steel blinds and a temporary sign, and when Bilara put the coffee on, and brought in the mail, they were back in business. But the apartment was another story, up to six weeks or more.

Sell it, he said. I'll find a new place.

I have a realtor, George Glosworth said, that morning. He'll get you an apartment. He already had an offer for *this* place. It's unbelievable, the prices today.

You won't find better than Fifty-seventh. I know what the prices are. But I'm not selling. When I do, I'll let you know.

Bilara found a small apartment on East Sixty-third, but when the agent heard his name and asked about the bombs, she had to tell him, and that finished it, and it happened three times in a couple of days, and he told her, Quit. I'll stay at the hotel.

But when George Glosworth came in with the paper for new insurance cover, he knew he had to think again.

You see, George said. These bastards don't know where to stop. They don't get you the first time, they try again till they get the pay-off. Has to be taken into consideration. That's the reason for the up. It's no act of God.

I believe I have to try another business.

Look. Could I ask you a question? Just what sort of money's tied up in this?

Around three million dollars. Or more.

George whistled.

You're the bottleneck? Baby, how'll you look at Riverside, all those hundred-dollar wreaths?

You mean I won't be around for any new business?

Not till they collect.

You don't think I can win?

The money says, No. You're going to be in business how long? Till they get you? Then they can sell. They're gunning down their own guys in restaurants. For how much? Why not you? Listen. You, instead of three million? How long do you last?

I won't take out insurance. Everything goes to the bank, except the current exhibit. Every artist insures his own. I had enough.

Careful how you go home.

George, after all these years, I have to say, you're a real help.

Mr. Paul. I told you. I know the trade.

George, we did business a long time. What're the odds?

I'll tell you. This is what we call risk policy. I don't go further. I like to see you healthy. It's costing somebody three million. For how long?

Jonathan Cole came in with the rolled umbrella, the black hat and overcoat, drunk in the old style, upstanding, an odd pull-away instantly corrected, the eyes not always on target, the smile a mite too gracious, spittle at the corners of the mouth, and the job of barbering must have cost ten dollars plus.

They tell me I was selling pictures belonging to my aunts, he said, feet astride in the office doorway. They're all older than me. I'll go before any of them. Why would I want to sell their property?

We know nothing about it, he said. Do please sit down. Have a drink. What pictures are these?

Oh, well, you know how it is. One dies, the other goes to live with the other. Pretty soon you have five of them living together. All got everything they had. That's plenty. But what's this, I'm selling anything belonging to them?

I wouldn't take the slightest damn notice.

You don't know anything about it?

I heard a rumor, yes. But there was no back-up. I called your Long Island address. I heard nothing more.

Well, now, wait a minute, here. These babes have between them something over eighty old masters. All bought in the last century. I said why hang on to them? Sell them, travel, donate, anything. But why just clutch them? What's the use? Watch your coffins go down the stairs? Do what I did. Go around the world. Spend it. Feels good.

So *they* said?

Took a little time. First, one. Then the other. Finally they all want to sell. When could they send them? I'd ask you out. But it's a pilgrimage.

You can see for yourself we're not in the best shape. But I'll take care of them.

That procession of pictures, in every kind of frame, gold, white, or cream-rococo, with dust in the whorls, and verdigris over the little metal tabs naming the artist and the dates, all came in on that Saturday morning, and the new blinds rattled down, the doors were locked, and within thirty minutes a committee of four agreed that they were forgeries, especially well done, and good enough to pass as originals.

Henny Fuld, Joe Rabin, and Henri Tameur went over the list, and signed, and went into the buffet served by Kumeli.

You're goddam lucky, Henri said. I could have been fishing in Alaska. Wish I was.

Never mind about Alaska, Henny said, through potato salad. How many other people bought this? Plain crap.

Not crap, Henri said. Has its price. You have to prove it.

Look, Joe Rabin said. Don't let's talk nonsense. These are eighty-odd supposed masters. All got a price. We all stupid? Mean to tell me these people had these pieces all along, published in the private catalogs, and nobody ever spotted them?

You have something, Henri said. They don't look all that old to me. Henny?

That paint looks kind of new. Could have been restored? Who *is* this guy Cole? I've heard the name. Paul, do *you* know?

Heir to a hell of a big fortune, he said. In real estate. Never sold. Probably not much cash, but that can come. When all the aunts die. These pictures are supposed to be their combined property. I don't believe it.

So what are you going to do? Henri asked, spreading mustard on roast beef. Should I tell you? You already had something like thirty fakes—they say—out of this gallery. Now you have this bunch. Get the same name. Where there's smoke?

I never knew any woman who didn't take care of good things, he said. *All* these, the combined property of *five* women? All of top families? Probably had servants all their lives? So they let the labels grow mould? And all that dust? No, *sir*. These are fakes. Bilara, you check the pictures against the documents, put in a call to Inspector Hanrahan, and another to Mr. Cole. Kumeli, you call the trucking company for a job to Long Island, and then see if you can find anybody in George Glosworth's office. Or call him at home. I'm here all day.

In the long Bedouin linen dress, Rivka came in, shoulders-down tired, and dropped in the chair almost with a grunt.

Take off your shoes, he said. You look beat. I'll fix you a drink. I didn't see you for days. What's been going on?

I could die here. Nobody'd ever know.

Prevailing wind's away from you. I'll tell Chom to call around and see we don't have a corpse. I'll see it's properly buried.

It?

What else?

Why, that's un*feel*ing. You mean, I die, and you call me that? *It?* Would you like people to call *you* that?

I don't see why not? What have I got? Life? No. Sex? No. Anything? No. Clay. Dust. What else? What's your trouble?

Well, she said, looking through the open doorway.

Here's your drink. Well, what?

She put hands to her face, and the beautiful reddish hair fell over.

I thought I had the ideas, she said. Goddammit, I don't. They don't work out.

He leaned against the doorway. There was only the darkness. Not a star.

You're up against the problem of all artists, he said. What are you going to do? How are you going to do it? Who did it before? How are you going to do it differently? When you all line up, how do *you* stand out? What, exactly, do *you* want to do?

Make flowers. Windows. Anything. In glass.

Why don't you?

They're no good.

You've been here how long? A couple of months?

About that. More.

What do you expect to do in that time?

You're making fun of me.

He went over, and knelt beside her, breathing the sweet of her hair.

Rivka, listen to me, he said. How long do you suppose it took to dream up this place? All the planning. The work. There are still more than thirty workmen every day just building. Gardens, pools, tree planting. A couple more years won't see it finished. If I could go out that door and wave a wand, would I have to wait? Or will it all happen in that flash? Don't you think I haven't put my head in my hands a few times? What do *any* of us have to go on, except hope, and patience? Are you different? Do you expect to have ideas and dreams without time interfering? Do your fingers obey? If your brain doesn't tell you what to do, where are you going? So some poor little pathetic pair-of-teats comes in here and moans because the flowers won't grow? Get back there and start thinking, goddammit. Start working. Sweat. I'll be down there Sunday. See if I have a corpse, or flowers. Flowers, I love. A corpse, I'll bury. Get out of here.

She went out of the chair as a sprinter leaves the blocks, and stood a sacred, still moment in the doorway, hands on the jambs, and he saw the beauty of waist, thighs, legs he seemed to have missed before.

Came here for help, she whispered. I came to *you*.

He heard her running down the path, jumping the steps in strides, knowing he must order lights along the way, hoping she might not fall and scar those legs, instantly aware of a lit mote of want, trying to imagine her naked, scorning himself in the same instant, wondering if he should follow her, and hearing, No.

Here's Mr. Cole on the line, Bilara said. He sound like they got him nail' down.

What in the name of Christ's own hell are all these goddam pictures you sent me? Cole shouted. Some sort of a stupid joke?

I return the consignment you sent me.

I sent you? *I* did? There isn't a single one—not one—I sent you. Not one son-of-a-bitch belongs in this house. They're not our property. I told the driver to load them back on and deliver them to you.

Is he still there?

Right here.

Ask him, please, to take them to your local police and

deliver them as unclaimed lost property, and I'll go around
to the Sixteenth Precinct and file a complaint. You'd better
go with him. Give the name of the trucking company you
used. They could have been switched. Do you have the
provenance on all of your own pictures? Documents, so
forth?

Certainly. Jesus. Let me call my lawyer. Let me know,
will you?

That terrifying paralysis of arms, legs, the numbing at the
base of the skull, attacked, a feeling of terror that struck,
defied movement, made him mute.

Bilara poured straight scotch.

You trust Mr. Cole? she asked, in the small voice.

Bilara, I trust *you*. Now, what *about* him?

You want it without the sugar? He's a no-good. Never did
a lick of work. Women kept him. How come he send the
pictures here, and all we get's a load of fakes? How do you
switch eighty-odd pictures? A whole gang must have worked
on it. It took Kumeli, Sam, the three guys from next door,
the truck driver and the other guy with him, and me, the
best part of an hour to get them *in* here. Now swap this load
for another the same size. What time they leave the Cole
house?

You should have been a cop.

Only have to look at guys like that. Inside, I throw up.
Simon Legree, just a step away. Now, this guy, Cole, *he* like
to fry my ass on a stove. *That's* for sure.

I'd like to fry your ass with a kiss. Or two.

Mr. Paul, any time please you. I never knew kiss-my-ass
sound so good.

Bilara, we always had to work together. Sometimes we
slept in the same place. You made it plain, keep the hands
off. I did. Did you mean we wasted time?

No, Mr. Paul. Nobody waste time. When you find out

what to *do* with time, it's beautiful. You *can't* waste it. Just goes *on*.

But.

He had an eye for Kumeli. She topped Bilara by a couple of inches, half the width anywhere, with little breasts barely a shadow, and always in the background, looking down if he talked to her, never saying anything. Yet she was sharp, never had to be told twice, got it first time and right, and he knew she looked to him. She came from Liberia, and a family in Virginia, and she got some degree at a college in Florida was about all he remembered. She was smart in appearance, in approach, and she never did less than a solid day's work, and he never forgot he never went to college and never got a degree.

Near her, he felt the electric charge. She always looked away.

Mr. Paul you now have twenty-nine artists in residence, sixteen in temporary quarters, and three just got here, Yehudit said, opening the meeting. I believe they'll all move in. That's forty-eight in all. We're limited to fifty. The other two can come in any day. What happens after?

Tents, he said. Till we get the buildings up. We haven't got a sculptor in marble. We're never likely to turn out anything like the Three Graces. With all the beautiful women in Israel? Nobody loves, any more. It's a disappointment. If I could see one of our people, out of our new country—that's so *old*—produce anything to stand beside the Greeks, or the Florentines, the Venetians, the rest, I'd die happy. After all, we have a lot of the Greek in us. Generations of our women were raped. When's that genius going to look at us? I want to find it. Take care of it. I'd love to find a sculptor in marble. What else?

We need an hotel, Yehudit said. Two offers to build here. Return them. We don't want any of the rot of letting beds. Let them come, and go. This place is for work. Not tourists. Enlarge the hostel, fine.

But tourists spend money.

Pack the item, and go.

They like to see people work.

Everybody does. So long as they're not.

Boaz wants money for granite. And transport.

Lend it.

Rivka needs more moulds.

Get them.

Lot of money.

Does it matter?

She's had more than anyone else.

She has more talent. In her own line.

Take her a long time to pay back.

How long do you live?

Yes. That's another question. Where do we bury our people? Including you and me?

Talk about it later. But if anything happens to me, I want to be cremated. Here's where I want to be. We ought to have the right sort of oven here.

Oh, my God. Remembering the holocaust?

They went in there alive.

*Ter*rible thing to say. How can you even *men*tion ovens?

If I couldn't, would we *be* here? Ask yourself. It was their sacrifice. Who *were* they? All those grey people. Ghosts. They all had a name. Somebody *loved* them. They all *loved* somebody. How do we think of them? Holocaust? *Is* it a fitting term? A fry-up?

Mr. Paul, Kumeli said, when he came in late that afternoon. Bilara went around to the Sixteenth Precinct. They have all those pictures around there. They still don't have the owner. They wanted her to witness they all got sent back from here. She said they didn't. She wouldn't sign.

Great. Put the blinds down. Lock up. I don't want this place open after sundown. No call from Mr. Cole?

No, sir.

I don't understand a lot of things. How a man of family can act like that. Abuse his position. Forget his name.

Mr. Fuld said it don't matter. It's the money. Show 'm the money.

Mr. Fuld?

Yes, sir. He went around there with Bilara.

That was good of him. I like that. We all need help. How do *you* live, here?"

She clasped her hands, looking through the dark window. I'm sharing, she whispered.

With a man?

Oh, *no!*

Oh. Happy?

She shrugged, smiled.

You have to be, else you're not. If you're not, nobody help you.

If you ever need help, you have only to ask me.

I like to dance.

Dance? You want to train to be a dancer?

No. I dance. I like to dance for you.

Here?

No. Here's work.

Yehudit, in the shortest blue shorts and a blue minibra, had a Renoiresque, ample, florid quality though without a roll or any start of a bulge, and her tan in shadow made her a deep gold, all in all, anybody's eyeful, and her smile of perfect teeth seemed a fanfaronade to putting down the long black folio.

We got him, she said, in triumph. I knew if we prayed hard enough.

Who?

Your sculptor. He's Italian. Outside Naples, there. I'm no judge. I think what I've seen of his stuff is just beautiful. But I don't know anything.

You'll do. Where *is* this stuff?

Coming off the truck.

Didn't take long? Hallmark of the artist. They make up their minds, it's done. How long, between application and now?

Six weeks. The Consul-General took a hand. Look at this.

She held up a photograph, a carving, in marble, of a girl reaching for a bunch of grapes, with a serpent coiling about the vine. A marker showed it to be life-size.

Wonderful, he said. Let him settle in. I'll see him.

He has a daughter. You're going to forget me.

Doubt it.

Sure?

Appeal? Pathos? Fear?

He put out a hand, touched the bounteous thigh.

I'll break a rule, he said. No mauling in working hours. I'm *sure*.

The smile repaid.

There's Sam Ravicz on the line, Bilara said.

That you, Sam? How're you doing?

Why, Mr. Paul, I'm doing great. You remember you talked about a place around here? Well, a friend of mine, a

furnishing store, got the corner along the street, he's going
out of business. Fair price. You want to see it?

Right now, Sam. Miss Tancy's going to be up there in the
next thirty minutes. I'll be there this afternoon. Around
four?

You see, Mr. Paul, it's real difficult for a single gal to live
in New York, Kumeli said, from the kitchen, that evening. I
mean, without a family to hang onto. Every time you turn
around, somebody want to use you. Else you're no date.
Just a waste of money. That's all. No talk. Just action, action.
Get the panties off. Let's go. Well, I can't.

Moral scruples? Religious?

Physical. I was a cripple. When I was six, we were in
Monrovia. My daddy was maritime superintendent, and he
up-anchored and went to Baltimore for me to have treatment. Saved my life, all right. But I have a bone deforma-
tion below there. Has a name. I forget it. Nobody get in. I
was *the* wallflower. No dates. Nothing. The word got
around. Couldn't get in her with an oil rig. You got used
to it. Lots of kind people took me out. What I hear, I didn't
miss an awful lot.

Pretty sure you're right. Or wrong. Depending.

On what?

How you feel. You want it, you want it. You don't, you
don't.

Too easy. You don't have the chimney, you don't have a
fire. That's me.

So you dance?

Right. How you get rid of it? Throw it off? Pills? Drugs?
Fool with yourself?

The voice echoed off the kitchen's tiled walls, seemed
to float.

What did *you* do?

Found somebody.

Why am *I* here?

Only way to *get* you here.

He put the drink aside, and stood.

Now tell me, he said. I came here to see you dance. What's this?

I'll dance. Please sit down. She going to be here any minute. Mr. Paul, *please* let me fix you another drink. She be so angry I let you go.

That key scratched in the door, and Kumeli side-skipped out of the kitchen, linked her fingers, and stood, waiting, and somebody shut the door, rough breaths of an overcoat taken off, and Bilara paced in, without surprise, kissed, softly, both cheeks, standing tip-toe, and Kumeli, taller, kissed her forehead.

We finally managed to get you here, Bilara said, tranquil, happy. I thought we never would. Kumeli told you about herself? Yeah. Well, that's my trouble, too. So when we met up, and found out, why, we stayed met, and I never was so happy. Well, that's why we had to get you to come on up. Let me fix myself a drink.

I never knew you did.

Only here. And only one. We don't go to any bars. I have to get some courage to tell you.

What?

Kumeli and me. We don't want to go to Israel.

Changed your minds? All right. But I'll want you there for minimum one month anyway. You have to train that staff. Nobody else can. I don't have the time.

That's good as done. Far's we concerned. But they got a color bar over there.

First I heard of it.

Them black Hebrews? Got thrown out?

Well, in the first place, they were *not* Hebrews by any standard, and you'll be tourists. You'll have three months on your passports. Second place, I have a proposition. Kumeli, how do you look when you dance?

That comes after, Bilara said, in the small, lazy voice. We did a little cooking, and we have a bottle of that French wine you like, but we kind of like to hear the proposition. You never laid a hand on me. Except once. And I couldn't tell you.

How long since you and Kumeli met?

Oh, few months. But we only got to talking a couple weeks ago. That's when she moved in. This place's my Daddy's. We have the top floor. Through there we have the studio. Modern ballet. For the kids. Doing fine. But I can't get any kind of smoke in the art classes.

Try nudes.

She shook her head.

I don't want no cat-house in here, she said. Mr. Blantyre got angry one day. He said these people are turning art into pornography. A naked woman, like a naked table or a naked flower isn't art. It's what an artist can *do* with them. *That's* art. He kind of directed my life. My Daddy was his mailman, first. Then he moved into office lunches. Then he had his own place. And he went on from there. Got 'm all over. Could I ask what the proposition is?

That corner building up there at a hundred and ninth?

It's good. Elevator to the third floor. Built solid. Location's fine. But it's out of the money. Wrong nabe. What's it for?

That's where you start the first gallery of copyists' art, and the first all-black gallery. You know enough.

Bilara looked across at Kumeli, but she was looking down at her hands in her lap.

Black artists thrown in with a bunch of white fakes? she said, sitting up. I don't *like* that.

Bilara, it's going to take a long time, the way we're going, till enough black creative artists can take home the price the white fake gets for *his* work. The white fake went to art school. He had to learn. He hasn't got it? So, start copying. A thousand dollars or more for a month's work? Why not? If he's good, it's a whole lot more. But *you* don't have to tell any fairy tales. You don't have to be anything except honest. This is a copy. That's all you have to say. But it's the best copy you'll ever see. Only an expert'll tell the difference. In a while, the dealers are going to bless you. You'll clean up the market. You'll sell it for what it *is*. *Not* a fake. A copy, of a master. But so well done that only a so-called expert could tell the difference. Stop using the word "fake." It's not a fake. It's a copy.

Tho white painters going to give me their work? They going to trust *me?* I'm *black.*

Bilara, look. When there's a sale, there's money. Where there's money, there's trade. Where does a black artist get a fair shake? Most of them are so goddam shy, they won't go near *any* gallery. So? You have a special room. The public go to you for a fine picture. It*is* a fine picture. You don't deal in daubs. It's a real, good copy. You could challenge an expert. All right. But in the black artists' room, you have originals. You can bring the prices up. Pretty soon, you get the name. How did Mr. Blantyre start? I'll tell you. With prints. Then home-grown American painters. Who gave a damn for *them* before he started the Reid? Began showing? Who knew about them? It was all imported. It's imported, so it *has* to be good? Start there. This is home-grown. *This* is

American. This is *Negro*. Come and buy it. Give the *black* artist a chance to live. And *be*. Don't like the idea?

Bilara moved the long legs, and stroked her hair.

Mr. Paul, she said, lazily. I believe we *both* going to dance.

Sam, the cleaner, messenger, and part-time coffee-maker, came in that morning and stood in the doorway, well-dressed, even smart in an old-fashioned way, in gifts of clothing over many years.

The wife died this morning, Mr. Paul, he said. I can have the day off?

Ah, Sam. I'm sorry. Why certainly. Why didn't you say something before?

I didn't know. I didn't live with her a long time.

So why do you need the day off? Funeral?

No. It's, I believe I ought to remember her. The way she was. I like to. She was real beautiful, Mr. Paul. Only. Well. She kind of lost her mind. She was in this place, there, the past twenty years. She never knew me.

So what have you been doing? Marry again?

Ah, no. What's the use, you marry again? Same thing happen?

Think I know what you mean. Sam, I believe we ought to talk about your pension.

Sam nodded, looking at the stairway to the first floor.

That's right, Mr. Paul. I been here over forty years. I believe it come time.

What made you think so?

Sam shook his head, pulling up Mr. Blantyre's ex-trousers, sharply creased.

I just heard word going round this place closing down.

He always thought of Sam as some sort of gentle lunatic.

Mr. Blantyre said, back there, You have to give thanks you
were born in your right senses. Sam's been with me a long
time. Be kind to him. Let him feel he's looked after. Give
him a little present now and again. If you wore a suit or a
pair of shoes long enough, hand them over. Shirts, ties,
socks, what the hell. Make him feel *want*ed. Make him feel
as if he's *part* of this world. Bring him *in*to it. Let him know
that if he only dusts pictures, or cleans windows or makes
coffee, goddammit, nobody could do it better, and if *he*
didn't, you'd feel a loss. Take care of Sam. He's wise in his
own way.

What's the word going round, Sam?

He knew Sam got in with all the other messengers, and
he knew the sort of gossip, because for many years he had
lived Sam's day-to-day existence, knew the same streets,
made the same coffee, brought the same mail. When he was
out, Sam was in. And when Sam was in, he was out.

Why should this place be closing down, Sam?

I don't know, sir. It don't have the name it did.

What do you mean?

I don't believe we got what we had.

Could you tell me a little about that, Sam? Why don't you
sit down?

No, sir. I feel I just don't be*long* any more. I use' to be top
man. I knew it. I *act* that way. I'm Reid Gallery. I don't have
to say shucks to nobody. But just lately they telling me I'm
carrying around a bunch of fakes. Me? Fakes? Mr. Blantyre's man? *Me? Reid* Gallery? *Fakes?* Mr. Paul, they
laughing at me. Giving me the sign. I was younger, I fight
them. But I'm old. Don't have it.

He broke in the face, at the knees, and he wept, feeling
blind for the wall, leaning.

Go to him, son, Mr. Blantyre said, in the gentle voice. Go

to him. Let him know somebody's around. He always faced the goddamnedest toughest world. He never had the warmth of a woman's arms. Never knew a real kind word except in here. Reid Gallery was his life. He *knew* what he was working for. Go to him. Dry his tears. He's crying for *us*.

Resting the sobbing head, putting a hand on shaking shoulders, knowing he held the kindly years of Mr. Blantyre's life, he saw Bilara in the doorway, almost an angelic vision, nodded her over, and she took Sam sweet as a mama, in wordless croon, walking him away to her office.

He sat at the desk, staring at the restored Rowlandson. Everything was restored. Every item in place.

All as it was.

But it was not.

Wise in his own way, Sam knew in the heart.

If Sam knew, then who else? Who might be persuaded? Why? For what reason?

Mr. Paul, Yehudit said, in her business voice. Chom Vissel's gone to the hospital. Nurse took him. Something in the stomach. Who's going to take care of the dogs?

Surely we have somebody? Why won't Toni or some of the others?

The dogs won't eat.

Loyalty?

Or love?

Dogs?

Well, Mr. Paul. I have to tell you. Dogs *can* become awfully fond. You didn't know it? I have two. I'd never be without them. Why don't you come on down and see them? We could go to Toni's for something to eat, and take them *their* supper in a bag. They're the luckiest dogs around. Bones, *this* size. Won't you? I mean, come on down? I make a pretty good cup of coffee.

No scotch?

Can't afford it.

Bring my own?

At least I have ice and glasses. And music.

Her voice faltered. Instantly the air seemed scarlet, savagely redolent of blood, an electric pulse that brought the bright sunlight to shimmer, clearing to sharp awareness of the garden's quiet, the pale-goldish stone strictly laid in the path's downward curve, doves billing in flowering almonds, and a flash of carp among the stone pool's water-lilies.

Do you feel lonely here?

Oh, Mr. Paul, *no*. Never. I've found something here I always looked for. If ever I had to leave I believe I'd *kill* myself.

Won't happen while I'm here.

There was a rumor you were selling.

That's all it was. Where did *you* hear it?

Nurse Sokolow told me she got it in Haifa.

You've seen the correspondence. Did you tell her it was rubbish?

Yes. But you *can* change your mind.

Have you asked yourself? If I sold, where am I going? How do you sell a dream? What do you do with yourself when you wake up? Naked, with money, is that something to *be*?

It's a lot of money.

What do you *do* with it? Buy gee-gaws? Start someplace else? What *for*?

I'll say this. You made a lot of people happy. Isn't a happier place, or happier people in this world. It's in the work. I think it's beautiful, the things they're turning out. And Tsahali, she's going to be big. How's this?

She offered the inside of her elbow, and he sniffed, and

looked at a smile in deep blue eyes, in sunshine almost the gentian in the dye shop, and gentle flesh held its own wide space of wonder.

You're beautiful, he said. How do you think a drop of that under each breast might hit me?

She laughed the large white teeth in a natural mouth. Bring the scotch and find out, she said. Around eight?

Mr. Paul, this is Bilara, the small voice said. I know it's early, but Mr. Weil's office called last night. You get the message?

To call this morning? Yes.

It's real urgent. You want me to call him, fix a time?

Do that. Soon's you like.

Weil's early-morning eyes flung him off-base, the fearful, facing a haunt of grief.

You have problems, he said, sitting at the desk, opening the folio. First, the question of a series of sales in the past ten—fifteen years. The terra-cotta figurines, whatever you call them. Other deals here. Plus the thirty-odd fakes. Then the Cole robbery, and the enquiry into the Etruscan business. Then Chinese and Japanese, and the medieval Persian stuff. Well. A whole lot of things I don't understand. But I have to. First, there's a long report here from the Vatican about your part in selling stolen Church property over a period back to World War Two.

Never.

It's all here, in detail. Then a report from Interpol linking you with the sale of stolen statues and paintings, a number of them, and forging documents. Provenance, you call them?

So far as this gallery's concerned, *not*.

Read the reports. It all adds up to pretty damning testimony. Cole's suing you for attempting to palm off a lot of inferior artwork for the consignment he sent you. This gallery appears to be a center of shady deals. Hard thing to say. But read this stuff. I'd like to know who's behind it. I'll find out where De Ruysker's got their instructions. Somebody's getting at you.

I can guess.

Better tell me.

Jonathan Cole. I always thought he was a sort of gentleman farmer and part-time playboy-drunk. Lately I'm not so sure. He *could* be a front. Any paper you have there I can meet, no trouble. I'd like to know why I'm singled out. Nobody else. Just me. And this gallery.

Well. There's first of all a hell of a lot of money here. You're supposed to have it. Ergo?

All I had was sales commission. The robberies? I know as much as you.

Let's have it clean. Clean's a hound's tooth. No shenanigans *any*where? I mean, *any*where? I just want to warn you the FBI's in on this. They'll want to talk to you. But why?

List what you've mentioned. It's well into the tens of millions of dollars. Don't have to look further. Cole's nonsense is nothing more than blackmail. He can't prove what went into that truck. I can prove what came out of it, and where it went.

But this happened twice.

And both loads went around to the Sixteenth Precinct. I wouldn't have them here. Those files will give you all the details. My accountants will give you the figures. I haven't a worry in the world.

But cold snakes writhed in the gut. He remembered the terra-cotta *bozzettos,* models of the statues, supposedly by

Canova, and their provenance, in a pouch of tooled red and green Venetian leather. All were excellent copies. They might even have been from the same cast. But they were no more original than pastry models of Rockefeller Center. He sold because the buyer wanted them at any price, and at that price he sold, and later heard they had gone to Osaka, to the collection of Tuni Tamoshito, an industrialist. Many other works in statuary, stone, marble, and bronze, and at least two hundred canvases had gone there over the years. He had to admit to himself that too often a certain laxity had been permitted in standards set by Mr. Blantyre, especially where deals were made outside the United States and beyond Europe. There had never seemed any risk. But items began coming back to be exchanged or resold, and because prices went up, more publicity resulted, and closer scrutiny by competing dealers raised doubts in the trade and among collectors. Fortunately the papers had always been in order, which dispelled most misgiving, though not the trade gossip.

There lay the danger.

It was evident in the folio. Read by anyone outside the dealers association, it seemed, as Weil had called it, a damning indictment. Yet each statement could be rebutted, and fact put in place of fiction, hard supporting evidence instead of hints to the contrary.

Luckily they were no more than hints, or accusation without basis, especially in the Bishop Petretti Eldonado's report, which made a charge that the Reid Gallery had sold over a period of years more than five hundred works stolen from the Church in various parts of the world. Jonathan Cole's collection—which always supposedly had been his grandfather's—was there as recent pillage from Cerveteri, with the tomb ornaments, and the bases, the ossuaries, the bronzes, the Roman frescoes, oils, figurines.

Bilara and Kumeli between them got it all out of the files, and in a couple of weeks had a report, entirely factual, which demolished the Bishop's nonsense, and Lucien Weil said it was a triumph of honest fact over noisome gossip.

He, only he, knew that it was not.

It was carefully concocted garbage.

But ignoring the shade of Mr. Blantyre, he had to hate himself in forgetting the ethic, disregarding the strait honor of that honest man, becoming something less—remembering that gentle voice—constantly, joltingly, remembering that gentle voice—Remember, son. There *are* shits in this business—and having to live with the idea that he was one.

He knew it.

If nobody else knew it.

For the money.

Prestige, that cunt-word, meaning—in the moment—more important sales than anyone else.

More money.

Himself, and desecrating the Temple of Nelda's raised knee.

Where he browsed, and met himself, and hated. The only beauty he could know, and touch, and feel, was innocent.

He was unworthy.

There are shits, my son.

He was one.

The raised knee of a woman in love was his temple. But he was unclean, tried to buy, had to bribe, and he hated, not himself, but her.

The new house gave him the warmest feeling every time he went up, and that was four and five times a day, if only to see the growing beauty of the garden, and Kate, with Chom and a team of Druse gardeners planting trees, and

Arab masons setting the paving stones, building the fountains, laying the stairways, and placing the huge circular millstones flat on waist-high pedestals, to be planted in the axle-space with a blue glow of gentian, and in others, giant heartsease of one color, a mauve here, yellow there, coral, red, purple, and an innocence of white, and alyssum ruffled white among the cracks in the paving stones, with dwarf pinks, and Sweet William in beds along the walls, and flowering rock plants caressed the high buttressed walls down to the rose garden, the herbarium, and—Kate's suggestion—her especial pride, a rock garden, with every flower, plant, shrub, and tree mentioned in the Bible.

A fountain's rosette whispered prismatic splendor among the Della Robbia cupids in the atrium, a wide marble surround held cushions for sunbathing, and rooms opened under the colonnade, the largest, facing the Mediterranean, a checkerboard of red and white tiles, a dull red Bedouin rug stretching the length, and a canted window, allowing two majestic views, divided by a portico and double-door of silver, probably stolen from a Peruvian church, part of an exchange deal that cost him only his initials on the sales slip.

The staircase to the second floor was finished except for the baluster rail, a beautiful pseudo-S of red lacquer, from Siam, perhaps twelfth century, with supports in red, gold, and black, and a dragon's head on the ascent, nubbed to the nostrils by many a generation of pilgrims' playful rub-of-the-palm, hoping for health, love, and money. The roof garden had been planted with all the small flowers, and lilies, in beds with broken sculpture surrounds, and shallow pools floated water-lilies, and miniature bulrushes, and all kinds of coral fish swam and flashed a lazy delicacy of wondrous color.

The dream began to live.

Down below, on all sides of the hill, artists were busy, and from weekly reports, happy. The gallery's sales figures went up week by week. Forward orders took most into months of work, and a majority into more than a year. Tsahali, in the perfumery, now called The Alembic, had at least a two-year backlog, but she refused to move to larger quarters, or to employ more than the four girls helping her, and he agreed, because the glass-blowers were in the same state, of piled-up orders and the confining hours of the day, with little hope of more flasks unless she decided to let some company turn out one type, but she refused, and again, he agreed.

One, and only one, was the rule.

Bilara called that night to make a final report on empty racks, lack of stock in the strongroom, the bank's bare vault, and simple walls.

I sent off Mr. Gluck's last check this morning, Mr. Paul, the small voice smiled. We got the visas. Airline tickets, everything all set. The new owner was around this morning with his decorator. Can you imagine this gallery a health-food hang-out?

I'm too sad to want to think about it.

We been crying all this month. Only reason they kind of dried up, the tears I mean, that's *our* gallery up there. That guy you sent sure has the ideas. It's just shaping up beautiful. Oh, and Mr. Ravicz, the paint shop, he's going to put in a stand, and we get five percent of the sales. We can't sit still, waiting to get in there.

I'm happy about that. Bilara, what was your final sale?

Well, sir. *I'm* happy to tell you it was a toss-up between the *or*iginal Eakins—strictly home-grown—and that fake David you never liked.

Which one's that?

"Madame Récamier."

But that's Gérard, surely?

No sir, Mr. Paul. That's David. And I hit him for seven thousand five, and he thought he got a bargain. Eakins really went in the money, and *he* was final sale. I don't think I *bear* closing down on a *fake*.

A *copy*. Think of your new business. And my memory must be going. I always would have sworn that "Récamier" was by Gérard.

Well, sir. Mr. Blantyre knocked that in my head the first couple months I was here. He said she was the biggest whore in Europe, and if David saw her like that many times, he must have sampled the goods. Lucky bastard, he called him.

I must be one. To have someone like you taking care of things. You've been great, Bilara. You two going to dance for me again when you get here?

Any time, Mr. Paul, sir. We sure enjoyed the last time.

David should have seen *you* two. That *would* have been something to paint. He wasn't such a lucky bastard, after all. *I'm* the one.

You going to be again, just's soon's we get there.

That's a promise?

Sure *is*.

So get here soon. The canvases are all waiting for you to hang them. And the girls here are waiting to learn. Give Kumeli a hug for me. One for you.

I got it, Mr. Paul. Give it right back. Double. In spades. *Two* of us.

The first visit of the two FBI men passed without much in the way of worry, although it was always present, and those cold snakes in the gut chased each other through the endless hours of that week, while every file and all the provenance went under steady appraisal, with constant reference to the thick folio they brought with them. Neither accepted Bilara's offer of coffee, or his, of a drink, and they came in and went out, the original nameless and faceless, at a little past nine o'clock in the morning and a few minutes after six o'clock at night.

The second visit was not so pleasant. From the sound of their talk, they were Ivy Leaguers, and they looked like Brooks Brothers with a dash of Knize, but they sounded like rented hell. Many questions, going back before his time he had no answer for, though he began to see that Mr. Blantyre, too, had sometimes nodded. Questions about Rembrandts, Gainsboroughs, Vermeers, Toulouse-Lautrecs went over his head. He remembered delivering some of them, but the filed records gave no help.

We come to this man you insist on calling the Name, one of them said. What's the idea of that?

The original owner of this gallery gave that promise. I won't break it. That name will not be mentioned.

It's in all of these newspapers. Why not?

In this gallery, no.

All right. He had this collection. All fakes. Bought here.

They were not. He bought the originals here. You ought to be out looking for *them*. Let me give you an address.

He wrote the address of Sam Ravicz.

See him, he said. Ask him to take you to the paint factory, out near the Amboys. Open your eyes.

Seems to some of us Mr. Blantyre didn't always keep his on the odd spitball, the senior said. They put a few right past him.

Look at the provenance. What are you going to argue about? Who's the umpire?

It shut them up.

But he still had questions to answer. The collection of Etruscan bronzes and funerary ornaments were all, apparently, sold in the past few years by fly-by-night grave robbers. Jonathan Cole and his aunts were a figment, and the Long Island telephone number was a gas station.

How do you get caught this way? one of the agents said. Couldn't you take the trouble to check?

Look, I have a business here. I don't have a detective agency. This Cole guy comes in, wants to buy or sell, I buy or sell. He's on the books since before I started working here. What do I have to check?

You ought to know who you're dealing with.

Maybe I should check on you?

The first anniversary of the Hill brought up all the Druse and Arab workmen and their families from the villages, and everybody came out to welcome them, among their donkeys, all in floral garlands, groomed, with scrubbed hooves, carrying the old people and children up to Toni's, with pipe and drum music, and a bar free to all, and a lamb, duck, and turkey-poult grill.

Next year I shall entertain you in my house, he told Azma'uta's father. Before that, I shall invite you on the night when I open the house. When the garden is ready. When the chairs are in the rooms. When I sleep under my own roof.

It is important, Azma'uta translated for her father. A man without his own roof has nothing. Even a Bedouin has a tent. But you have no woman.

I have women when I want them.

They do not protect your name.

I do not require the patronage of women. Simply the service of their bodies.

Your name suffers.

Where? Among which kind? Anything to respect?

How do you acknowledge the meaning of respect?

I know the meaning. But which mind should I look into? Do we all agree? Respect in your mind may be contempt in another's. I follow what I think.

It's enough?

For the moment, yes. A glass of champagne?

Thank you. My father does not drink alcohol.

Yehudit read the accounts, that Friday noon, and put everybody in a good humor, except David Shalkovsky, the sculptor in bronze. All twenty-odd of his statues were almost ready, but the money was held in escrow until they were delivered, and he said he was broke and dependent on his neighbors for meals.

What happened with Toni? Yehudit asked him. He'll feed you. So will Dov.

I'm strictly kosher, he said. I'm a be*liev*er.

So why are you making images?

I'm not. God made man in His *own* image. I'm making them the way *I* want. But I keep the law. He's selling meat up there with the blood in it, and ice cream and rice pudding and stuff, after. I won't eat in a kitchen like that. And I don't like Dov's place. He's selling hamburgers and franks down there. In a milk bar?

Talk to Rabbi Berezhkoy. Everything's in order.

Not for me. He's known to be Reform.

Yehudit looked around.

Mr. Paul, she said. Do you have anything to say?

Nothing. I'm not in this. But let's have this clear. This is a place strictly for artists. Religion doesn't count except with the individual. I'm not interested in what a man believes or how he worships. I want to see how he *works*. What he produces. *That's* important. If the Lord God hadn't worked six days, would we be here? Did He observe dietary laws? *Were* there any? So why fool around with them today? Do an honest day's work. Rest on the Sabbath, if that's what you want to do. If not, work. As I do. And enjoy it. After all, do fish take a day off? Cows stop giving milk? Mothers don't give the teat to babies? We don't urinate, do whatever else we have to do? Stop the nonsense. If our friend, Mr. Shalkovsky, doesn't like what we're doing here, I'll put him and his goddam statues on a truck, and dump him where he pleases.

This is Israel, Shalkovsky shouted. You can't *say* that, here.

I said it. I say it again. This place is for artists. If there's anything an artist worships, it's the image. The image is *his* image of the world round about. No room, no time, for anything else. You don't like it, you know what to do. Yehudit'll help. So will Chom.

He went over to Tiberias with Yehudit and sailed on Lake Kinneret, and fished a couple of fingerlings, and wished he had let them enjoy their time, and steamed in the hot springs, and ate simple meals of wonderful fish at lakeside cookshops. They left it all to the tourists after a couple of days, taking the slow way back in a feeling of utter relief that he had someplace to go, almost not of the world, but only the world he had dreamed and worked for, where others before his time had dreamed and worked, made possible for him to live in, with their sweat, and privation, and the war-death and mutilation of their young men, and in the heart-sacrifice of their women. Yehudit told him all that, pointing to the memorials, the land's limits before the Six-Day War, the Arab villages, the Israeli settlements, the new roads.

Listen, he said. How do you know so much about it?

She looked at him in surprise.

I was in the army, she said, as if hurt. You didn't read my record?

I look at people's eyes. I like them, or I don't. Paper means nothing.

Well. At the end of this month, I go back for forty-five days. Perhaps less.

Don't you get tired of it?

She shrugged.

It's no good being tired. If the army isn't trained, they come in and murder us. You like that? You think the Arabs are very kind? And I suppose while I'm away, you'll find another girl?

She'll have to be good. No. I don't think so.

You only say it.

I don't see anyone else like you.

A woman in bed, it's the same.

Wrong. Are all men the same to you?

All? The three I have known, no. They put it in, they ub-ub-ub, and they go to sleep. It's enough?

I'm like that?

She smiled, away, at the hills.

No.

And if I took another woman, you'd go?

She looked her doubt, shook the fair head, shrugged.

No. I think you would be, you know, *kind*. Not sly. Open. Then I think I could bear it. It's in the nature of the beast. I mean, me. I need the outlet.

I'm an outlet?

Of course. Aren't I? For you?

And what happens when my black girls get here?

She moved, sighed, lifted her hands, let them fall.

I shall be jealous.

No need. There's no action. They'll dance for me. That's all.

Dance?

They run a ballet school. Saturdays and Sundays, and in the evenings. It's for children, first. Youngsters have the weekends.

They could start one here.

His turn to shake his head, leaning back to light a cigaret.

Blacks only, and I agree, he said. They have their own rhythms, their own outlook. That's what I'm waiting for. The black artist in the graphic arts. Dancing, music, they almost broke through, except in the classics. I'm waiting for the first real soloist in what *we* call the classics. Singers they have. I'm waiting for the composers. That's why I don't want them starting anything here. We have to go our own way. That's the next thing. Music. Every aspect. They've been neglected. Composers, musicians, where's the place for them to grow? Dramatists. Poets. They used to have patrons. They have to eat, pay rent. Exercise the talent.

Who's to judge if they've got any?

They will.

In that hot midafternoon, Ephraim Wirtz came up with a baked-clay *bozzetto,* about a yard long by a couple of foot, of what could only be Chom, and the dogs dancing all round.

This is that nut with the daughter, he said. Remember? The easy piece, almost got you? She posed for me. I could have done what I liked.

Nude?

'Course. I have the bronze almost ready. But I'd like to buy *this*.

Did she get paid for modelling?

No.

She'll be paid for it. Put the bronze down there in the biblical garden. Eve. How about Adam? I'll pay *you*. What's this worth to you?

It's a beautiful job. I'll blow it up twenty times. I'd say two thousand dollars.

So I'll give him a check for two-five.

Twenty-five? That's all?

Two thousand five hundred. Get clearance and receipts through Yehudit. But remember. I don't want him up here. Or her. Clear? And the Chom group goes in the middle of the Plaza. Break up that space. Ask Kate to plant a site.

Beautiful. I'll *work* like a dog. Thank you, Mr. Paul.

Sunday morning, Kate took the keys, and with Chom and the team of Arabs in the truck, went down to the main store to bring all the furniture up to the house. He had no patience. He wanted to see everything in place, as in the plan of each room he had drawn for her, and then push here, change there, as he wanted it, as he had imagined.

Sam Ravicz was on the line just as he got to the hotel, and he took the call in the foyer.

Yes, Sam?

Oh, Mr. Paul? I thought I ought to let you know. But you won't say nothing about I told you? We went out to the Amboys. A whole gang went in. Rounded up everybody in there. Can you believe? More than two hundred canvases? Lot of stolen originals. That's not all. That place in back we never went in? They had statuary, pots, all kinds of stuff, restoring it. You know, they cast first, then they break it, and some other guy pieces it together. Restoring *fakes?* Greek, Roman, Chinese, the whole *megillah.* How do you *like* that?

Sam, do you have plenty of insurance?

Yes, *sir.* And I already got the idea to visit with my daughter in Cincinnati.

Make it a nice, lo-o-o-ng visit.

Calling from the airport. Be seeing you, Mr. Paul. Take care 'yourself.

Walter Sedrow, calling from San Francisco, had a painful, urgent note in his voice.

What's this we hear, you're the biggest fake dealer in the country? What's going on over there?

Nothing. It's a lot of verbal diarrhea.

It's in an article here. Well. Not quite that. But it says if you want a good fake, the Reid's the place to go.

Would you phone the editor for me? Tell him the Reid's closing down. But there's a gallery up at a Hundred and Ninth that won't sell anything but the finest copies of the masters, and original work by black artists. You might mention we never sold a fake, and if museums and collectors are finding they have to change labels on pictures bought forty and fifty years ago from Mr. Blantyre, and Duveen, and the rest, they were accepted then by the experts of that time. They didn't have our advantages. I mean, in the laboratory. I don't believe Mr. Blantyre cheated anybody in his whole life, including the Metropolitan or the Luberman, any more than I believe Duveen would deliberately cheat Andrew Mellon. It just didn't happen. But I *certainly* believe a copy could have been put in place of the original. *After* the sale.

Jesus. What gives you *that* idea?

The whole set-up. Men's names we all respected are being blackened. I don't like it. That's why I'm getting out.

Out?

I'm selling. You'll get the notice.

I'd like to make an offer.

I've *had* offers, but I turned them all down. There's a different kind of business coming in here. I believe Mr. Blantyre would agree.

What's happening to the staff?

Well, Sam's going to Henri Tameur. Laszlo's going to do some work for Bilara. I'm sick of it. I had enough. I'm *out*.

But where are you going? What'll you do?

I don't know. Just like to feel *clean*. That's all.

A buzzing telephone.

The clock showed three-twenty, green, in darkness, and Bilara sounded even tinier than usual.

Mr. Paul, you hear what happen? Wait till I tell you. Sam Ravicz' place just ashes. Sergeant Mackearn, he called couple minutes ago. We have guys tailing us from now on.

Good.

How about you?

I'm fine.

He like for you to leave town. But he don't want to say it to you.

I'm thinking about it, Bilara. See you in the morning.

I sure hope so.

Don't be frightened. Everything's fine.

Lucien Weil saw him in the morning, worried.

Legally, you have the paper, you're in the clear, he said. But the guys behind this can do just what they sweet please. You realize it? You can get hurt. If I had a lead to them, I might do a little string-pulling.

There's the widow of the Name.

She died. Don't you think I've covered all of that? Way I read it, the family let the boys take over, and they be-

lieve they have a lot of folding money tied up in those pictures. One picture to them's the same as any other. This is
original, this is a copy? But the *copy's* original. Not so? It
was painted by one man. So? It's original. You can't get
them to see there are years between the original idea, and
all the work, and the copy of today. To them, it's a picture.
That's worth a hundred thousand? Then so's this.

You're in touch with them?

In a manner of speaking.

Look. The difference is in the market. It depends who's
buying. Over there's a Tiepolo. Worth what? A million?
Why? It's the only one. That copy? Worth a thousand or
so. Why? It's a copy. Plenty of copyists'll turn out a wonderful job anywhere. But it's not the original. Get them to
see it.

Get *them* to see a cop's their long-lost brother.

All right. Mice on a wheel.

Suggest anything?

There's a gallery going to open soon up on a Hundred
and Ninth. It's going to sell copies. I believe it'll blot up
the market. If these people want to sell, that's where. *This*
gallery never will. I promise you.

I respect the decision. But you had *one* bomb. I believe
you have to be careful.

So far, I'm breathing. And it's not the first piece of advice.

But he told the switchboard no calls, and asked the desk
to make sure.

Buzz-buzz-zz-zz- buzz-zz- a thin ice-cold wire going in
the brain, and awake, he felt for the telephone.

One-fifty. I thought I asked you not to call me till seven-
thirty?

Mr. Denis. We have a Miss Bilara Tancy on the line. She
says she takes the responsibility. We told her.

Put her on, please.

Speak up.

Mr. Paul?

Bilara? What's wrong?

Mr. Paul, I hate to tell you this. They took us clean off of the front step. Didn't get a chance.

This Paul Denis? A man's voice. Insinuating?

Yes?

Look. We have these two crows here, see? They can get plucked and roast any time you say. We got around sixty-something pictures here we like you to sell, see? You want to sell, or you want maybe a package of bones?

No deal. Bring the two gals, *with* the pictures.

No funny stuff?

I don't think this *is* funny.

No police?

They going to do me any good? Just get the gals here. About the pictures, we talk. Solid.

O.K. How we fix this?

I'll go to the gallery right now, and I'll wait. But remember. My insurance won't cover what you bring in. It all has to be cataloged for sale.

By me, O.K. Won't be too long.

Are you Vanuzzi?

You stupid? Don't you never read the prints? He *lapsed*. This is somebody got a head don't belong on a calf. We're on our way. Listen. Second time around. Don't try no stand-up comic stuff. Else you be feeding the jokes strictly below sea level. Boxed.

Get the gals *here*. That's all. Rest's easy.

That strange paralysis of the arms and legs, an icefield in the neck, tears blinding, dry mouth, corrugated throat, bubbles about the heart, for the first time he felt in horror the oncoming of fear. Thought of Bilara or Kumeli hurt, or roughed up, or worse, made him feel sick enough to vomit. He felt as something more than a brother. More. Much more. He remembered their gentle beauty.

He got into clothes, called a cab, and went down Park Avenue praying, switched off the burglar alarm, unlocked the door, and went in, to familiar warmth, and the current exhibition of Surrealists.

He almost saw Mr. Blantyre sitting in the restored chair in front of the restored Rowlandson. He almost saw himself cleaning the carpets. He could feel the vibration of the Hoover. He put the coffeepot on, spooned out the grind, set the cups in the saucers, just as in the years of other days.

The calm days, when everything had a place.

Patrolmen tried the doors twice, but the new glass panes were one-way. No light could be seen outside.

He almost thought they had been joking, or he had dreamed, but then he heard the raps on the back door, and Bilara's voice, You there, Mr. Paul? Know me? with the pathos of a child needing help.

He let them in, and the girls fell on hands and knees, and Bilara's sobbing brought Kumeli to hold the shaken head in her lap. Both must have fought. Their clothes were torn.

O.K., a quiet voice said, to children. Here's the crows. Pictures coming in. What's the deal?

First, we get the gals straightened out, he said. Then I go over the pictures with you. We make two lists. You sign mine, and I sign yours. Then I want a document you are the legal owner, or entitled to deliver these for sale. I can't go against the terms of my license. Selling without a legal certificate's a penitentiary offense. You know that? Could I know your name? I have to write the checks.

Men were bringing in the pictures, stacking against the walls, going out, coming back, no hurry, no noise. They all seemed a copy of each other, clothing, faces, walk.

Call me Joe, the man said. And I don't want no checks, see? Cash. Bills.

Who signs the receipt? You have the tax man looking at you.

No taxes.

Go over and look at that license. Read the terms.

I believe we have to roast a couple of crows.

Do you any good?

Quit talking. How much?

Depends on the market. These are copies. We call them fakes.

You sold them.

Not on your life. I sold the originals. Different market.

But an electric blaze lit to white heat.

One of the men carrying four canvases turned them paint-side to the room. One was a Klee, another Van Gogh. Both originals. Instantly he wondered if some of the originals had been mixed with the copies. The number seemed to back the guess. Except for the two Modigliani. An area of doubt. Worth the risk. A gamble.

How much would you want to give me, cash? Joe said, back to him, watching the last four canvases stood against the far wall. I told you. No checks. No names. *Cash*.

Look. Understand what's going on. All of these have to find a market. Somebody who *wants* to buy. Put one over the fireplace. Price? Depends. A good copy'll fetch six hundred up. To about a thousand. If it's good.

These worth sixty-four thousand. Right?

Wrong. You have the market to consider. And most of

these can be in stock a couple of years. Cost you nothing but money. In premiums. Insurance.

How much?

I'd have to bring a couple more dealers over for an opinion.

I'm asking, *cash*.

Look. For me, this isn't even merchandise. It's nothing I could sell. In the open. I can't sell a fake. Don't you understand that? I have to find somebody wants to handle them. Let's say, outside, they're worth five hundred bucks each. You have sixty-four? That's thirty-two thousand. Listen, instead of snatching a couple of gals, why didn't you come see me? Do a deal in daylight? It's a reasonable business proposition. I could phone around.

How much, *cash?*

He thought for a moment. At least two out of sixty-odd were originals, and worth possibly two hundred thousand dollars-plus.

He felt in his pocket for the bunch of keys.

Look, in that safe I believe I have around twenty thousand dollars in bills. Don't take my word. You open the door. Look inside. Anything you find, you take. But you leave these gals alone, and you don't interfere in here again.

I don't want a goddam thing to do with it.

He tossed him the keys.

Open up.

The catcher's hand caught the ring in a slap!-jingle, and he went over to the safe, played with a few keys, turned, and the door squealed open, the cash drawer screeched, and the notes, bound in hundreds by the bank, were counted on to the desk.

Twenty-three thousand, Joe said, back to him. That's all?

You want some more, you come back tomorrow. Talk to

my insurance people. And the police. These are copies of what got stolen. You don't know? The FBI's in this.

I heard.

Get smart. Take the cash. I have to cover up. But listen. I don't want any more nonsense. For that reason I'm doing a deal with you. Costing me money I don't have.

So what's it doing in the safe?

Belongs to clients. Has to be paid over. Less commission. Transport. The insurance. All I want from you's a receipt and a guarantee. Follow?

No receipt. Nothing. I dumped them. Listen. I don't believe you be*long* up there, see? You got the FBI after you? So who's smart?

No more nonsense? Here, or with my two assistants?

No interest. I got what I want.

Good. Now, I'm going to do you a favor. The cops on this patrol call in around now. You go out the back door, you won't run into them. Listening?

I'm gone.

Bilara closed and locked the back door, leaning against it, and tears ran. Kumeli went to her.

Right off the front step, Bilara whispered. Could have been real bad.

All right, he said, purposely loud. But I'll tell you what's *good*. You have here the solid basis of your stock for the new gallery. You go up that side, I'll go up this. Put the originals in the middle.

It took a few minutes to sort twenty-eight of the original paintings, at a rough evaluation, more than two million dollars.

He dialled Henri Tameur's apartment and got him on the dozenth ring.

Henri?

Who's this?

Paul Denis. You want to slip into a pair of pants, and come on down to the Reid? Might interest you.

Something wrong?

Everything's bright. And so *right*.

He gave Kumeli a bill.

Take a cab. Go down to that all-nitery, bring us some coffee and toast. We'll have breakfast later. Bilara, you call my hotel and book yourself a double for a week. On my account.

They take color?

They better. Then see if Brink's is open. We want a truck to take these copies to a Hundred and Ninth. You have the keys? We'll take them up, put them in the strongroom. Ring the Glosworth office for insurance from tomorrow. Why don't you live in the apartment upstairs? Whole lot safer than where you are. Keep the school there, and live over the gallery. They're good rooms.

They sure are. You real kind, Mr. Paul.

Nothing of it.

They cataloged the originals, and started on the copies, and Kumeli got there just before Henri, and they all had a cup of coffee.

Coffee, they call this? Bilara said. Strictly out the bucket. That's out the back.

We ran out, he said. I made the last for myself.

You had a real tough night, Mr. Paul.

I did all right, Bilara. Henri, take a look at these. You want to sell them for me, usual commission, expenses?

Provenance come with them?

Bilara's going to dig it all out of the files.

Why wouldn't *you* want to sell them?

I estimate I have stock here might take three months

or so to clear. Then Bilara moves to the other gallery. I already sold the freehold here. I want the hell out.

Know where you're going?

I have an idea.

Know when?

When I finished here.

Eli Gartry's lawyer gave him the papers in a red morocco wallet, put his pen away, and picked up the cigar.

I didn't see it, but from the photographs and ground plans it's a pretty nice property, he said. Glad you got it. When do you think of going?

Any time I have things in order.

Yehudit, in khaki uniform, with a short skirt showing her beautiful legs well above the knee, and a jacket smothering in khaki wrinkles the beauty up above, came into the office that morning, tucking a paratroop maroon beret under an epaulette.

I got my orders, she said.

I'll miss you.

I wish I thought so.

Aeons of yearning women, brilliance in the blue glance, a shadow of nipples among the wrinkles, a belt pulled to a nothing-waist, appeal, a yearn, a woman, helpless except in herself, and strict for service to her people, what? A sweet-pretty, splendrous in bed. What?

Ask the question.

There she is. A woman.

Beautiful.

A soldier?

He put his arms around her.

Telephone often, he said. Anything you want, call me.

You have any friends you want to bring, I'll send a car. Nothing you want you can't get. I'll always be here.

Nobody's going to take my place?

Not even your desk. There'll be fresh flowers on it every day. I'll see to it. Azma'uta's going to work from her own office. How long does this Army business go on? How many years?

I won't put up rank till I get there. That's the main reason. I can train a squad of senior girls and examine others for grades. That's the second. What's called a sensitive area. I didn't know I was so fond of you. Or how sorry I'd be to leave. I'll hitch to Tel Aviv and get the bus.

Hell you will. I already ordered the car. Take him where you want.

She folded her lips between her teeth, looking off, at the Mediterranean's blue, flung an arm around his neck, kissed his cheek, pulled away, and ran, taking the stairs in twos and threes, and he heard the sound of her heels on the tarmac below, and the car starting.

Instantly the loneliness closed, suffocant, almost a physical hurt.

Chom and the dogs led the team of Arabs across the Plaza, carrying up the last sections of the stained-glass window for the winter garden behind the house, overlooking the almost-completed biblical park, where Eve stood in provocation of missing Adam and the threat of the Tree, both, with the Serpent, in moulds down at Ephraim Wirtz's atelier.

But in the studio of Renzo Gianmarco, another Eve began to grow from a block of marble, and Vashti, his daughter, was model, a truly exotic beauty physically, perhaps eighteen or so, but her face had been crushed in a car smash, and the only time he saw her, for those few moments without the veil she always wore, he thought some giant hand might have smudged every feature to a pink-edged horror.

Nothing to do, Renzo told him, that first time. Four years ago. It was terrible. The plastic surgeon can do nothing. I modelled the mask for her. But there is no bone to build. Every time he operates, no improvement. Every time she wakes up, she cries. Cries. *Cries.* Her mother went blind. So I said, It's enough. The child refuses to see her friends? Refuses to continue her studies? What is there to do? We left London. We went to relations in Naples. I always had plenty of commissions. But it was still the same. She thought everybody was looking at her. Because she was ugly. But I said, It's the veil. They think you are a little nun. So they stare. But she had a terrible neurosis. Her mother, not much better. One day I was in a café—and I *bless* the day—*truly* I bless the day—and I spoke to some American tourists. They told me about this place. I went to our Consulate, and then we are here. You can*not*—I can*not*—express to you my gratitude—imagine how this wonderful place has changed our lives. We have peace. Complete. Quiet. Absolute. She can walk to the market. Nobody looks. My wife begins to see. And I work fourteen hours a day. Life is a pleasure once more.

No hope of improvement?

Renzo shook his head.

Why should we hope for more than we have? How many are so fortunate? So happy? We often say it's as if we came out of a terrible storm and found wonderful peace. We have *you* to thank.

I'm privileged. Artists are the only reason I've ever been able to do anything. But why did you call your daughter Vashti? Wasn't she thrown out by King What-was-his-name? For not doing as he wanted?

Ahasuerus. Xerxes. Yes. Why should she? I always admired her. If she didn't want to belly-dance in front of a lot of drunken old pricks, why not? She was a queen. She put her foot down. No. That's why we called our daughter Vashti. Long before this women's liberation nonsense.

You think so?

Of course. They still think industrialized. Male and female complement each other. It's not master and slave. It's man and woman. My daughter has no face. But she has the body of a goddess. I try to tell her. But it's vanity, you see. She wants the face she can't have. She wears a veil. It's the same sort of liberation. They are slaves to an even worse form of slavery. To themselves. They are their *own* slaves.

That last huddle with the FBI men strung out through ten never-ending days of misery. They wanted details not in the files. They had them in their own folio. He felt he was being punched around the ring. He called Berthold Gluck on the third night, and got him to fly to New York that Thursday. He came in with Joe Rabin and Henny Fuld, and Henny's messenger brought in the files.

Look, Berthold said. I'm in this business just over fifty years. My father, my grandfather before me. Henny and Joe, they both worked for my father before they went out on their own. We all know the Reid Gallery. Highest standard of integrity. If you want, I get my files out of storage.

How can you know what went on in *here?* the chief FBI man asked. All we want is the facts.

You'll get nothing else, Berthold said, in the mild voice. Everything sold was known all around. How do you keep track un*less* you know? Name, provenance, price, name of buyer. I'll take a bet. Any item you have there, I'll tell you straight off, who the original seller was, the price, and who's got it now, and where it was before. How much you like to lose?

Betting isn't my concern, the FBI man said. I don't doubt your knowledge for a moment. Or the integrity of anybody. What we're trying to do is verify certain information. So far, we're right on beam.

What's that mean? he asked. I haven't given the right information?

Not enough to counter the information we have.

Could we hear the for-instances? Berthold asked. We're all in this, you know? I'll call a meeting of our association. See what *they* have to say.

Well. There's a question of the Giottos. They were stolen from a church near Potenza.

Prove it, he said. Show me the church. This has all been gone over. Where *they* say the church was happens to be an empty lot. Want to see the photograph?

It's what it says here.

They have to do a hell of a lot more homework. We *did* ours. We sent a team all over Europe. Oh. And incidentally. You never heard of parish priests, or people around the churches doing a little fiddle on the side? You think it's easy to rob a church? Why not try? You'll find you're going to need help. Those little towns and villages, they all know each other. Strange guys come in? Everybody wants to know who they are. You can hide out in a church? Where? Ever been inside one? It's generally a massive key. How do you unlock the door to get out? What time? Who picks you up? Priests and sacristans are early risers. *Carabinieri—* their cops—are pretty good. Bakers and cooks? That's long before dawn. Customs? How do you get them out? How do you pass through Customs, *here?* Some of these guys in

New York know plenty. But you *have* Customs certificates. They're real, not forged.

Another thing, Berthold said, still mild. Who got first money, first sale? Why not see *him?* We're dealers. We sell on the evidence of our eyes, knowledge. What we know of the market.

Listen, Henny said, stroking the little grey mustache. Could I ask a question? What's all this *for?* Who's behind it? Who's interested?

Uncle Sam, the FBI man said. A whole lot of stuff's going out. Lot's coming in. We want to know *why.*

Somebody making a little on the side? Berthold asked.

Seems so.

Buying a cracked-up-put-together pot for a million-plus, I'll say so, Joe Rabin said. They better not come to *me.*

What's next? he asked.

The collection of stolen Etruscan statues. Or figurines.

You'll have to prove it.

We have the testimony.

How'd they get in the country?

That's what *we* have to find out.

Here?

Well, no. But somewhere we might find a lead.

I'm pretty damn sure the entire association across the country'll open their files for you, Berthold said. Anything you want to know. This kind of investigation affects all of us. I'm retired. But I have this feeling somebody's doubting my word. I don't *like* it.

Henny raised a finger.

Goes for me, he said. I find anybody doubting me, word or print, I'll *sue.*

He awoke in darkness, listening to the rattle of shutters,

the howling of Chom's dogs, and in a pause, the hum-and-gone of heavy truck traffic down on the Nazareth road.

Mr. Paul? Mr. Paul? the small voice echoed in the stairwell.

Yes? Who is it?

Mr. Paul, this is Nurse Sokolow. Could you come on down, please? Sorry to waken you like this.

With you in two minutes.

He put trousers on, and a dressing-gown, and hurried through the dark rooms to the staircase, and down, and opened the front door. Nurse Sokolow, a whitish blob in darkness, had Chom and the dogs with her, but the dogs were silent, and they all turned for the path down to the Plaza.

It's not so bad as I thought, she said. Boaz, that stonecutter down there, he had that girl in bed, and her father—

Wait a minute. *What* girl?

The one wears a veil. I don't even know the name right.

He had *her* in bed?

Seems so. Her father broke that big window, and went after him with a hammer. Well, this boy, Boaz, he's quite a size. He took the hammer off of him. But he had to hit. So the father's got to go to the hospital. Cut's too big for me to suture. Girl's in raving hysterics. I had to give her a shot. Then the mother went after Boaz with a knife. He broke her arm. I had to give *her* a shot. Now I find Boaz has a stab wound. Lower belly. I tell you, I had a great time, there, the past half-hour.

I'm sure you did. What can *I* do?

Well, everybody's up. They want to lynch Boaz. I got the guards to hold them off.

Splendid.

The crowd around Boaz's workshop started shouting

when he came into the light, and when he felt the glow on his face, he held out his arms for silence.

Why don't you please all go home to bed? he shouted. Are you making things any better?

He ought to be *stoned,* a woman's voice screamed from the darkness. Taking advantage of a poor little girl.

If she got in his bed, he took no more than what she gave him. She's her own woman. I don't want any moralists in this place. Understand me? Now, will you go on home? Or I'll throw the *lot* of you out. You're not in any goddam suburban hideout, here. You're in a place of your *own.* *Make* it so.

Lucien Weil's eyes might have wanted to say something else, but what they *were* saying made him laugh without hearing a word.

So what's funny? Lucien asked, standing there, grey pin-stripe, grey hair, black briefcase, white handkerchief alping in three peaks, yellow pad under arm, the whole legal bit.

You are, he said. You look like you wallowed in the gutters of despair. That's Mr. Blantyre's. What's bugging you?

What I'm worried about, and trying to avoid, is your arrest.

Arrest? *Me?*

On something like ten charges. False pretences, conniv-ance, just to mention a couple. We have to go into this. The whole question of faking. They raided places out there near the Amboys, and others in New Jersey. They found stolen paintings, and a whole lot of copies. They said you sold. You're the kingpin.

Well. Anybody can *say.* What they need is proof. Do they have any?

They have signed statements. Didn't you buy upwards of sixty just recently?

Yes. But they won't be on sale here. You go up to a Hundred and Ninth Street with Bilara. She'll show you where they're going to be sold, and generally tell you the story. All right, Bilara?

Fine with me, Mr. Paul. Going to be a call around eleven-thirty from Mr. Levin, the printer. He has the catalogs ready for the final go-over. I believe I *fly* back. Right there, the front page, *my* name? My daddy so proud, got rocks in his shoes, keep him on the ground. The Bi*lara Tancy Gallery*. Mhh. *My!*

The house seemed always to have been there, either because Chom had a touch with the hammer, or because the Arab masons outdid themselves in the careful selection and cutting of stone. The doors he bought in Zanzibar, huge, thick, mahogany, arched, studded in iron bolts, with bronze lion's-head handles. The iron gateway and railing were born under the hammer of Haim Prins, from Andorra, and the art of the Basque country was in them, and in the gateway separating the garden from the biblical park, calling aloud in the grilles over the lower-floor windows, and the circular wheel-spit in the hollow on the other side of the house, large enough to grill whole sheep, and at least a couple of bullocks, plus the sausages, breads, and etceteras. Altogether, a fine, comfortable place, and exactly as he had dreamed.

Rivka, up on the ladder, in the winter garden, a silhouette in shorts and bra, almost made a further pattern in her window, gently beating the leaden surround to fit the steel struts holding it to the frame.

How are we coming along? he called from the balcony.

Shan't be any time, now, she said, without looking round. Just this section. This apricot tone held me up. I couldn't get it. But I did.

Great.

You'll see it better tomorrow, when the canvas is all off and the sun shines in. About a little after eleven. It'll patch this entire floor.

Pleased with it?

Who's *ever* pleased?

The flat voice drooped. She seemed to have no life, except in the steady, dull, tapping of the hammer.

That sound reminds me of the heartbeats of a dying animal. *Boomp—boomp—boomp.*

Probably is. I don't see much to live for.

That's hard luck. I see plenty.

Wish I knew the secret.

No secret. A lot of people like you helped. *Your* work. *Your* sweat. *Your* ideas. Suddenly, the place is just beautiful. *Every*body—the muscle—and every mind and talent, they all got together. Why don't you see much to live for?

Oh, just leave me a*lone*. I want to *finish* this.

Finish it. *Then* come and have a drink.

What I *don't* want's a drink.

All right. *Be* bad-tempered. See how far it gets you.

All very well for you to talk.

Why not?

You can say what you like.

Can't *you*?

What good's it do?

What d'you *want* to do?

Oh. I don't know. Finish this, first. Then I'll see.

You have time. Anyway, you know where to come to talk things out. If you want.

All right. When I have this section finished, and the window in, and the canvas down, and everything just the way I want it. Then I'll come and talk.

That's the big mistake. The way *you* want it. Sometimes it won't happen that way.

Keep on trying till it *does*.

Damn right. I'm with you.

Walking away, her smile stayed in mind and seemed to brighten the corridor shadowed in sunset, and brought again the feeling that it was time to hang the pictures, stacked in corners in sixes and eights, friends, that might be staring closed-eyed reproach for long-undeserved neglect.

Mr. Paul, sir, Bilara said, with her especial I-found-something smile. I believe you better take another look at some of them copies up there. Seem to me you could have missed a few. So I brought them in the cab, you don't mind? I don't know what kind of a dealer I going to be, don't know a *fa*-uh-copy from the original?

She lined up ten canvases, and almost unbelievably she was right. Two Boudin, a Van Gogh, a Bosch, a Greuze, a Romney, a Fragonard, a Guardi, a Chagall, and a Rouault.

I have to hand it to you, Bilara, he said. You have a lot better eye than I ever thought. That's no insult. What I have to ask myself is, how the hell I came to pass them over. I believe it's time I quit this business. I don't know my own trade. I don't know copies from originals any more. That's tragic. Sell them here. The commission goes to you.

He went out that lunchtime, and went in Buccellati, and bought her a diamond bracelet, a delicate mist of stones that shone some part of her smile, and he realized that the blue velvet box held the only jewelry he had bought for a woman since the rubies he gave Nelda on that last birthday.

He felt wordlessly sad, thinking of that raised knee, some part of himself wishing, some other part snarling, somewhere the longing that never stopped, an ache without balm, a pain, never far from hurt.

There's Mr. Ginzfeld, the lawyer, on the line from Tel Aviv, Azma'uta called, running along the balcony. You could take it in the accountant's. Nobody there.

He seemed to know before he picked up the receiver.

Mr. Paul? the voice said. Dave Ginzfeld. This is real bad news. The office of Lucien Weil just got through. They're warning there *could* be extradition proceedings. You want to deal with this personally, or should we?

You deal with it. What's the charge?

Long's your arm. I'm waiting for the black and white. Then we know where we are. What do you suppose it could be? I mean, who's pressing charges?

You know as much as me. There's been talk I sold fakes. I never did. I have plenty of clients ready to stand up. Dealers of repute. I'm not afraid of anything anybody can say.

You sold your own gallery, right? And opened one for blacks? And selling copies?

Correct.

More profitable?

Nothing like it. I wanted to come to Israel.

But not till the FBI started asking about some deals?

Long before.

But you flew to Mexico, first. Then to Rio. Then South Africa. And up here. Did you know there was a warrant out for you around that time? The day of your departure, in fact?

I didn't. I was in Florida with Mr. Berthold Gluck. We

both flew down to Mexico City. Our association had the annual meeting there. I attended, and flew on. South African Airways fly the South Atlantic.

I have the details here. You want to resist extradition proceedings?

Certainly. I've done nothing. Never have.

Well. You'll get all the backing we can give you. I'll know more when I have the papers. I'll be in touch.

Sol Levin sent up the dummy for the Hill's first catalog, with ten illustrations in color, thirty in black and white, all on handmade paper, and letter-press taken from a series of books and art magazines in five languages.

It is wrong, Azma'uta said, sharp. Nothing in Arabic? Nothing in Hebrew? The languages of the country? Ridiculous.

All right. We have to get it translated. Who?

She clasped hands, lolling on the right foot, negligent, as only a woman magnificently sure of herself can be.

Chom Vissel, she said. He is a scholar. Aramaic. Hebrew. Arabic. Greek. Latin. English. French. German. Spanish. What you like.

Wait, he said. How do you know that?

She spread her arms, a lax Nike.

*Every*body knows. He writes letters for everybody. He earns extra money. He was professor.

He's well paid. Why does he need extra?

Ask.

You don't know?

Everybody knows.

Except me?

Of course. Why *should* you know? He pays for Arab children to have school. In the village.

Why don't I know this?

Let not thy right hand know what thy left hand? Remember?

You have that in Arabic, too?

Of course.

So why can't we get together? What's in the way? Why won't Arabs talk?

Ah, Mr. Paul. I wish we knew.

Look. Try to find out. I want to know.

It's the land, first.

But you've all got your *own* land. All around here. Haven't you?

Not the areas from the war of six days.

All you have to do is sit down and talk.

It is against *Shari'a*. The sacred law. We cannot discuss with infidels. It is forbidden.

You discuss with me? I'm an infidel.

But I am not a serious believer in Islam. I am modern. I have education. My father permitted. My grandfather will not speak to him. Or to me. For him, we are worse than dead.

So really what's keeping everybody apart is just old-fashioned religion?

It is why Chom started the school. Our children must be taught the subjects of this century. Not the Koran. But Western subjects are still forbidden to be taught by *Shari'a*.

I'd like to talk to Chom. Take a hand. That main store's vacant. We could start there. Desks. Blackboards. Easy.

The printer's shop reminded him of a woodcut. Heavy black beams held the roof, and pulls of posters in black and grey hung around the walls. The fonts were all in the big room, next door, and the place smelled of printers' ink, fresh paper, and coffee.

Chom don't want nothing to do with it, Sol said pointing

to the copy. He just wants to do what he's doing. Happy with the dogs. He told me he lost his wife and both his sons. He stopped being who he was. No interest. Did you know he was professor of Oriental languages in Latvia, someplace? Anyway, I'm getting the Hebrew done by the Rebbe, here. Berezhkoy? And the Arabic, a guy in Jerusalem. Ready this weekend. I just saw Gianmarco. Still got the bandage. I believe he feels better about things. I got the wedding invitations off this morning. Boy's out delivering.

I hope he didn't take it out on the girl?

Well. You know. He's pretty strict. Thought he been dishonored. Old stuff, these days. Any idea where the wedding's going to be?

Main gallery. We're trying to have the synagogue ready in time. But there's still a lot of stone to be cut. Long job.

Wife and me went up there last night. Going to be just beautiful. Entire place. I don't even want the day trip to Jerusalem. First time in my life I'm real happy.

Nice to hear.

He wondered how it might be to feel happy all the time, instead of just now and then, a flash, and gone. He knew too well what caused that unrest. But still he turned away from any thought, even from writing a letter, trying to think of it as something on the other end of the telephone for others to deal with, and, given a little chance, perhaps bury.

He promised himself a royal party that night, though even as he thought it, doubt nagged, and he knew he had no right to hope, and the day seemed to darken, and all he had done became dross, not worth the effort of a shrug.

Did we wake you up? Berthold said, on the line from New York clear as if he stood in the room. Look. The association

made me president of the enquiry. We had the entire afternoon with De Ruysker's people, and Lucien. I believe we
have it nailed down. The Italian fine arts people—the ones
stop works of art going out?—and the Spanish and a couple
more, plus the Vatican, they just come alive to it. There's a
long report tying you and the Reid Gallery in with years
of sales, all stolen Church or national property. Well, I just
had the association open the files. We've all had the same
type deals. Not just you. We have the record of where they
all come from, and where they are now. If there's been any
fraud, it's back home where they belong. Lucien believes
you're all the way out in the clear. Here, talk to him.

Paul? Just quit worrying. I don't think they have a case.
They certainly don't think so. The record's straight all the
way through. I'm preparing a report.

But where's the pressure coming from?

Well, now. Just let's think a moment. The guys not getting
their share of the gravy, d'you suppose? They'd like a lot of
it back there for the national archives? For resale? At
twenty–twenty-five percent? Or more? What the market'll
take? Who's kidding who? They just started sniffing the
money. Don't disturb yourself, Paul. We have it licked.
It's a clear line.

All right. But who's behind it, our end?

I believe somebody had one in the fire for you. Want to
laugh? I believe it could be the Mafia boys. Helped by
somebody at the Luberman–Hertz? I mention no names.
They have troubles of their own. That was where the FBI
came in. And there's a guy on the Church side. Boy, he
loves you. With true Christian charity. The bleeding heart,
you know? *Your* bleeding heart. And a cut throat?

I can guess.

Well, everything's squared. We know just where we are. Safe as tomorrow morning. You happier?

Ready to dance. And grateful. You have no idea.

Perhaps it was like Mr. Blantyre used to say, Why the worry? You can always imagine twice the purgatory you really have. We *all* have purgatory. Any time. We're all heading there. Hell bent. Why shake it out in front of you? Enjoy your life. That ought to be one of the Commandments. Instead, you get tied up with your neighbor's ox. And his ass? Who's interested?

But then, despite all the friendly assurance, he still had a feeling of strolling about blind in a trap sprung to hurt.

He changed a blade, and the phone rang, and the clock's numerals flipped to 7:16, and he felt that curious ripple near the heart.

Paul Denis.

David Coningsby. I'm in from the Coast. Could I see you? I'm at the Stanhope.

I have an appointment at nine. This afternoon?

Flying to Paris, two-fifteen.

All right. Let's say thirty minutes?

Right here? Appreciate it.

Whatever he thought or feared seemed underlined by Coningsby's face, puffy, dragged, eyes red-rimmed, fingers feeling the mouth, pinching the nose, and while the order was taken, he pretended a frown at the menu, if breakfast was never his meal.

All right, he said. Something on your mind?

Plenty. I want to sell the collection. As is.

Everything?

Just that.

Let's have it clear. No favorites you want to keep?

Don't want a goddam thing left in the house. I have all the art I want. I got a couple of pools, and the chicks to match. I can look at *them*. I had a couple of FBI guys there. Wanted to know where I got this and that. Look. I'm oil and gas. See what I mean? So I stopped off. Sell it.

Could I ask you what they wanted to know?

Where everything came from. I know there was something else behind it. I gave them the key to the file room. Help themselves. I went to Dallas a couple of days. They took off. Left a note. I don't like it. You got an art collection, so they're on your neck? Specially the Indian pieces. Sorry I ever touched the goddam things.

They're only beautiful.

That price, they ought to be. Suppose I can make any kind of a profit? Or leave a little skin?

We could do a whole lot better. Want me to take care of it?

Right this minute.

Tell your people the packers'll be there later today. Warn your attorney. He'll be responsible for check of each item. With the provenance. Get your insurance agent there. You'll want an attorney this end. And the insurance guy. The items go into bond at Kennedy. That's where I start work. Any idea, total outlay, including what others sold you?

Around six million.

Less than I figured. I'll see how close we come to seven. Or eight.

I knew I was right. Paul, I'm going to be so goddam happy. Just to know they're flying.

All right. Now tell me why.

The dark eyes flickered around the far wall. There

seemed crusts between the eyelashes. The waiter slid the tray on the table. The eyes followed it. The head shook.

I don't want to get into it. Leave it there. Sell. That's all I want.

Bilara must have been on the line all day. When he got back, near six o'clock, she had the calls, and the offers, on a pegged pad.

Mr. Sedrow's flying in tonight, she said. I reserved a table at Michael's Pub. He liked it the last time. He says the entire Coningsby job ought to be here Thursday, latest. I got hard offers here, Mr. Paul. They topping around sixty–seventy-five percent extra. I believe these people just crazy. Them Indian pieces? They going over the million— three. Each. Think of the kids don't get to eat lunch.

I'll go for one–four or five on the Indian lots, on up. Everything else, ante thirty percent on the offer. If I'm going out of business I can afford a little fun. Or pay my own price and keep them. Five years, they're worth double. Bilara, we missed a bet.

We did, Mr. Paul?

Listen. If this guy's stupid enough to strip his walls, what's he got instead? Whitewash? Look. He's a couple of hours TWA out of Paris. See if you can contact him by phone. Or have a call in at his hotel when he gets there.

What do I say?

Ah, Bilara. If he doesn't want what he's been buying, along with the Indian, Mogul, T'ang, and stuff, how about the neglected market? Native-born Afro-American. He likes being out front. Can't get out-fronter. Price can only go up. That's all he has to know. He could be *the* number one. He doesn't have to spend millions. Just enough to let a guy live. And then go on buying. Through your gallery.

But where's the work?

Up to you. How did Mr. Blantyre start the Reid? He went out and found the artists. Staked them. That's why he was always number one. American artists never forgot him. Think black painters'll ever forget you?

Walter Sedrow called him from the Tuscany just after six, and they met at Michael's Pub at eight, starting with a Pimm's, hayforking small talk.

What's with Coningsby? Walter asked, in a pause. Told me he was selling out through you. Pretty nice, I'd say. But why?

He didn't like a call from the FBI.

Didn't tell me that. But it's no surprise. That's Br'er Rabbit in the lion's den. He'd show the scut.

But what the hell, why?

First place, his name's Conesco. Roberto. His daddy got tossed out in '46, was it? Planeload of the mob got dumped in Italy. Lucky Luciano, and them. Poor bastards. Well, Coningsby and his ma were native-born. They stayed on. He started young. Got up there in oil and gas. Front man for the mob. Investments, property, all like that. Very smart. Then the art collection. That was a goddam joke.

Six million or more? A joke?

Why not? He's pay-off man for the West Coast. Guy wants cash fast, he gives him a picture, tells him the dealer to go to. Dealer gets in touch, he buys it back, everybody happy.

It's probably the Pimm's. I'm confused. What's the idea of all that?

Transparent rims turned moon eyes.

He doesn't have to keep cash in the house or office, one. Two, no record of any cash transaction. Three, no names. A check to a known dealer. Picture donated to a museum. Tax deductible. Buying art? Who's interested? A few art nuts? The dealer? Sure. Ten, fifteen, up to thirty percent. Provenance? Supplied. Know what? The mob just loves us.

So why sell the entire golden goose?

FBI got into it. Smuggled stuff? Illegal entry? No clearance from Customs? The higher-ups—the granddaddies—won't go for it. Too near to home. Questions. Everybody in the act. They don't like it. So-oooo? Sell. But in your case, just let me stick two cents' worth in. I hope you'll examine this lot in bond. If you find a fake, or any item you have notice was stolen, throw out the entire consignment, and let the press boys know.

My granny already told me how to suck eggs.

Fine. She tell you how to spit out the eggshells?

Meaning?

Your name's part of the deal. Another Reid Gallery fake job?

Walter, who d'you suppose is behind all this?

The mob. Who else? Why's he come to you?

More to come?

You're still right side up and taking nourishment. And I could do with another scotch.

The waiter served two lamb chops, watercress, new potatoes, and a silver galleon of mint sauce, and while the wine poured, somebody plugged in a telephone.

Mr. Paul? This Bilara. Mr. Coningsby, he like the idea. I have an appointment when he's back. Next week. Either Monday or Tuesday.

Take somebody along from Lucien Weil's office. You need witnesses.

Yes, sir, Mr. Paul. On your way home, you want to drop by the Sixteenth Precinct? Inspector Hanrahan called just before we closed. Wants you to identify a couple of guys. Wouldn't tell me who.

I'll be there inside the hour. Thanks, Bilara.

Who could they be? Walter said, slicing down the bone. Passing stolen goods, maybe? I have them all the time. If the price is right, I buy. Nuts.

You can be in trouble.

Walter raised an eyebrow, a shoulder, in a chew.

Let the rest worry. You have to worry about the way the Reid Gallery's tied in with a lot of funny deals.

My feeling, it's the mob. I wouldn't give them the outlets they wanted. Or the price.

Nobody else seems to have that problem.

True. They didn't accept the deals I did. Without knowing. You can get sucked in.

I'll say. At a million-plus? One shot? At thirty percent? Try *me*.

Wasn't Mr. Blantyre's ethic.

Walter put down the bone, carefully wiped his fingers, and transparent rims ran odd, pale circles over his cheekbones.

That was *his* time, he said, lifting the glass. Here's to him. The greatest. But that ethic doesn't exist any more. Wherever you want to look. Museums, collections, galleries, they don't have it. Don't live by it. You *do*, or you get *done*. Won't happen to *me*. Remember this Watergate nonsense?

Hell's that got to do with it?

Bunch of creeps crawling in and out of each other's intestinal tracts? You did, no I didn't, yes you did, no I didn't? I *deal*. That's the price. No crap.

So where am I different?

Walter turned his head.

I hope it's so, he said. *If* so, why the talk?

He saw him into a cab for Kennedy, and took another to the Sixteenth Precinct. He felt numb. Without Mr. Blantyre to remember, with the ethic gone, the spine seemed to have been pulled out of all he had ever known or worked for.

The space inside the Precinct seemed huge, warm with the breath of crime, and the sergeant behind the desk looked down at him as if he knew that the ethic no longer had existence, far less any value.

'Spector Hanrahan? Up the stairs. Second floor, first left.

In shirt-sleeves and shoulder-holster, the Inspector took a bunch of keys from the hook, and in a midge-cloud of small talk, led out along the corridor, to the third floor, and a row of barred cell doors.

Sergeant, he called. Bring them two birds out, will you? This way.

They went in a long room, with a platform.

Just want you to look at these two, the Inspector said. Routine, that's all. If you ever saw them before, and where.

What are they charged with?

No charge, yet. Couple of drunks. Five–six-day bat. Dried out in Bellevue. They got rolled. Couple of reasons, I thought you be interested. Blue-chip cons, the pair of them.

The two walked on the platform, white-lit, in shirts, jeans, sleep-drowsed, but staring, here, there, the faceless, nameless, in horrid scent of bathos. He heard Meir Gershon's voice telling him about the Rabbi Hillel's saying, If I am not for myself, who is for me? And if I am for myself alone, what, then, am I?

Recognize them, Mr. Denis?

The one on the left is Brother Canopus. As I know him. On the right, Brother Philochorus. Look. I have an idea. If bail's allowed, I'm on tap. They might just have a few answers.

Tomorrow, ten o'clock. Up to the magistrate.

I'd like to get them on my side. If they can get a square meal from the outside, coffee, cigarets, here's the saver.

He passed a bill.

Gee, Mr. Denis. They going to hang up *your* picture.

Round at the gallery, he called Lucien Weil, and got him away from a bridge game.

I believe these two worked inside on the outside, if you know what I mean? he said. They might give us a couple of pointers.

What sort?

Who was who. The police just found out they have a truckload of stuff in a garage, here. They have the papers, Customs dockets, all in order. Mexican and U.S., and out-go from Peru. That takes planning. Did they have an address to report? A number to call? Date? Time? I'd like them milked. I'll pay for the defence.

I'll handle it. I'll bring them to the gallery.

No. Your office.

I'll call you.

He got the call just after midday, and went to an airless hive of attorneys' offices on Forty-second Street, trying to stop breathing disinfectant up to the fifteenth floor.

Lucien, the two monks, serene, smiling, two men, probably junior lawyers, and two secretaries sat about a desk.

They're out on five hundred each, Lucien said. Till the cops had time to check on that truckload. I warned them what happens if they don't show up tomorrow morning. Now, I don't have a lot of time.

Don't take on, Brother Canopus said. We don't have a case to answer. Drunk's not a crime. It's a pleasure we'll pay for. And five days' garage dues. We're clean.

Listen to me, he said. You can earn some real money just

answering questions. I'll take care of all fees and court dues. Who was Father Brant?

Poor guy died not long ago. He was the goose.

Goose?

You won't get near a place, they got a goose there. Raise more hell 'n any dog. That was Father Brant. Unfrocked priest. Specialist in the Black. I mean, the Mass.

It destroyed him, Brother Philochorus said, almost happily. I told him it would.

But are you two real monks?

We were, Brother Canopus said. It's been thirty-odd years since we were. A little matter of instructing the nuns in the niceties of the organ. Manual, of course. We were novices together. We matured quick enough. Known as the organ involuntaries. I doubt there was a virgin in the place. Saving y' presence, ladies. Except for the one on the altar. Who wants plaster?

Who was Brant working for?

O, the Devil his own self, Brother Philochorus said. See it in his eye. Anything to make a buck. Buy an animal. Or a newborn child. Unwanted. People like to see it. They pay. He was over the country with it.

With what?

The second Mass, of course. Black.

But what did he have to do with you?

Took orders like the rest of us. Any church stuff, they gave to him.

They?

Well, you get the idea. The boss, and them.

Who was the boss?

Mr. Wix.

He found curious relief in hearing the Name, out in the open, stripped.

All right. How did this whole thing operate?

Shaken head, raised hands.

We only got orders. From the other guy after Brant died. We had plenty to be sorry about, believe me.

Gospel, Brother Philochorus said. I never liked the man. Never one of us. Name of Cole. A glib one. Put everybody here under the table. Whisky.

Where is he, now?

Either Mexico or Canada. He'll not come in till he's sure he's safe. Way it always was.

Know anything about the Amboys?

Sure. We lived there the past fifteen years. Used to be a school. Then a Navy dump. Wix had four places out there. Two in Poughkeepsie.

What goes on?

Where the work gets done. Pictures. Pots. Furniture. Everything in the fake line. The truckload we've got? It'll get copied. You'll never tell which is the fake. We do the running. Collecting, delivering. Nobody's going to stop a couple of monks.

Didn't anybody try?

Oh, well, sure. But we have the Latin. And we carry a pocket Communion set. Put up a better Mass than any Cardinal. We've given the Unction. A paying job, that one. We did well enough, did we not?

We did, Brother Philochorus said. Always gave the best of satisfaction. There's a lot of money in death, no doubt. But I'll take the travel anytime at all. Spain, now. Or let's say, Portugal.

I won't say we didn't do a fine bit of good for ourselves, bringing the stuff back. Greece, too. Italy, I think they know us a little *too* well, would you not say?

I would. Going back there might constitute an error. For

the time being. There's enquiries, you might say. Myself, I'd call it prurient curiosity.

Enquiries about what?

What we took out.

Illegally?

Others were in it, Brother Canopus said, at large. Not a thousand miles from the nearest church. Or tomb. Don't forget confessions are heard. They're remembered. Priests don't have the tenderest life. They can use a little extra. Some of the younger want to throw it off and marry. What's a better idea than looking the other way and pocketing enough to build and furnish a house somewhere? And then throw the holy calling aside and—uh—and crawl in a double bed. Saving y' presence, ladies.

Shame on you, Brother Canopus said. I'm looking for a bolt from the sky.

Keep looking.

You were always a mocker. You'll suffer, later. I'll be on m' knees for you.

They're the wrong shape.

Just a moment, he said. Do you know anything about the return of a number of canvases to my gallery? The Reid?

Oh, sure. We refused the job. Why? We were known to you. You have a black woman there. A monster. We took the Mexican job instead. You see, when the man Wix died, everything got flung. That's what. *Flung*. No sense out of anybody. He ran his own business. His own self. It was like the Irish Parliament, there. Every son of sin on his flat feet in a bellow, and not a whoreson listening. Saving y' presence, ladies. Am I not right, Brother Philochorus?

Never holier truth. Those pictures we saw, yes, original or copy, a matter for strict doubt. Even we couldn't tell. Least of all the ones that took charge.

You mean the mob? Lucien said. Did they interfere?

They took control from the moment, Brother Canopus said. They offered a hundred for each canvas delivered to the Reid. Lot of money? We got more going to Mexico. No chance of being recognized. We got Peruvian Customs dockets off the ship at Ensenada, down there. Mexican near Tijuana and U.S. at the frontier. All paid, all clear. We never work dishonest. If there's a buck to be paid over and above, for a favor, let's say, we'll pay it and glad to. Saves bad feeling.

Just a moment, he said. What was the reason for bringing the pictures you mentioned back to my gallery?

Oh, now, look, Brother Canopus said, turning shoulders in distaste. Before this time we had men in charge. Knew their business. Moment the boss died, they were off. Who's left? Did they know the difference between a hole in the ground or anywhere else? Could they see any difference between an original and a copy? If I can't, why should they? Any price is good. Why should they believe that a lot less than a yard of paint on canvas is worth a cool, sweet million?

You're saying that nobody there knows anything about the job?

Or what else? The top men scooted. They didn't like the FBI in there. Listen. There's a lot of stuff piled up. They've a pottery at one of the Poughkeepsie dumps. They grind bits of old vases and use the powder to make a big one. They mix the colors from earths got from a long way underground in Greece. We've fine line artists in this country. Look, they have this carbon nonsense. Now they have this carbo-luminescence, and what more. It's supposed to do what? The way it's being done, will you ever find out?

The FBI probably will.

I'm sorry about it. The places out at the Amboys, anyway.
The artist got a chance, there. There was patience to it. And
love. Aren't they the old Greeks reborn? The Etruscans?
Who paints, who carves, who makes anything at all, and
it's not in love? So much love to give. Who to give it to?
And so many spit on the floor.

All right, Lucien said, and stood. I had your bank accounts checked. The documents on this truckload are all
in order. Pre-Columbian art and Peruvian ecclesiastical
stuff. Maybe Mr. Denis, here, can help find a market.

No trouble.

With what we've got, and what we might get, we'd try
to buy that coach house and the garden, Brother Canopus
said. Establish our own order. The Penitent and Dishev-
elled. Monastic regime. We've our own refectory. Wine
cellar. Library. Sixteen of us. We'd have to find the others.
We're a couple of simple ones. Is a coach house and a
garden too much to ask? And the nuns to go with it?

If I can read, and tend the garden, and visit the wine
cellar here and there, and play the organ, why would I want
to live any other way? Except the Lord God in His mercy
lets me?

You've a joyous argument there, Brother Canopus said.
Add me in.

The house without lights reminded him of dreams those
years ago, of walking in shadow, knowing where he was
because he built it, able to feel around furniture, to bookshelves, across carpets, to the bar, to the dining-room,
out to the kitchen, the breakfast terrace and garden, and
down the backstair to the herbarium, and on, to the rose
arbor, and the lanes of pergolas, and all the way around,

through the main garden and along to the front doorway.

A shape, white down one side, stood outside the gate.

Who is it?

Rivka. I could hear you telephoning. But nobody answered the bell.

No electricity. It'll be on at the end of the week. Want to talk?

Yes.

Come in the side gate. It's open.

She laughed.

If I find one door locked, I never try another, she said, and walked through. That should tell you something about me.

All right. If I find a door locked, I walk away. Tell you any more?

You're so much stronger, she said, walking in front, to the doorway. Nothing seems to affect you. What are you using for lights?

Reach for one. On the side table. Candles upstairs. Turn right. On up.

He poured drinks in the terrace bar, and took them out. She wore a long white Arab robe, lying back on the chaise.

Moon's coming up in twenty minutes, he said. It's something to see, from here.

Pity it's not on my window side. Did you see it with the sun coming through?

Never saw anything like it.

You really mean that?

Would I say it?

You never say anything you don't mean?

I try not.

I wish I could be like that. *Lechaim*.

Lechaim. How's the drink?

Just right. Mr. Paul. I have to tell you. I had an abortion.

He drank a little, reached for a cigaret.

Here?

Oh, no. Four years ago. But I never felt good about it. I don't wear anything. Don't take the pill. I'm plain *me*. I always had an awful feeling about that time. I shouldn't have gone through with it. But what would my mother have said? It's like the ceramic business. First, I thought ceramics. But then I went for glass. I knew I was right. Know it now. That window told me everything. I have the career I always wanted.

Did you sample many men?

No. I did not. And I'm not answering any questions.

Your privilege. But why tell me?

I'd like to have your baby. No marriage. Nothing like that. Just me, and whoever it happens to be. Boy or girl, fine.

Look, Rivka. You're a lovely girl. There are younger men. Why me?

I told you. Force of character, first. Imagination. Creative ability. I can go on.

Ever told anybody else about the abortion?

Oh, why, *no*. Of *course* not.

You trust me?

Why not?

Well. There's gossip.

You don't. I didn't come up here without being pretty sure. I wouldn't want just anybody's baby. I don't want to think of being married. Tied down.

But if you have a baby, aren't you tied, anyway?

I know a good nurse. I'm free, except for the feeding. That, yes.

You ready to go to bed?

Yes.

He got up, and walked into the dark room, looking at the Mediterranean's blue glow, and the lights of the fisherboats.

That calm voice, simple words, plain honesty, stuck the knife deep in a hurt not to be told in any form of speech. Son, Mr. Blantyre's gentle voice seemed to say, You always have to try to look for grace. It's a solid part of art and honesty. Grace *cannot*, can *never* be, *dis*honest.

Rivka, you can be just a little wrong about me, he said, hearing his voice resound in the room's corners. I've never really *been* dishonest. I've never stolen in my life, that's true. But I've cheated. As long as it looked safe. I allowed others to. I've been part of deals I knew weren't just right. Professional license, let's call it? But not strictly honest, the way I was taught. I can't snake out of it any longer. I tried for years not to tell the truth. I mean, about myself. *To* myself. But you've made it easy. I don't know what the block was, before. But if someone like you can come in here and tell me she wants my baby, I have to look at myself. He or she'll take over here after we've gone. It's a great idea. Part of the dream. It'll come true, just as this house and the entire place came true. But it was only a dream, not long ago. Do I sound sane?

Love it.

I have to go back to New York. If I have any charges against me, from any quarter, I'll face them. Lies aren't part of any dream. I won't be part *of* them. I'll come back here clean as you are. Clean as a child. Are you going to be patient, and wait?

I'll wait all you want while you're gone. But does that mean I have to be patient *now*?

He went out, and took her by the hand, and she leaned against him, and he put an arm about her, and led her down

the short flight to his study, felt around the table and arm-
chairs, found the telephone, struck a match, and Rivka held
it while he dialled the number.

No reply from Lucien Weil.

He dialled Berthold Gluck.

No reply.

We're six hours behind, he said. So it's around six-thirty?
I'll tell you who. For a thousand, gold.

Bilara answered on the second ring.

Bet you don't know who this is, he said.

I sure don't, Mr. Paul, sir. I was just praying either you
call, or walk right in the door. You know something? I sold
two of my black painter's pictures. You know how I feel?
I done crossed over into Jordan. And I'm *singing*.

Congratulations. How about the copies?

Sold eight. Pretty good. Seven hundred, top. The other
dealers sending guys here. But the blacks went for a
thousand–two, and nine hundred. I believe we beginning to
get the name.

Keep at it. How would you like to see me in a couple of
days?

Oh, Mr. Paul. Listen, the guy had this place, the furniture? He sold us a lot of things. Leather furniture. Just like
you had in the apartment. So we said, why don't we buy a
few pieces, and get that decorator guy to remodel that big
room on the second floor? We painted, and we got it just
the way we wanted it. You got your own place, kitchen,
bathroom, everything. It's something to see. And us. We
just waiting. And you know what waiting *is?* Picking your
damn nails. I got mine all ruined.

Watch for my cable. And call Mr. Weil in the morning.
Tell him I'll be in New York day after tomorrow. You going
to cook bacon and eggs?

Any time, Mr. Paul, sir. But for the night you get here, we got a chicken from Kumeli's daddy, one pound more, he ain't no chicken, he's a dragon. With mushroom and chestnuts, sage, thyme and onion stuffing, and cranberry sauce, and brussels sprouts the size the top of my thumb, and baked potato. How that sound?

I'll bring the wine. Bilara, it's good to have friends.

Come right on home, Mr. Paul. We waiting.

P1